DIAL BOOKS
An imprint of Penguin Group (USA) Inc.
Published by The Penguin Group
Penguin Group (USA) Inc., 375 Hudson Street, New York, NY 10014, U.S.A.
Penguin Group (Canada), 90 Eglinton Avenue East, Suite 700, Toronto,
Ontario, Canada M4P 2Y3 (a division of Pearson Penguin Canada Inc.)
Penguin Books Ltd, 80 Strand, London WC2R 0RL, England
Penguin Ireland, 25 St. Stephen's Green, Dublin 2, Ireland
(a division of Penguin Books Ltd)
Penguin Group (Australia), 250 Camberwell Road, Camberwell, Victoria 3124, Australia (a
division of Pearson Australia Group Pty Ltd)
Penguin Books India Pvt Ltd, 11 Community Centre, Panchsheel Park,
New Delhi - 110 017, India
Penguin Group (NZ), 67 Apollo Drive, Rosedale, Auckland 0632,
New Zealand (a division of Pearson New Zealand Ltd)
Penguin Books (South Africa) (Pty) Ltd, 24 Sturdee Avenue,
Rosebank, Johannesburg 2196, South Africa
Penguin Books Ltd, Registered Offices: 80 Strand,
London WC2R 0RL, England

Book Design by Jasmin Rubero
Text set in Garth Graphic Std
Printed in the U.S.A.

10 9 8 7 6 5 4 3 2 1

Library of Congress Cataloging-in-Publication Data
John, Antony.
Thou shalt not road trip / by Antony John.
p.   cm.
Summary: Sixteen-year-old Luke Dorsey is sent on a cross-country tour to promote his
bestselling spiritual self-help guide accompanied by his agnostic older brother and former
girlfriend Fran, from whom he learns some things about salvation.
ISBN 978-0-8037-3434-0 (hardcover)
[1. Faith—Fiction. 2. Interpersonal relations—Fiction. 3. Christian life—Fiction.
4. Authors—Fiction. 5. Brothers—Fiction. 6. Automobile travel—Fiction.] I. Title.
PZ7.J6216Th 2012
[Fic]—dc23
2011015535

THOU SHALT N[OT]

ROAD TRIP

ANTONY JOHN

DIAL BOOKS
an imprint of Penguin Group (USA) Inc.

To Ted Malawer and Liz Waniewski.
Everybody needs an A-team. You're mine.

SATURDAY, JUNE 14

7. For there were two brothers. And yea, one was shorter than the other, and weaker. 8. And though he bestowed upon his big brother gifts of kindness and thoughtfulness and love, yet did the taller boy mock him, lamenting, "Why art thou so short? Art thou a leprechaun?" 9. And the shorter brother was too much afeared to speak. 10. So the stronger boy laughed, and cried, "What art thou good for? What can thou do that cannot be done far better by a boy of true stature, whose mind and body are strong?" 11. And though he was still afeared, yet the smaller boy recalled the events of the previous evening, and so girded his loins and spake thus: "Remember thee, 'tis easier for a short man to pass through the eye of a cat flap when he misseth curfew, and thereby to avoid parental detection and retribution." 12. And the taller brother knew that it was true, and shutteth up.

2:20 P.M.
Lambert–St. Louis International Airport, St. Louis, Missouri

Letitia is biting the inside of her mouth. Her left eyebrow is arched. I get the feeling she thinks my e-ticket is a fake, but I don't panic. After all, Pastor Mike—legendary host of TV's *The Pastor Mike Show*—called my journey a "pilgrimage." How can a *pilgrimage* go wrong before it has even started?

"Your bag's thirty-two pounds over the limit," says Letitia, smacking her gum.

"I'm sorry?"

"You can be as sorry as you like, honey. Don't change a thing. That'll be an extra seventy-five bucks."

I remove the case from the scale and open it carefully. Inside are dozens of hardback copies of my book—*Hallelujah: A Spiritual Chronicle of a Sixteen-Year-Old St. Louisan*. My editor complained that the title lacked "punch," so the cover just says *Hallelujah*.

I transfer ten copies to my second case, and return the original case to the scale.

"Still twenty-two pounds over," says Letitia.

The man next in line groans. He mutters to the lady beside him, but I don't hear what he says. I won't try to hear either, because eavesdropping is sinful, and I need to be good. Plus, I don't think he's being complimentary.

I move more books to the second case and the scale shows that it's now just under the maximum allowable weight. I smile at Letitia, who rolls her eyes and drums her fingers. I drag the second case onto the scale.

"Twenty-eight over."

Mental math tells me I won't be able to avoid going over the limit, so I pull out the credit card that my publicist, Colin, gave me for all book tour expenses.

Letitia studies it along with my ID. "Wait! Not *the* Luke Dorsey?"

I glance over my shoulder in case there's another sixteen-year-old Luke Dorsey beside me.

"I saw your interview on *The Pastor Mike Show*," she gushes. "The passage you read about the two brothers—that inspired me. I know you said it was written for kids and all, but my sister's taller than me and she thinks she's the big boss lady, so I said 'Just you wait 'til you need to get through the cat flap, sister.' And you know what, honey? She *shutteth up!*"

Letitia reaches under her desk and retrieves a copy

of my book. The cover is worn, as though she has read it several times. I guess I ought to be impressed, but instead I'm just uncomfortable. "Would you autograph it for me?" she asks, voice shaking.

"Uh, sure."

It's not the first book I've signed, not by a long shot, but I'm still not sure what to write. In the end I settle for: *To Letitia, who embraces the light.*

She nods like a bobblehead doll, and hands back the credit card without charging a fee. I'm about to accept it too, but stop myself just in time. "I have to pay," I tell her.

"Oh, forget about it."

"I can't. It'd be stealing. And stealing is—"

She gasps. "A sin, yes. It was evil of me to suggest it. Please pray for me." She runs my card through the machine and hands me the slip of paper to sign.

"I, uh, pray for everyone," I say—kind of a lame response, but she seems satisfied.

"Are you done yet, book boy?" asks the impatient guy behind me.

Letitia casts him a withering look. "Hey, mister, you shut your Goddamned mouth. This boy here's Luke Dorsey."

The heckler looks shell-shocked—his mouth flaps open and shut like he has been struck dumb. When he repeats my name, a silence descends upon the mass of travelers. Their lines part like the Red Sea.

As I shuffle between them, people reach out and touch my new blue blazer. I think Pastor Mike mentioned that something like this might happen, but that doesn't make it any less weird.

By the time I reach my parents at the security checkpoint, I've crossed myself ten times and signed three more copies. I'm sweating so badly, I take off my blazer and place it beside my backpack. All around me, people continue to stare, but now they're checking out my parents as well. Mom and Dad are almost sixty, but look even older. They're dressed in their Sunday best, even though it's Saturday. Most people probably figure they're my grandparents. Happens all the time.

Dad clamps a hand on my shoulder. "Are you sure you're all right with this, Luke?"

"Yeah," I say, though my voice betrays me. "I'm on a pilgrimage, right?"

"If you say so, son. But once you get to Los Angeles, it'll just be you and your brother. It's a great responsibility." He bites his lip. I can see he's having second thoughts about this. "I can take off work if you'd like me to come."

"Me too," interjects Mom. "Perhaps that would be

best," she adds, nodding at Dad. "After all, not every path is as straight and narrow as it might seem."

To be honest, I wish they would come. Pilgrimage or not, I feel like I'm caught in a whirlwind. Everywhere I go, people stop me. Every time I try to relax, there's something I need to do, to write, to say. How is my brother going to help with that?

Yet, as soon as these thoughts cross my mind, I feel ashamed for my lack of faith. Faith is what inspired me to start writing *Hallelujah* in the first place. Which means that faith has brought me here. Surely faith will see me through.

"I'll be fine. Honestly," I say. My parents still don't seem convinced. Since I have no idea how else to reassure them, I go with Default Setting Number One: a quotation from Psalms: "'Yea, though I walk through the valley of the shadow of death, I will fear no evil.' Psalm twenty-three, verse four."

Mom frowns. "I wasn't suggesting you're going to get knocked off, sweetie. I just meant—"

I raise my hand to stop her. I know she cares about me, and she's worried, but she's really freaking me out. If I don't go now, I'm afraid I might not go at all.

I kiss each of them once on the cheek, grab my backpack, and stride toward the security checkpoint. I don't look back the whole time I'm in line. Finally, when I'm through security, I give my parents a single courageous nod. They're standing in the same spot, jumping up and down, waving madly. In Dad's right hand is my blazer.

5:50 P.M.
Los Angeles International Airport, Los Angeles, California

My brother, Matt, isn't waiting in the baggage claim area, which is surprising. It's not like him to flake out on me. As the minutes tick by, I'm not sure what to do first: call my parents for help, or get a taxi to my book signing.

Before I have to decide, Matt appears. He's wearing a tight black T-shirt that shows off his not-inconsiderable muscles. Curly light brown hair flops over the lenses of his aviator sunglasses.

"I told Mom and Dad I'd meet you at the curb," he says. "To save on parking."

"They didn't tell me."

"Evidently." He hugs me in a way that involves almost no body contact. "Another thing, just so I've said it: I never called you a freakin' leprechaun."

"I never said you did."

"What about that part in your book?"

Before I can tell him it had nothing to do with him, a family shuffles toward us. "Are you Luke Dorsey?" asks the father.

"Uh, yes. Yes, I am."

He nods for a second and then shakes his head. I'm not sure what this gesture means. "Is it true you wrote *Hallelujah* in two weeks?"

"Yeah. Well, more like two and a half. But, you know, Handel composed *Messiah* in two weeks, and that's a lot more work."

"Isn't it amazing how God inspires us?"

I nod because it's true—I had felt inspired when I started *Hallelujah* a year ago. School was out for the summer, and it was blisteringly hot, so I huddled beside the lone a/c vent in my bedroom and wrote. Over ten days and 150 pages the words just flooded out: an offering of thanks for my impossibly good fortune. No wonder that first part of the book was so humorous; what could I possibly have complained about? The momentum kept me writing through the church retreat, when words were harder to come by, and the jokes ran out—when I felt betrayed and alone. When everything changed.

"Modest too, see?" the guy tells his family.

I want to say thank you, only I don't want him to

think I agree. Instead I just glance at Matt. Behind the sunglasses, his brows are furrowed so hard he looks constipated.

"Well, I should let you get on with your good work," he continues. "I just wanted to tell you that you are one amazing human being. To have done so much already, had so many adventures . . ."

I'm not sure what he means by "adventures," but he doesn't seem to expect a response. So I shake his hand, and Matt and I head toward the exit, wheeling my cases behind us.

"Does that happen a lot?" he asks.

"Kind of."

"Wow." He makes a grunting sound. "That's seriously weird. I just can't imagine adults reading your book. Kids, sure. But *adults* . . . I guess it really is this big deal, huh?"

"Hmm. It's hard to believe."

"Sure is. I know the reviewers like that whole blend of humor and spiritual lessons and stuff, but . . . I don't know . . . it just feels kind of freaky to me. Like, one minute you're cracking one-liners, the next you sound like a suicidal version of Gandhi."

There's an explanation for that, but I'm not going to share it with Matt. Besides, once my editor mixed up the humorous and serious parts of the book, they balanced each other well. At least, that's what everyone said.

"And don't even get me started on your interview on *The Pastor Mike Show*," Matt continues.

"Why? What was wrong with it?"

Before he can critique my performance, we leave the terminal and get slammed by a wall of smoggy heat. Just in front of us, a female police officer is writing a ticket for a rusty car parked illegally against the curb.

"No, no," cries Matt, hurrying to her side. "Please, no. I'm just the humble escort for one of our nation's spiritual leaders."

The officer looks up. She's wearing sunglasses too, so I can't read her expression. "Are you talking to me?"

"Yes, officer." Matt grabs my arm and pushes me forward. "This is Luke Dorsey, author of the acclaimed book *Hallelujah,* and this is his current mode of vehicular transportation. Give him a ticket and his vital work will be compromised."

I thought high school was humiliating, but Matt's really raising the stakes. Uncertain travel plans and freaky silent families I can deal with, but I've always drawn the line at lying to police officers.

I wait for her to chew us out, but instead she leans against the car for support and points a shaking finger toward herself. "You see this face?" she asks, voice trembling. "This is the face of someone who doesn't give a crap." She slaps the ticket on the windshield and busts out laughing.

"So much for saving on parking." Matt snatches the ticket from the windshield and hands it to me. "Here you go. Your first tour expense."

6:10 P.M.
Somewhere in Los Angeles, California

Matt stops at the nearest gas station. It's kind of a relief when he turns off the engine, because his car is possibly the noisiest vehicle in Los Angeles, which is really saying something. "Where's that credit card they gave you?" he asks.

"What?"

"Mom and Dad said your publicist gave you a credit card for tour expenses."

"Well, yeah, but . . ."

"Gas is a legitimate expense, bro. Seeing as how it's your tour and all."

He's right. But this will be the third expense of the day, and the last thing I want to do is upset Colin, my publicist. Perhaps it's time I straighten everything out.

"Do you have a cell phone?" I ask.

Matt pulls one from his jeans pocket and hands it

to me. I take Colin's business card from my wallet and dial the number.

"Yes?" comes the voice, hidden behind a mask of static.

"Colin, it's Luke Dorsey."

"Luke, my boy. Are you at the store already?"

"Uh, no. But we're close," I lie.

"Great. How are you doing?"

"I'm good. But I have a question about expenses. See, I had to pay an extra baggage fee for being over the weight limit. And then we got a parking ticket at the airport. And now we're at a gas station—"

"Luke, Luke! Sorry to interrupt, but I trust you, okay? Besides, the way this puppy's selling, you could've gone a hundred pounds over the weight limit and we'd handle it. Did I tell you we've already begun a fifth printing? *Fifth printing* . . . and the book's only been out a week. Amazon has twenty-two thousand copies on backorder. The indie bookstores in New York are putting crucifix bookmarks in each copy. And Barnes and Noble is giving away *I've been touched by Luke and it was divine!* decals with the purchase of three copies."

"Uh . . ."

"I know. Amazing, huh? So give yourself a break. Oh, one more thing: Can I reach you on this phone during the tour?"

"Hold on, it's my brother's phone. I'll ask him."

Matt nods, because he's been eavesdropping the whole time. "Yeah, but it's a pay-as-you-go phone," he stage-whispers, tapping my credit card helpfully. "You'll need to add minutes."

"My brother says yes."

"Great. Tell him to keep it charged; it's the only way I'll be able to contact you while I'm out of town. Oh, and remember what I told you about these events: Arrive early, smile lots, talk to everyone. You have a story to tell, and people want to listen. Just be yourself, okay?"

"Okay." I hang up and hand Matt his phone, although I still hesitate before handing over the credit card.

He rolls his eyes. "Luke, my last paycheck from the café will be waiting when we get back to St. Louis, but that's not much help right now. So let's get comfortable using this card, okay? Otherwise, what's the point in having it?"

I hand it over, and Matt gets out. He doesn't rejoin me for five minutes. For a small car, this thing has a huge gas tank.

When he restarts the engine, there's a new clanging sound. He turns up the hip-hop on his stereo, but it can't drown out the noise. We lurch to the edge of the forecourt and wait for a gap in the traffic. The car shudders in time with the clanging. I can feel my teeth vibrating in my skull.

And then, suddenly, everything is quiet: no clanging; no booming bass. It's such a dramatic change that I can even hear the gentle in and out of our breaths as we share the same polluted L.A. air.

A car horn blares behind us. "Street's clear," I say.

Matt nods as he turns the key over and over. Eventually the street fills with traffic again. "Ah, crap," he groans. "That damned mechanic said this might happen."

"Said what might happen?"

He grabs my backpack from the backseat and pats my shoulder. "Don't sweat it, okay. It's only two miles to the bookstore. We'll make it easily if we run."

7:15 P.M.
Born-Again Bookshop, Manhattan Beach, California

It is not two miles. We do not make it easily. Matt's knowledge of Manhattan Beach is significantly less encyclopedic than he thinks. And the whole way we don't pass a single other pedestrian. In the city where everybody drives everywhere, St. Louis's most out-of-shape kid is warming up for his first event with a half-marathon. Sheesh!

When we finally arrive—fifteen minutes after the event should have started—the place is in disarray. A line streams out the door and people are arguing. Worse still, paramedics carrying a stretcher are attempting to fight their way through the mob, which isn't moving one bit.

"Let them through!" I cry.

At first there's silence, and then a faint murmuring. All eyes are on me, and it's clear that even though I'm drenched in sweat, everyone knows who I am. To my surprise they move aside, allowing the stretcher to snake through at last.

The poor person being carted off is an old lady in a brown wool suit. She wears an oxygen mask, but as she passes beside me I recognize her face. "Yvonne?"

The lady on the stretcher shakes like she's having a seizure.

"Yvonne Thomas?" I say, jogging to keep up with the paramedics. "I saw your profile on the Born-Again Bookshop website. You're a legend. W-what happened?"

Yvonne opens her eyes. Studies me for a moment. Makes the connection . . . and sits bolt upright and rips off the oxygen mask in one smooth movement.

"Thank you, gentlemen, that will be all," she trills.

The paramedics exchange glances. "Lie down, ma'am," says the oldest. He has a kind face and a gravelly voice. "We've got you now."

Yvonne glances at the line around her bookstore. "The hell you have!" She swings her legs over the side of the moving stretcher, but when she tries to stand she has to lean against me for support. She's shaking like a cartoon skeleton. "Luke Dorsey, you . . . you saved me!"

The paramedics freeze and the crowd falls silent again. I wait for someone to cry *gotcha!* and for the hidden camera crew to emerge so we can all share a laugh. Meanwhile, I have an eighty-year-old lady hanging in my arms. If I hold her too tightly, I'm afraid she'll break.

She turns to face the crowd. "Did you see that?" she asks them. "Well, *did* you?"

The murmuring resumes, a low-pitched hum that grows and grows until the crowd has whipped itself into a frenzy.

She shouts over them: "Nothing this boy says could possibly speak louder than his actions. There will be no talk, no questions. We must simply be grateful we were here to witness this . . . this *miracle*."

I can't believe she just said that—it's obviously untrue. Even Yvonne hesitates like she knows she overstepped her mark and wants to take it back. I wait for someone to call her out, but the longer the silence goes on, the harder it is for anyone to break it. In the end, the word stands: *miracle*. It makes me queasy.

Yvonne tries to let go of me, but her legs aren't up to supporting her. "Please form an orderly line," she continues. "We are Christians, after all. And don't waste this opportunity to buy copies of *Hallelujah* for your friends, and your children, and your friends' children, and . . . anyone you *care* about." She leans heavily on the word *care,* which gives everyone a chance to count the bills in their wallets. Some of them sigh as they pull out credit cards.

When she turns to face me, she sniffs the air. "You stink," she hisses. "Even worse, you're fifteen minutes late for your own signing. I swear . . . kids today!"

She pulls herself up to her full five feet and tells me to escort her into the store.

8:20 P.M.
Born-Again Bookshop,
Manhattan Beach, California

My hand is cramping. Actually, my hand began cramping half an hour ago, and my signature isn't just illegible now, it's not even my signature. Not really. I just draw a line, add a circle, and finish with a wave-like squiggle that has a pleasingly artistic quality.

Some of the customers stare at the squiggle for quite a long time. I think they're trying to see how it correlates to my name. I feel kind of guilty, but not for long, because Yvonne drives away anyone who outstays their allotted ten seconds.

It didn't start out like this. I tried speaking to everyone in line, but I kept writing down things they said, instead of my inspiring line: *It's time to be moved!* And then Yvonne literally began moving people. Sometimes forcibly. So I kept it to just a signature.

Then the squiggle.

Several people in line try to shake my hand, but it has cramped up badly, and I can't seem to unclench the Sharpie. It's like they're fused together. I'm afraid the best I'll be able to do is to make sure it's firmly capped before I go to bed tonight.

Little by little the line shortens, and finally there's only one person left. For the first time in over an hour I feel my shoulders relaxing. My breathing slows along with my pulse. I'm suddenly aware that two time zones separate St. Louis from Los Angeles, and I'm exhausted.

I summon a brave smile for the last customer of the day. Then I wonder if I'm daydreaming. It's a girl: about my age, with long blond hair and perfect white teeth. She's wearing a blouse with a high frilly collar, and the wooden cross hanging from a cord around her neck is just about the largest one I've ever seen on a human being. When she leans over the table it swings forward and bumps my nose.

"Oh, my! Please forgive me," she says. She looks at the cross apologetically, shakes her head, and turns to leave.

"Don't go," I say, my voice cracking.

She bites her lip, but stays. She presses the cross against her chest, like she's instructing it to stay put. Her chest is not small.

I force my eyes up to her face again. "I-I'm Luke," I say.

She offers her hand. "Teresa." She has a gentle handshake: warm fingers like silk.

"Like Mother Teresa."

"Exactly. Isn't she extraordinary? I mean, dead now, I guess. Very dead. But still, a perfect role model." Teresa is babbling, which makes me think she might actually be nervous. I know exactly how she feels. "My mother says good role models are vital. That's why she gave me your book."

I can feel my face flushing red. "Oh. Well, I-I just write what the good Lord inspires me to write."

"That's so wise." She places her copy of *Hallelujah* on the table. "Would you write something inspirational for me?" she asks.

"Absolutely. I mean, I'll *try*."

I look at the title page at the front of the book. It's very white and empty. It needs to be filled with something inspirational, but my hand is begging me not to write another word.

Meanwhile, Teresa fingers her cross again. As she leans forward I catch a faint scent of peaches. She's waiting to be inspired.

Unfortunately, my brain has gone into lockdown.

To Teresa—

I hope that writing her name will create some momentum, but the pen just hovers an inch above the page. My hand is shaking, and I'm sweating again.

Teresa places her hand on the table. Her skin is porcelain white, nails a soft pink color.

I push the pen against the page and write: *Seek and ye shall find me.*

When I look up, I can tell she's disappointed.

Keep the faith, I add hurriedly. *For like your namesake, you are destined for beautification.*

Teresa stares at the page. "Beautification? Am I ugly?"

She points to the word, and I can't even breathe anymore. Before I can grovel an apology, she laughs gently, a tinkling sound that lets me know she's kidding. "Beatification. I get it. . . . Hey, you want to get a coffee? It'd be so great to talk to you."

She's lovely, and I did just mess up her book, and it has been a year since I even wanted to hang out with a girl, but still . . .

I look to Yvonne for advice, but my bodyguard has gone now that the line has ended. I don't know if it's usual for authors to share coffee with beautiful girls who attend their signings. I mean, not that we'd be *sharing* the coffee, just that we'd both be drinking it. Separate cups of it. At the same time.

Before I can mumble a response, I notice Matt standing across the room, watching me. When we make eye contact, he raises his thumbs, and I turn bright red.

It's a sign: I shouldn't be thinking what I'm thinking.

"I'm touched, Teresa, but . . . no, I can't. I'm really tired, and I have another signing tomorrow." The expression on her face just about kills me. She looks crushed. "I need to be at my freshest to, you know, do God's work," I add.

This time she nods. "Yes, of course. Well, until tomorrow, then."

It's not until she's gone that I realize what she just said.

9:50 P.M.
Freshman Residence Hall, University of Southern California, Los Angeles, California

Matt doesn't talk to me on the ride home. He doesn't speak as he hands the taxi driver my credit card. I'm not even sure he knows I'm there until we arrive back at his residence hall and walk up two flights of stairs.

"You're not planning to become a monk, are you?" he asks.

"What?"

"It's a fair question, 'cause that girl at the signing was totally into you. And underneath the weird stuff, she was actually pretty hot. Plus, you both have that born-again thing going."

He shoves the dorm room door with his shoulder and stumbles in. Somehow the university has managed to squeeze two beds inside, and it's clear that Matt's roommate isn't around, so I'll even have somewhere to sleep. Given our track record since leaving the airport, I'd half expected Matt to announce that we'd be camping out in cardboard boxes under the Santa Monica pier.

When the door is closed behind us, Matt turns to face me. "All I'm saying is, it's becoming a habit with you."

"A *habit*?"

"You know what I'm talking about. Freshman year, you and Fran were *this* close to dating. Anyone could see how much you wanted her. But you completely blew her off."

I should have known that's where this was headed. It's the same thing he brought up every time we talked on the phone last fall. It's the reason we've barely spoken since Christmas.

"I didn't blow her off, Matt. Fran was the one who got weird. If you saw the way she looks, you'd understand."

That silences him, but only for a moment. "So it's okay to judge a book by its cover, huh? Is that one of the lessons in *your* book?"

As soon as he says it, I feel ashamed and outwitted. Then again, he's taken advantage of my greatest weakness: Frances Embree, formerly one-half of the St. Louis city debate championship pair, and one-half of the organizational committee for our church's youth group, and one-half of . . . well, quite a lot of stuff actually.

"Seriously, Luke, you two were best friends."

"I don't want to talk about it. It's none of your business."

Matt nods. "In a way, no. But as long as I'm dating her sister, it's hard for the two of us to switch it off. You know how close they are."

Unlike us, I guess he means. Although if it weren't for Fran, Matt and I would still be close. It's yet another reason I resent her.

"How is Alexis?" I ask.

"Alex is cool."

"That's it? Your girlfriend is *cool?*"

He flops onto his bed and studies his hands. "She's always working. I think Caltech is kicking her butt. I figured we'd hang out most weekends, but she's always in the lab or something. I got us tickets to the USC-UCLA football game, and she bailed on me. Can you believe it?"

Truth is, yes, I can. Alex was always more interested in participating in sports than watching them, and everything came a distant second to schoolwork. Being at Caltech wouldn't have changed that. Still, I don't think Matt wants to hear it, so I pretend it was a rhetorical question and say nothing at all.

"Look, I'm not trying to pressure you," Matt continues, "but the situation with you and Fran hasn't exactly helped things between me and Alex this year."

"So you kept telling me. But Fran never tried to stay friends with me either, remember?"

"No, but it's harder for her. Since she changed, I mean."

"Changed?" I almost laugh. "Have you *seen* her?"

"Yeah. Photos, anyway. And I'm not saying the punk version of Fran is as hot as the original. I know you dug that whole prim-and-proper thing, with the cute bob and the matching sweater sets and color-coordinated hair bands. I get it, I really do."

Okay, so he's right about that. She was a vision back then: pretty, with a smile that could melt me. But she was so much more. She had boundless energy and wasn't afraid to laugh. She was the peaceful protestor, supporter of the oppressed. At lunch, she insisted we sit with the least popular kids—the ones who sat at mostly empty tables on the edges of the cafeteria. Now she has one of those tables to herself.

"You're thinking about her right now, aren't you?" Matt asks.

"No," I say. It's not even a lie, because that version of Fran doesn't really exist anymore.

"I'm just saying, you of all people ought to be able to look past the hair—"

"The *purple* hair?"

"Yeah, the purple hair. And the piercings—"

"All of them?"

"Yeah, Luke, all of them."

"Do you know how many there are?"

"No, I don't." Matt sighs, but then a smile creeps across his face. "But if you do, you might want to think about what that means."

I ignore the challenge in his voice, and play my trump card: "What about the tattoos, huh? She made crazy lines along her forearms, Matt. Tell me: Who does that to herself?"

Matt shrugs. He looks tired. "I don't know, Luke. But you would, if you'd ever bothered to ask."

He doesn't know what he's talking about, but it's late and I haven't got the energy to argue anymore. So I brush my teeth and say my prayers—thanks that my parents love me; thanks that my plane arrived safely; thanks that I didn't have a fatal heart attack running across Los Angeles—and try to find a position on the lumpy bed where the springs don't dig into my ribs. Finally, exhausted, I recall this evening's event, and everyone's words of support and appreciation. For some reason, though, my mind keeps returning to another image: a shy girl with long blond hair and an irresistible smile. And as I fall into sleep, my brain runs wild with thoughts you won't find anywhere in *Hallelujah*.

SUNDAY, JUNE 15

Mishaps 9: 15–17

15. But the boy barely recognized her, for though she was similar, yet did she appear strange, as though winged messengers had taken the ends of her hair and flown upwards and outwards with it. 16. And the girl responded not, even though he was staring at her with both his eyebrows furrowed tightly. 17. And though he was silent, the boy was wise, and wondered to himself if indeed she was not the same girl. But she was not.

8:10 A.M.
Freshman Residence Hall, University of Southern California, Los Angeles, California

"You snore."

I hear the words, but my eyes won't open. I don't even know where I am; only that something is digging into my back.

"Seriously," the voice continues, "you're like a freakin' foghorn or something."

I stretch and my calf muscles cramp up. The pain is so sharp that my eyes snap open. Matt towers over me. He doesn't look happy.

"We are so not sharing a room on this trip, understand?"

I nod vacantly.

"Fine. As long as we're agreed on that." He reaches into his pocket, pulls out his cell phone, and drops it next to my head. "You'd better call that Colin guy to let him know."

That really gets my attention. I don't want to ask Colin for more money already. Besides, it's Sunday morning. He's probably at church.

"Why didn't you wake me?" I ask.

Matt narrows his eyes. "You're the star of the show, Luke. I'm just the chauffeur. Plus . . ." His voice trails off.

"What?"

"I feel bad about my car breaking down. I called Mom and Dad earlier to say you got here okay, and they asked about the signing. I probably should've kept my mouth shut, but I told them we were late and . . . well, let's just say they didn't exactly see the funny side."

"It wasn't your fault."

"Maybe not. But the mechanic warned me my car was on life support. I just couldn't afford to get it fixed. I should've gotten us a taxi." He shrugs. "Anyway, it won't happen again. This tour is a big deal, so we'll get a rental car with the top AAA coverage and everything."

"Thanks, Matt. That's really . . . Hold on. Who's paying for the rental car?"

Matt reaches down and presses a button on his cell phone. "Go ahead. I've already got Colin on speed dial."

I grab the phone, and hear Colin's husky voice: "Luke, is that you?" He doesn't sound as patient as he did last night. I can even hear a voice in the background—probably his pastor giving the sermon. Or perhaps it's more than one voice—a choir singing. "Luke?"

"Uh, yeah. Look, I'm really sorry to bother you, but my brother says he won't sleep with me."

There's silence on the other end. I overhear Colin telling someone to go ahead without him. I can't believe he might be missing Communion because of me.

"He won't *sleep* with you?" repeats Colin slowly.

"That's right."

"Are you sure it's me you should be calling?"

"I think so. Who else can give me permission to get separate hotel rooms? He says I snore."

"Oh!" Colin chuckles, a sound like dislodged phlegm. "Yeah, yeah, Luke. Sure, whatever, that's fine."

"Thanks."

"No problem. I take it *you* slept well though, right?"

"I guess."

"You *guess*? Finest room in Pasadena and you *guess*?" Colin clicks his tongue. "Well, just don't go all diva on me, okay?"

I wonder if we're having different conversations, or if he just has a weird sense of humor.

"Uh, okay. Although . . . well, there's something else too. My brother's car broke down last night, so we'll need to rent one."

Colin pauses. "Ooookay. That's fine. Yeah, that's completely fine." Another pause. "Seriously now: Are you sure your brother's up to this?"

I glance at Matt. He's slouching in his desk chair, sleep-deprived because *I* kept him awake. "Yes," I say. "Why wouldn't he be?"

"Well, I've already heard you were late to yesterday's event. Looked like crap too—I've seen the photos. If it weren't for that *miracle,* I'd be giving you an earful right now."

"Sorry."

"That's okay. It was your first event. But you've got to arrive early from now on. An hour is good; gives you a chance to relax and chat to the booksellers. And whatever happens, stick to the schedule. We already factored in a free day tomorrow, but after that it's one event per day. It's a tough itinerary. And I still feel bad for bailing on the original plan—"

"You shouldn't. I know you're heading out on tour tomorrow."

"Yeah, but I told you and your parents I'd be going on *your* tour, not Martha McCrawley's."

"She's a top author."

"And so are you. So if you're worried, tell me now. None of the other publicists are available, but I'll find you an escort in each city. It's the least I can do."

I hadn't really considered myself a top author before, and it's true that someone with knowledge of the tour stops would be helpful. But I've already asked for so much from Colin. Besides, everything that has gone wrong so far has been an accident.

"We'll be okay, Colin. Really."

"All right. Then get the car, reserve an extra room, and make sure your brother knows that schedule by heart. If your events continue to be overcrowded, I might have to do some last-minute venue switching too, in which case I'll call you on this phone, okay?"

"Okay."

"Good. One more thing: While I'm on the road, I won't always be available. So as far as these expenses go, I trust you to keep them reasonable." He laughs suddenly, so loud that I wonder what the rest of the congregation thinks. "You wrote *Hallelujah*, for Christ's sake, you know?"

I expect to hear outraged cries from Colin's fellow churchgoers, but there's no sound at all.

"Well," he continues, "I'd love to stay and chat, but there's three guys waiting for me to tee off. And we've still got sixteen holes to go, plus a date with José Cuervo, so . . ."

"Oh, sure."

He hangs up without saying good-bye.

Matt crosses the room and sits on the edge of my bed. He taps Colin's credit card against his palm. "This is going to be a busy week, Luke. So why don't you leave all the crap to me? Buying food, paying for gas, checking in with the parents—I can take care of it."

"Okay. I'd appreciate that."

Matt gives me a thumbs-up and heads for the door. I'm dozing again before it closes behind him.

10:55 A.M.
Freshman Residence Hall, University of Southern California, Los Angeles, California

I have a signing at one p.m. Two hours ought to be enough to get anywhere in L.A., but after yesterday's debacle, I'm not so sure.

Matt strides in carrying a box of doughnuts and a cup of coffee. Sweat glistens on his forehead. When he opens the box, I can see the residue of the four doughnuts he has already eaten.

"Man, it's hot out there," he groans. "And don't get me started on finding a rental car on Sunday morning. Seriously, everywhere was closed. We go on and on about separation of church and state, then shut down half the country for religious stuff." He looks up suddenly. "No offense."

"What do you mean, *no offense?*"

"I'm just saying . . . Here, have a coffee: white, one sugar. And a doughnut. You must be hungry."

I am hungry, and I'm dying for the coffee. But I can't help glancing at my watch.

Matt *tsks*. "I'll get you to your signing, all right? I've taken care of everything now, so there won't be any hold-ups."

"What did you need to take care of?"

"The rental car and stuff."

"What stuff?"

"Just . . . stuff."

He pushes the box at me, so I take a doughnut and wash it down with the coffee.

"Good, huh?" he says. "Right, so now the bad news. I went to pick up your cases, but someone had broken into the car and taken them."

I choke on the doughnut. By the time I manage to stop coughing, Matt's already heading toward the door.

I grab my backpack and follow. "What do you mean—*taken?*"

"Stolen."

"How?"

"I don't know—probably jimmied the locks." He pulls the door closed behind us. "I'm not thrilled about it either, but it was just books, right? Worst-case scenario, we'll claim on your travel insurance and buy some more copies. It'll make your sales look great."

"So you're a business major now?"

Matt ignores the sarcasm and hurries along the corridor. He takes the stairs two at a time, and it's all I can do to keep up with him. At the bottom of the staircase I see a Camry parked outside. It's decadent, but at least it's not the hulking yellow Hummer in the neighboring spot.

The car reminds me of the previous evening, and running several miles. I glance at my watch again.

Matt stops beside the Camry. "Will you please stop looking at your watch? Anyway, what are you worried about? On *The Pastor Mike Show* you said this was a *pilgrimage*."

"What? No. Pastor Mike said that."

"Uh, no. Definitely you." Matt looks puzzled. "You have seen the interview, right? I mean, you said some pretty interesting things."

"No. Mom and Dad only get basic cable."

"Ever heard of YouTube?"

"We don't have Internet access either."

"Still?" Matt shakes his head. "Do they have any idea how weird that is?"

"It's not weird. They just like to keep things simple."

"Pretending the twenty-first century hasn't started doesn't keep things simple."

If I weren't so hung up about my bags being stolen, I'd probably agree. "It's fine. I just use the computers at school."

"During summer break?" He's got me there. "Listen, bro. It's okay to criticize Mom and Dad. Sure, they love us, and they're supportive and stuff—doesn't mean they're right about everything. They wouldn't let me play football because it's too violent, but they've sent you off on tour without even giving you a cell phone. In some states, that constitutes child endangerment." He pulls out the car key. "You appeared on national TV, bro, and you haven't even been able to check out your Oscar-winning performance yet. That's just wrong. Hey, maybe you can watch it on Alex's laptop when we pick you up from the signing."

"What do you mean, Oscar— Wait! Alex will be at the signing?"

"No. We'll meet you after, once we've packed all her stuff into the car."

"Alex is coming on tour with us?"

"Yeah. Didn't Mom and Dad tell you?"

"No. I thought it was just us."

I turn away to hide my disappointment. When I pull the passenger door handle, I set off the alarm.

"What are you doing?" Matt cries.

"Opening the door," I shout over the wailing alarm.

"That's not our car. You think all Alex's stuff is going to fit in there?"

"So which one is ours?"

Matt presses a button on his key and the Hummer's doors unlock with a click.

12:05 P.M.
Somewhere in north Los Angeles, California (I can see the Hollywood sign)

The Hummer has leather seats and an interior that's more luxurious than any vehicle I've ever seen. It is quite possibly the most inappropriate form of transportation Matt could have chosen.

It's also quiet, but I won't break the icy silence. I want Matt to know I'm annoyed about the Alex situation, and my cases being stolen. Even though the coffee he gave me was excellent.

After twenty minutes, Matt pulls up at a large store with a bright neon sign proclaiming that this is THE CHRISTIAN WAREHOUSE.

Matt points at the sign. "The Christian Warehouse,

where you can buy new and used Christians at or below invoice price." He busts out laughing.

"Have some respect, Matt," I say quietly. "It's Sunday."

"I know, *Luke*." He's serious again. "The *Sabbath*. The *Day of Rest*," he says in a deep voice like he's narrating a movie trailer. "So what the hell are you doing selling your books on a Sunday? Or is this a ruse? Maybe you're planning to hop in there and overturn a few tables instead, huh?"

"I didn't make the schedule. I asked Colin not to arrange anything for Sunday, but he said I should think of it as kind of like a Bible study group."

"And you bought that?" Matt shakes his head and points to the handle on my door. "I'll be back in a couple hours. Break a leg."

He takes off as soon as the door latches behind me.

I'm early, thank goodness, but that doesn't mean I'm first to arrive. Large groups are congregating in the parking lot, exchanging hugs and kisses as though a Sunday event is the social high point of their weekend. Come to think of it, I'm kind of jealous—that's how church used to feel to me.

I keep my head down and push through the main doors. As I approach the help desk a middle-aged guy darts forward and clasps my right hand. It still aches from all the autographs last night, but I try not to grimace.

"Luke, Luke, Luke," he says. "My name is Bradley, and I am humbled by your presence."

I'm not exactly comfortable about him being *humbled,* but I nod and extricate my hand. Meanwhile, people are gravitating toward me like I'm the last remaining human in a zombie movie. "Is there somewhere I can sit?" I ask.

"Sure. Follow me."

Bradley leads me to the staff room, and then disappears for half an hour. By the time he returns, I'm getting nervous.

"Ready?" he asks.

I smile ambivalently and follow him through the door. The crowd is staggering: At least two hundred people are crammed into a corner of the store, and only half of them are sitting. Thunderous applause accompanies me all the way up to the tiny stage.

Bradley begins by telling everyone who I am ("as if you don't know") and reminding them to get a copy of my book ("a life-changing read"). When it's my turn to speak, I have no idea what to say.

He only waits a moment before throwing me a lifeline. "So, Luke, can you tell us how you came to write this wonderful book?"

Okay, this I can answer. As long as I remember to breathe.

"Yes, um . . . so, Andy—he's the pastor at my church—asked everyone from the youth group to write modern-day parables for the kids in Sunday school . . ."

A lady at the front is adjusting her hearing aid. I need to slow down.

"And so I wrote a few, and some longer passages too, and before long I'd filled a hundred pages. It only took a few days. And Andy really liked the first few pages, and said I should keep going. So I did. Well, until church retreat, anyway. It was harder there. But I still kept going until I had nothing left to say . . ."

There are a lot of furrowed brows. People look as though they're being asked to follow the complex plot of a psychological thriller. I really should have rehearsed this.

"At the end of the retreat I gave the first part of the book to Andy, and he made all these great comments. So I gave him the rest. But what I didn't know is that Andy went to theology school with Pastor Mike. Well, he mailed a copy to Pastor Mike, who said he liked it too, and told me about some publishers that might be interested in it. Turns out he was right, because one of them offered to publish the book, and they even gave me an advance—"

"How much?" someone calls out.

No one approves of the interruption, but no one tells me not to answer either.

"I don't know," I say honestly. "My parents put it in a trust fund for me. They said it'd pay for most of freshman year if I go to Mizzou . . . most of the first month if I go to Duke."

Everyone laughs. I hadn't meant it to be a joke—it's what my parents actually said—but the laughter takes the edge off the atmosphere.

"Anyway," I continue, "*Hallelujah* is out there now, and it seems as though people like it. It's kind of amazing, actually. I hadn't expected any of this."

There are several raised hands, so I guess my introductory remarks are officially over. Bradley passes a microphone to the woman nearest him.

"H-hello, Luke," she says, her voice low and trembling. "I j-just wanted to say that . . . the world being the way it is . . . people hating and war and stuff . . . I think it's really important you're doing this." She hands the microphone back.

When I imagined all the things that people might say or ask—*How relevant is a book of contemporary parables? Is theology school the next step? When's the sequel?*—her comment definitely wasn't on the list. I'm not even sure what she means by "this," but when I smile and nod my head, everyone claps as though I've explained the meaning of life.

The microphone makes its way to an elderly man near the back. As he thanks Bradley, his rasping voice is amplified. "Luke, I have a question," he says. "I love the didactic parts of *Hallelujah*—the 'lessons,' as you call them. They're to-the-point, and they remind us that the world isn't all sweetness and light. But there's all that humor too. Now, don't get me wrong, I'm not opposed to humor, *per se*. Humor is fun. Humor is what makes people laugh. Without humor, the world would be a lot less funny. But is a spiritual self-help guide really the place for laughs?"

This question elicits a chorus of disapproving tongue clicks, and my throat tightens. I knew someone would ask me this—even Matt said the balance of humor and serious sections felt off-kilter—but I still don't have a satisfactory answer.

Then an odd thing happens: As I follow everyone's eyes, I realize that the hostility is aimed at the old guy, not at me. Apparently I don't need to answer at all, because on the issue of funny vs. not-funny, Team Luke is winning hands down.

Dad told me that answering questions would feel like a debate competition: weird objections that I'd have to analyze and deflect. But he was wrong. The audience is completely behind me, as if the scores have already come in and I've been declared winner.

"The humor, Luke," repeats the old guy, but quieter this time.

More tongue clicks.

"Well, Andy wanted this book to appeal to the kids in Sunday school," I explain. "So I thought about what I disliked most in Sunday school, and realized it was the way everything seemed so serious, even when we were talking about great things. I didn't want the kids at my church to think that's the way it has to be. I wanted them to laugh, because I used to laugh a lot. I guess that's why I figured humor had a place in *Hallelujah*."

He cocks his eyebrow. "You *thought*? What do you think now?"

I think I wish he hadn't asked. "I think . . . the response has been amazing."

He clearly expects more, but he must be tired of playing the role of party pooper, because he gives up the microphone. As other members of the audience clamor to have their say, I realize I might just get through this after all.

"Why *Hallelujah*?" someone asks.

"Because it's a joyful word," I reply.

"Are you like some kind of superhero or something?" asks someone else.

"Uh . . . no."

"Do you have a girlfriend?"

"No."

"A boyfriend?"

"No."

"Want one?"

Bradley grabs the microphone. "My goodness," he says. "It's time for the book signing already!"

2:20 P.M.
The Christian Warehouse,
Los Angeles, California

My fingers are shaking so hard, I can't grip the pen anymore. Signing my name is torture, and every time the pile of books in front of me gets smaller, someone brings out a new box. They've got about twenty more boxes ready to go too. I think there are at least twenty books in a box. That means there could be four hundred books. A little voice at the back of my mind is telling me I ought to be grateful, that it's a Very Good Thing to sell this many books. But my hand is begging me to stop.

I have enormous sympathy for my hand.

I inscribe books to Joe and Joseph and Joshua and Jeremiah, to Mary and Mariah and Maddy and Martha.

One by one the customers stand before me, their voices oddly distant. I try to reply, but quite soon the best I can manage is a bland smile. It seems to satisfy them all the same.

Eventually the line thins out. When the last person steps up, I recognize her immediately.

"Hello again," says Teresa sheepishly.

"Hello . . . again," I say, grinning stupidly.

She looks different today, so pretty it takes my breath away. She's wearing a gray knee-length skirt and white silk blouse, a single string of pearls around her neck.

"It's good to see you again," she says.

"It's good to see *you* again," I reply. My voice sounds higher than usual, like I'm going through puberty in reverse.

Teresa hands me a copy of my book. "I forgot to buy one for my mother." She sighs. "I'm so forgetful."

"I'm so forgetful too." Oh no, I did it again. "I mean, sometimes. Not always. Sometimes I remember."

Teresa nods slowly. "Right. So my mother's name is Gilda."

"Okay." I take the book from her before I make an even bigger dork of myself, and try to think of something to write. Eventually I settle on: *To Gilda, Teresa's mother.* On the page it seems a lot less intelligent than it did in my head.

Teresa looks at the inscription, brows furrowed. I can't tell if she's having trouble reading my handwriting, or if she thinks she's simply misread it. Or maybe she's coming to the conclusion that I'm a moron.

As she bends over to get a closer look, her fingers brush against mine. It's like an electrical current passing between us, and my breath catches. When I look up, I'm at eye level with her chest.

Someone beside us coughs, and we turn at once. "Oh, sorry," says the new arrival.

For a moment I think I must be hallucinating. I want to believe I'm dreaming; or having a nightmare, more like. Just as long as this new girl isn't really here.

"Sorry, Luke," says the girl again, looking genuinely contrite. "I didn't mean to interrupt you while you were staring at this girl's boobs."

I can't breathe. My face, already red, burns with the power of a thousand suns.

"Oh!" gasps Teresa. "I never intended . . . I'm so sorry."

"No, no, no. My fault," I say. "Teresa, this is—"

"Fran," announces the arrival, giving a brief wave. The sleeves of her combat jacket are frayed at the ends. Her fingernails are black. "I'm a close friend of Luke's since . . ." She puffs out her cheeks and winds a strand of shoulder-length purple hair around her finger. "Well, years. We were practically inseparable, weren't we, Luke?"

Fran waits for confirmation, but I can't form words.

Meanwhile, Teresa is staring at Fran like she's a particularly puzzling piece of art. "I see," she murmurs. Then she turns to me again, mouth twisted into an anxious smile. "So, um, would you be able to chat today? You were tired yesterday, but today . . . well, it's still early, and this morning I read a passage in *Hallelujah* that I'd love to discuss, and there's a coffee shop across the street." She almost trips over the words, like she's been building herself up to say these things.

Before I can reply, Fran grabs my bottle of water and downs it in one go. When she's done, she seems surprised that I'm watching her.

"What?" she asks. "Oh, wait, you want my permission, is that it?" She shrugs. "Yeah, you two should totally go out on a date. You'll make such a cute couple. And don't listen to all that stuff about how long-distance relationships never work. If anyone can make it work, it's you, Luke."

For a moment there's nothing but silence. I can't even look Teresa in the eye anymore.

"I didn't mean . . ." Teresa covers her mouth with

her hand. "That was really un-Christian of you," she tells Fran.

Teresa looks at me again, but there's no way I can say yes now. With nothing left to say, she holds out her hand and we shake. Then she turns and walks away. I want to take in every last footstep, but Fran is watching me.

"What are you doing here?" I ask.

"I've been visiting my sister," she says flatly. "Nice to see you too, by the way."

I re-cap my Sharpie and stand up. "Well, I hope you've had a lovely time."

"Sure have. I'll tell you all about it on the way home."

"Don't bother. Just tell Matt to come pick me up once he's dropped you off."

Fran pauses. "You sure about that? It's going to take him a while to get to St. Louis and back."

Then she watches me closely as her words sink in.

2:45 P.M.
Parking lot of the Christian Warehouse, Los Angeles, California

Matt is giving me a look. It says: *This is not my fault. Please don't make a scene. Or ask me why Fran is here. Or why I agreed to let her come with us.*

I give Matt a look too, through which I attempt to communicate the following: *I'm seriously unhappy. I'm dreading this. It's fortunate that one of the commandments is "Thou shalt not kill."*

But I don't say anything. At all. I should be on the fast track to sainthood for this.

In response, Matt shifts his weight from foot to foot, and pretends to adjust the cases in the trunk until Alex arrives to save him. She has a mile-wide smile and the large eyes of a Disney princess. Kind of like Fran—before she changed.

"How are you doing, Luke?" Alex wraps me up in a burrito hug. "I read your book. You must be so proud. How are your lovely parents?"

"They're dinosaurs," interjects Matt. "Completely out of touch with reality. What's lovely about that?"

Alex cocks an eyebrow. "Hey, any time you want to swap, just let me know. At least your parents talk to each other."

Matt's had even more firsthand experience with Fran and Alex's overbearing parents than I have. "Point taken," he says quickly.

Alex hugs me again. "Oh, it's so good to see you," she says with such affection that I wonder if we've been best friends without me knowing it. "So, hey, Matt's all over your schedule, and I just know we'll be in great shape. The next signing isn't until Tuesday. And Flagstaff is only seven hours away."

"Good." It's reassuring to know that Alex is on top of things too. She's the most organized person I've ever met.

"Still, no use in wasting time. So let's hit the road and see how far we get, huh?"

"Suits me," I say.

A moment later she claims shotgun, relegating me to the backseat. I climb in and discover that Fran is already there. We exchange the briefest of looks and push ourselves against opposite doors, so there's at least a yard of leather seat between us.

"You kids play nicely now, okay?" says Alex. She concludes her teasing by pecking Matt on the cheek. It makes the distance between Fran and me feel even greater.

As soon as Matt can navigate our behemoth of a vehicle out of the tiny parking lot, we grind along the supersized L.A. streets and throw ourselves into the white-knuckle rapids of the Foothill Freeway. I wonder aloud how anyone can bear to drive in the city. Matt tells me to be thankful it's Sunday, otherwise the traffic wouldn't be so light.

At the other end of the backseat, Fran stares out the window at the L.A. sprawl. I can see her reflected in the glass, and when she notices me watching her, she turns to face me.

"Yeah?" she says. It's an accusation, not a question.

"Nothing," I say.

By the time I dare to look out her side of the car again, an hour later, we're on Interstate 15, heading north through the San Bernardino Mountains.

"I wish we had time to stop at Lake Arrowhead," says Alex. "It's so beautiful up in the mountains. The water's cold, but it feels great."

Matt shuffles in his seat. "When did you go to Lake Arrowhead?"

"A couple weekends ago."

"Huh." He breathes deeply. "I didn't know that."

"It was just some people from the lab. You're not upset, are you?"

"What? No! Anyway, we can make a trip there this fall, right?"

"Uh-huh."

Alex takes his hand and squeezes it. But when Matt reaches across to squeeze her back, she reaches for a guidebook, and his hand just hangs in the space between them.

5:25 P.M.
I-40 at Ludlow, California

Matt pulls off Interstate 40 near a town called Ludlow. We stop for gas, but afterward we don't head back toward the interstate. Before I can ask where we're going, Alex pulls out her guidebook and clears her throat.

"Ludlow, California," she says, voice brimming with excitement. "Gateway to prealignment Route 66. Former water stop for the Atlantic and Pacific Railroad, the town grew following the discovery of iron ore in the nearby hills. Route 66 gave the town a fresh start, and businesses moved to accommodate travelers. These buildings can still be seen today."

When she's done, she peers over her shoulder as though she's expecting applause. But we're passing between the boarded-up skeletons of the Ludlow café and garage now, and applause is the last thing on my mind. Other buildings cling to the road too, unnamed, but equally dead. It's a ghost town in the truest sense of the word.

"Um, Matt," I say, "why are we on Route 66?"

"Route 66 is a national treasure, Luke. It's a spiritual experience. You of all people should appreciate that."

I gawk as we pass the last shell of a building. There's nothing but an eerily vast expanse of sand-colored wilderness before us. "But we're in the middle of nowhere."

"Yes, we are. Smack bang in the middle. If nowhere has a geographical center, this is probably it. But look around you—have you ever seen anything like it?"

"Well, no," I admit, "but then, I hadn't exactly seen anything like the scenery from I-40 either."

"We'll stop for a break at Amboy," says Alex, who clearly doesn't like the direction of our conversation. She taps her guidebook. "It says here that Amboy is a Route 66 . . . *oh!*"

"What?" asks Fran.

"Funnily enough, it's another ghost town," explains Alex. "Official population, twenty; actual population, four. Maintained in its weathered state for use as a motion picture location."

"Hold on, how do you *maintain* a weathered state?" I ask.

"You resist the temptation to make improvements," says Fran.

"Sounds like your kind of place."

Fran shakes her head and looks away, so I do the same. For the next twenty-five miles I watch the Mojave Desert drift by.

Amboy is as small and ghostly as advertised. It's impossible to miss it, because the buildings here are the first we've seen in miles, and the ground is so flat that I can tell there won't be any more for several miles after this. All the same, I can't help wondering why the town exists at all.

Matt pulls over by a sleek building with a giant neon sign: ROY'S MOTEL CAFÉ. As soon as we stop, he and Alex pile out and start taking photos.

I step out into blazing heat and a stiff wind. Fran wanders toward an enormous canopy and shelters beneath it. Since it's the only shade around—the café clearly isn't open—I join her there.

"I thought you'd want to get away from me for a few minutes," she says, studying her nails.

I decide to play innocent. "Why?"

"You know why." She looks up, eyes blazing. Even a thick application of eyeliner can't hide those eyes: sky blue, almost translucent. I've spent quite a lot of my life dreaming of those eyes. "Please don't stare," she says.

"Sorry." Instinctively I turn red, which is really annoying. "If you don't like it, why do you have purple hair?"

"What did you say?"

"I'm not being mean," I add hurriedly. "It's just . . . you have to know people are going to stare."

She doesn't say a word, but her fingers gravitate to the cascade of hoops in her right ear. She fiddles with them as she shakes her head.

"I'm not judging you, Fran. I just want to understand." I can't even tell if she's hearing me. "You used to like debate."

"That's what you think this is—*debate*?"

The sharpness of her voice makes me hesitate. "Sort of."

"You can stop trying now, Luke. I'm sure it'd look good for you to save a few souls while you're on tour, but you don't need to feel responsible for me, okay? I'm just trying to get a ride home, that's all."

"What were you doing in L.A. anyway?"

She leans against a wall. "Visiting Alex. Believe it or not, my parents were happy to see me disappear for a couple weeks."

I have no idea how to respond to that. Thankfully, I don't have to; Matt jogs over and hands each of us a granola bar.

"What's this?" I ask.

"A snack. Or maybe dinner," he says. "Depends

how much progress we make. Got to make hay while the sun shines and all that, you know?"

No, I don't. But it ends my conversation with Fran, and I'm grateful for that. We only spoke for a minute, but I'm more exhausted now than I was at any time during this afternoon's event.

When we start driving again, I make a pillow from a balled-up towel and close my eyes. As the car purrs through the unchanging landscape, my thoughts return to Fran: why she shut me out and won't talk to me about anything that matters anymore. It's so depressing that it's a relief when, at last, I fall asleep.

11:10 P.M.
Tailfin Motel, Route 66, Arizona

I wake up when the car stops. There's a neon sign outside my window announcing that we've arrived at the Tailfin Motel. There are no other cars here. I've seen movies set in places like this, and they rarely end well for the main characters.

"Colin booked us rooms *here*?" I ask.

"What's wrong with it?" replies Matt. "You want us to drive through the night instead?"

"No. I just want to make sure I got our plans right." I wait for Fran and Alex to get out. "Speaking of which, is there anyone *else* you're planning on picking up?"

He lowers his voice. "What do you want me to do? Ditch Fran in the middle of the desert?"

"That'd be a good start."

As soon as the words are out, I want to take them back.

"You willing to share that thought with your fans at the next event? Or do you save the nasty stuff for family and former friends?"

"I'm sorry. I didn't mean it."

"Yes, you did. You just don't want to admit it."

He heads inside while I grab my backpack and stumble along behind him.

The foyer is small and cramped. Lightbulbs flicker uncertainly. Matt nods his head in the direction of the only corridor and stops at the first of two open doors, where Alex is waiting for him.

"It's not exactly the Empress Pasadena," she says.

Matt kisses her on the cheek. "Hey, it's got a bed. That's all we need."

He punches my arm in what I assume is an undergraduate gesture of farewell, and disappears inside.

There's a framed print just inside the door of the next room: a photo of the motel by day, dirt-brown mountains rising in the distance. It's an alien landscape, not so different from Ludlow and Amboy.

"Your bed's there." Fran's voice drags me around. She's here, in this room—as though she's planning to stay.

"What are you doing here?"

"I'm getting ready for bed." She sounds bored. "You?"

"But . . . you can't . . . I mean, not here. Not with me."

"I'm not going to share your bed, Luke. There's two, see? I have standards."

I run out of the room and bang on Matt's door. A long while later, it opens. Matt's already shirtless, which reveals his unnecessarily muscular chest.

"What's up?" he asks.

"I can't use that room."

"Why not?"

"Why do you think?" I whisper. "Because Fran is in there."

"So? There are two beds."

"Uh-uh. Can't do it."

Matt rolls his eyes. "You're sharing a room with her, bro—not a bed. If it's such a big deal, get another room."

"What'll I tell Colin? That the two of us need *three* rooms? I think he'll work out we have company, don't you?"

Matt sighs. "What do you want me to do? I mean,

you can use our spare bed, but if you keep Alex awake all night with your snoring, she's gonna be really pissed. And I should probably warn you that Alex and me, uh . . . kiss a lot."

He pulls a face like the thought of kissing grosses him out, and I take a step back. By the time I've gathered my wits he has closed the door and locked it.

In the other room, Fran is sitting on the far bed with her back against the headboard. There's a tiny bottle of a clear liquid in her right hand. Every few seconds, she sips from it robotically.

"What's that?"

"It's um . . ." She squints at the label. "Huh! It's vodka. Who knew?"

"You're sixteen. What are you thinking?"

"I'm thinking that since I started drinking this little bottle, I no longer feel like sticking my fist through the window. You should be pleased."

I'm cemented to the spot, unable to take a step toward the Girl Formerly Known As Fran. She responds with a roll of her black-rimmed eyes and another long swig from the bottle.

"Are you trying to get drunk?"

"Trying, no. Succeeding, yes."

"Why?"

"Because drunks feel less."

"Feel less *what*? What happened to you?" My brain

is wired, but my voice is barely a whisper. "What went wrong?"

"Rhetorical question. Love–fifteen," she says, reprising a game we used to play when we practiced debating.

"Please, Fran. We used to talk all the time, remember? In Andy's office—plans for events, and fund raisers, and Bible study programs, and retreats, and Sunday school excursions. We prayed together. We made a difference together. How could you throw that away?"

"Presumption of guilt. Love–thirty."

So this is how it's going to be. It breaks my heart, but at least I've had a year to get over the shock.

"I'm not going to fight you, Fran. No matter how rude you are."

"That's a personal attack. Love–forty."

"But you *were* rude this afternoon. What you said to me and Teresa, that was unfair."

"Why? I was only telling you what you wanted to hear." She forces the corners of her mouth into a smile, but doesn't look at me. "Such a shame you blew it. She was completely your type—couldn't have been more perfect for you if she'd tried."

"She's no different than you used to be. Are you trying to tell me this is an improvement?"

"This?" Fran's eyes lock on mine. "Is that how you

think of me now? Not even a *person* anymore." Her voice is raw, and I know I've finally elicited a genuine response. On some awful level it feels like progress.

"Don't forget—I *know* you, Fran. I'm willing to help if you'll let me. I *want* to help. But not when you're drunk."

Fran downs the rest of the bottle. When she's done she claps her hands together in mocking applause. "The prosecution rests, Your Honor."

"I'm not the prosecution."

"Course you're not."

"You know what, forget it. I'm not staying when you're like this. I'll sleep in the hallway."

Fran jumps up and hurries past me. *"Mais non!* You're the famous author. The celebrity. You can't be roughing it on the floor. You deserve feather pillows and fresh sheets and flights of angels singing freakin' lullabies." She barrels out of the room.

I hate hearing the venom in her words. I hate feeling defensive. But most of all, I hate how relieved I am to see her leave. "You're wasting a break point," I remind her.

She stops dead and turns to face me, lank hair draped across her eyes. "You know, it's possible to lose even when you win. Anyway, I can tell when I'm not wanted. I've had a lot of practice this year."

Fran shuffles down the corridor and turns the corner, out of sight. I don't know where—or even if—she's planning to sleep. I'm worried about her, and in the silence of the room I wonder if I could have handled things differently. The author of *Hallelujah* ought to do better than that.

I guess I should follow her; but what would I say? She doesn't want me around—I've had a year to work that out—and so maybe it's best if I give her space, let her cool off.

I brush my teeth and head to bed. But all I can think about is Fran as she used to be: the carefree smile, the entrancing eyes, the breezy movements of a dancer. And I don't sleep at all. Not because I can't, but because I don't want to.

Sleep would mean letting go of that vision.

MONDAY, JUNE 16

Realizations 6: 5–9

5. And then he found a quiet place, where there was very little noise; almost silent, with no noise at all. 6. Except for the idling buses just outside the wide-open windows. And the screaming students released from school for the day. And the jackhammer from the construction site across the street. And the airplane circling overhead, preparing to land. 7. Thus did he realize that it wasn't actually silent. Not technically, anyway. But yet did it seem so to him. 8. And in that moment he realized the silence was not around him, but inside him. 9. And he thought, "Whoa. That's actually pretty cool."

5:30 A.M.
Tailfin Motel, Route 66, Arizona

Matt doesn't settle for knocking on my door; he hammers it repeatedly until I stagger out of bed and unlock it for him. Outside, the sun is just beginning to rise.

"Dude, you look like crap," he says.

"I only just went to sleep."

"Oh yeah?" He raises an eyebrow. "You and Fran made up then, huh?"

"What? Oh, my—*no!*" I try to wash the thought away. "She's not even here. She left last night."

"And you *let her*?"

"What was I supposed to do?"

"Stop her!" He grips the doorframe. "She's sixteen, and we're in the middle of freakin' nowhere. What if something's happened to her?"

He's got me worried now. I pull on yesterday's clothes, and together we sprint along the corridor, but there's no sign of her. The foyer is empty too. We run outside and scan the parking lot; still no sign of her. We approach the Hummer and peer through the windows.

Fran is fast asleep, sprawled across the massive backseat.

"Guess I forgot to lock the car," Matt says.

I'm about to bang on the window when he stops me.

"Let her sleep, bro. Whatever's going on with you two, tiredness isn't going to help."

"So why did you wake *me* up? It's dawn."

Matt thinks about this. "Arizona's a beautiful state. I'd hate to miss out on seeing it. Besides, there's this great detour—"

"*Detour?* What do you mean, detour?"

Matt raises his hands. "It's sixty miles, I swear. It's so worth it."

I'm suspicious of the word *detour,* but as there's no signing today, I decide to let it slide. All the same, as I head back inside to grab my stuff, I can't help wondering how a sixty-mile detour could ever require a 5:30 a.m. start.

6:30 A.M.
Peach Springs, Arizona

After breakfast in Peach Springs we hit the road again. The yawning emptiness of Route 66 stretches before us. I'm ready to get to Flagstaff, check into the hotel, and finally get some sleep.

Instead we take a left turn.

"This isn't Route 66," I say.

"No," says Matt, "it isn't. This is the detour I told you about."

"I thought Route 66 *was* the detour."

"Nope. This is Highway 18. Beautiful, huh?"

Beautiful isn't the word I'd use. *Remote,* perhaps. Or *scary.* If this stretch of road had one of those Route 66 neon signs, it would probably say *Abandon hope, all ye who enter here.*

Alex interrupts my thoughts by cracking open her guidebook. "This sixty-mile stretch used to be a two-day journey in the nineteenth century," she reads aloud. "Microclimates mean that you can pass from warm sunshine to snow in the space of only a few miles." She pauses so we can share her excitement.

Okay, maybe *scary* isn't strong enough. This is the kind of road where you can break down and the search-and-rescue crews won't find your decomposed body for months.

It doesn't take me long to lose my bearings. The road hugs cedar-covered hills, and is engulfed by giant pines as it rises to higher elevations. Every now and then there's a break in the trees and I can see clear through to the mountains beyond.

We push on through the wilderness, slowing down occasionally to gawk at a few ruined buildings dotting the roadside. Just as the sameness is lulling me to sleep, the trees end, the road descends, and we're on a plain. It's like a first grader drew a map where the woods stop dead at the line where the plains start.

"That's incredible," says Fran, speaking for the first time all day. "It's like someone drew a line and said 'trees here, plains there.'"

It's as though she read my mind. But then, we used to think alike all the time; it was uncanny.

Fran turns to me. "It *is* amazing . . . isn't it?"

I don't know if she really means for me to answer that; she sure didn't care much for my opinion yesterday. When I shrug, she purses her lips and mimes opening a cell phone. "Hey, it's God," she says, holding out the imaginary phone. "He says if you can't appreciate this, then what's the point?"

"The point of *what*?"

She looks away and studies the landscape. "Of everything."

Alex hastily reopens her book. "This kind of open range is rare, and sometimes— Oh, it says that cattle have right-of-way, so slow down, Matt."

Matt grunts and lets the speed fall by about one mile per hour.

Out here it's impossible to get a sense of scale. The mountains on the horizon could be in another state, for all I know. The highway is still deserted. We haven't passed another car all day.

In yet another dramatic change of scenery, the road swings left and right and the plains give way to solid rock walls and plunging gorges. I check my seat belt as we pass within a few feet of a seemingly bottomless drop.

"It says here that the road eventually passes through sheer rock walls and deep gorges," says Alex, head still buried in her guidebook.

For a moment no one responds, but then Matt starts laughing, and I do too. Even Fran snorts. "Well, thank God for the guidebook," says Matt. "We'd be screwed without it."

Alex looks up suddenly and takes in her surroundings. When she makes the connection, she laughs. And then we're all laughing together, sharing in her silliness. It's such a relief. Maybe this detour is a good thing after all.

We slow down, and Matt announces that we've arrived. I can see he's right—we're in a parking lot, and ours isn't the only vehicle here, not by a long shot. But we're still in the middle of nowhere.

We all clamber out. "Uh, Matt, where are we?" I ask.

"The end of the road. The rest is on foot, so get your hiking shoes on."

"What hiking shoes?"

"Sneakers, then. Just not those," he says, pointing at my black leather shoes. "Oh, and I'd only bring a toothbrush and a change of clothes, if I were you. Just what you absolutely need for an overnight stay."

"A *what*?" Even Fran seems surprised.

"Just trust me, okay?" Matt sounds simultaneously amused and irritated.

"What about my book signing?"

"It's not until tomorrow. Hey, you'll thank me for this."

I'm pretty sure I will *not* be thanking him, but the alternative is to spend the rest of the day and night by myself in a parking lot in the desert. So I grab my whole backpack—no way I'll risk leaving it in the car—and accept when he offers me a liter of Gatorade, and then another. And another.

"Exactly how far is this place, Matt?" I ask.

"Not far. I just don't want you getting dehydrated."

I take a sip from one of the bottles. It's lemon-lime, my favorite. "Thanks."

"Hey, no worries." He claps a hand on my back. "Gotta look after my little bro, right? Anyway, I couldn't afford to get you airlifted out of here even if I wanted to."

9:40 A.M.
Havasupai Trail, Supai, Arizona

Fran is enjoying this, I can tell. The first mile of rapidly descending switchbacks was just a gentle warm-up for her, whereas I feel as though my knees have been used for batting practice. My quad muscles provide all the stability of Jell-O.

Now that the rocky path has leveled out somewhat, Fran's calves, toned from another year of cross-country running, flex with each step. She peers over her shoulder at frequent intervals to check that I'm not lagging too far behind—or maybe to check that I *am*. I'm not in the right shape to be doing this. My gym teacher says I have the physique of a long-distance runner, but he just means that I'm skinny as

72

a rail. You wouldn't be able to find my calves with a microscope. I have the cardiovascular fitness of an obese guinea pig. And I've already downed two liters of Gatorade just to stop from keeling over.

"Easy, bro," Matt shouts as I uncap my last bottle.

"I'm thirsty," I fire back. "Anyway, it can't be much farther, right?"

Matt opens his mouth, closes it again, and finally settles for an ambivalent shrug.

"Right, Matt?"

He stops walking and waits for me to catch up. "Think of all that our Lord endured," he says solemnly. "And you're getting worked up about a four-hour hike?"

"Hold on, did you just say *four hours*?"

Matt shakes his head in disgust. "And you call yourself a Christian." He chuckles as he rejoins the others just ahead of us.

"I can't hike for four hours, Matt. Not in this heat."

Alex and Fran turn away from the brewing argument.

"Then just sit by the path," he says. "There's a mule train that passes by every day."

"You mean, I could hitch a ride?"

"Sure." He scratches his chin. "Unless there's no room, in which case you'll be vulture fodder by lunchtime."

Now that he mentions it, there are large birds flying overhead, and odd sounds echoing around the rust-red canyon. The path ahead of me is clear, and I have company, but on my own I'd be dead meat before nightfall.

"Come on," says Fran. She pats my arm, and then stares at her hand as though it acted without her permission. "Remember the cat flap, Luke. What goes around comes around."

Is she really comparing this situation to a passage from *Hallelujah*? Especially *that* passage. Our house doesn't even have a cat flap, and I've never broken curfew. Is she suggesting I deserve this somehow?

"Thanks for the support," I say, and Fran half smiles, like she can't even detect the sarcasm in my voice.

11:50 A.M.
Havasupai Lodge, Supai, Arizona

I'm out of Gatorade and I've consumed two of Matt's energy bars by the time the village of Supai comes into view. It's nestled on a plain between canyon walls—beautiful, in a remote way.

I slump down on a step as Matt heads inside the lodge. A few minutes later he emerges and leads us to our rooms. We check out the first of the two neighboring rooms: no TV, no phone. We're in the land that time forgot.

I claim the bed nearest the door and flop down onto it.

Matt clears his throat. "We'll meet in the café in thirty minutes. Got to get our energy levels back."

Being horizontal feels really good. "I might be in the shower," I tell him.

"Don't bother. You'll be sweating like a pig again this afternoon."

"Why?" I look up, but Matt and Alex are leaving the room. "Why, Matt?"

There's no reply. Meanwhile, Fran makes herself comfortable on the other bed.

"We can't share a room again," I tell her. "It isn't right."

"I couldn't agree more," she says. "But it's your turn to sleep in the car tonight." She claps her hands. "Hey, if you set off now, you'll be there by nightfall."

She laughs as she tugs at her gray vest top. It's sleeveless, and her shoulders are tan. If I ignore her ink-blemished arms and focus on just her shoulders, I can almost picture the way she used to be.

"You know, I wrote a book too," she says. Her words

are softer than usual, less assured. "I was like you—got carried away with Andy's assignment. Wrote a hundred and eleven pages."

"I-I didn't know that."

She stares at the wall, lost in thought. "No one does. No one's ever read it."

"Why not?"

"By the time I finished it, I wasn't going to church anymore. I wanted to show it to Andy, to talk it through—I think that would've helped—but he was busy with *Hallelujah*."

"Which you don't like."

Now she makes eye contact. "What makes you say that?"

"Just a guess. Did you watch the Pastor Mike interview?"

"No. Why should I?"

I sit up and rummage through my bag in search of something to eat, but there's nothing there. I'm practically wasting away, thanks to Matthew Dorsey's sadistic weight loss program. "You hate this whole tour, don't you?"

"I never said that. But now you mention it, why *did* you want your book published?"

It's a simple question, but the answer is complicated: because Pastor Mike said I should; because I was flattered; because the publisher paid me. Only, I don't want to get into all that—not with Fran, anyway—so I go with one of Pastor Mike's famous catchphrases instead: "It's the job of every Christian to spread God's word."

"They're not God's words, Luke. They're yours." She runs a finger along the black lines on her left arm. "Did the Sunday school kids like it?"

"I don't know. I haven't had a chance to ask."

"But you wrote it for them."

Again, I wish it were that straightforward. At the time, I believed I was writing it for them. But really, *Hallelujah* was more like my spiritual journal: 150 pages of euphoria, followed by 100 pages of despondency. No one suspects that, because my editor rearranged every section. But *I* know. After editing the book for six months, I even begged him to take out the funny passages—told him they didn't feel real to me anymore—but he refused. He said they were dynamite, and people needed optimism, and no one would buy a 100-page book. So I stopped arguing. Now it feels like he put those words in my mouth. As for the Sunday school kids, I guess I haven't thought about them in weeks.

Fran is watching me.

"I've been really busy," I tell her.

"Yeah. I guess you have. And hey, your book's on course to be a best seller. But I can't stop worrying about who you've become."

"Hold on. *You're* worried about who *I've* become?"

She smiles. "See what I mean? A year ago you never would've said that. Or even thought it. Because a year ago you didn't feel superior to anyone."

"What makes you so sure I do now?"

She takes a swig of Gatorade and places it deliberately on the nightstand beside her. "Good point. Fifteen–love. Or maybe we'll just give you the game. Unless, you know . . . I'm right, and you do feel superior to me, even if you can't admit it."

She's quiet then, and the chilly silence gives me all the time I need to work out that she's absolutely right.

3:20 P.M.
Havasu Falls, Supai, Arizona

It's all Alex's fault.

Matt, I can ignore. He's the one who dragged me from my room and onto yet another dusty path, pushing me like one of those hyperactive personal trainers on TV infomercials. I can pretty much tune him out. But Alex . . .

"Come on, Luke," she says, my personal preppy cheerleader with the perfect perky ponytail. "We're almost there."

"Almost where?" I say, more breath than words.

"Wherever Matt is taking us."

She is Matt's messenger—just a go-between—but I can't be angry with her, and she knows it. Ahead of us, Matt bounds forward, eyes shifting from left to right in search of something I can't see.

And then, finally, he stops.

And points.

Alex runs to join him. She gazes at the scene before us, entranced.

I can see why too. It's a vision from a movie: A waterfall cascades down a sheer cliff face, into a circular lake so blue I'd swear I can see the bottom. Actually, it's not blue—it's turquoise. And as the spray from the waterfall catches the afternoon sun and sparkles like jewels, I know it's the most astonishing place I've ever been.

Alex doesn't speak, but she and Fran lean against each other, heads touching. Fran is smiling too; not a big smile, but enough that I know she's content.

Whatever else has been said today, we're at peace right now, all four of us. And in spite of the throbbing in my legs, I'm glad I got to see this.

"I could read from the guidebook," says Alex.

"Or you could just stay absolutely still and quiet," replies Fran.

Alex nods. "Yeah. Maybe I'll do that."

"And in that moment he realized the silence was not around him, but inside him," says Matt, reciting a line from *Hallelujah*. "And he thought, 'Whoa. That's actually pretty cool.'"

I glance at Matt, but he won't meet my eyes. I can't believe he just quoted me perfectly.

"What on earth are you talking about?" asks Alex.

"Just being reflective," he says.

I can't tell how far down the lake is, but it has to be the clearest water I've ever seen. Compared to the Mississippi back home in St. Louis, it's glassy. Then again, everything looks clean compared to the Mississippi.

"I have to go down," says Fran.

"To the water?" I ask. "How? There's no path."

"Sure there is." She and Alex pull apart, and Fran walks on a little way. Then she points. "See, there's a path right here. Easy."

I'm sure we're not supposed to go down there,

but Matt and Alex have decided this is a kissing moment, and I'm not hanging around for that. So I traipse along behind Fran, feet slipping, hands grasping for support. In the back of my mind is the nagging thought that I'm supposed to be on a *book tour,* for Pete's sake. But when I glance up and take in the scene before me, I forget about everything but the pure and awesome beauty of the sky and rocks and water.

Fran sprints the final yards and kneels beside the lake, cupping water and letting it slip through her fingers. "I've never seen anything like this," she says.

Neither have I. The world has been stilled here. The waterfall sounds like a parent hushing a child, and the other sounds merge together harmoniously. The sun feels reassuringly warm against my back.

I close my eyes and lose track of time. For weeks now, I've been preparing for the release of *Hallelujah,* and the TV interview with Pastor Mike, and the tour. My entire life has revolved around this book. Maybe it is the job of every Christian to spread God's word—to reach out to others—but no one warned me how exhausting it would be; or how it would feel to lose faith in my own words. I haven't slept well, eaten well, even *thought* well. I haven't felt inspired.

But now, as I stand here in my own paradise, I feel

the tension melting away. Even Fran is silent. I open my eyes to see what she's doing.

She's sitting on a rock, removing her shoes and socks.

"What are you doing?" I ask drowsily.

"I'm going to swim behind the falls."

Behind her, the sound of the movie-set waterfall seems to shift: no longer a lullaby, but a roar of warning. It pulls me back to the present. "That's crazy."

"No, it's not. Alex said it's possible."

"But look at it." Fran removes her shorts; it's hard for me to concentrate. "The falls are . . ."

"Are what?"

"Are . . ." I can see her underwear. "Are . . ." Her underwear is green. "Are . . . *dangerous*," I say so loudly that her eyes flick up.

"Not if you don't come with me, they aren't. And I don't expect you to."

"It's irresponsible to swim alone."

"You're not responsible for me, Luke. Anyway, if I don't make it back, just think of the extra room you'll have on the backseat. This could be a win-win for you."

I hate that she said that. It's cruel. So is undressing in front of me. I don't know where to look anymore. I was so relaxed, and now she's messed everything up.

"What happened to you, Fran?" I ask.

She folds her slender arms into her body, hiding the black marks on her forearms. "Things changed. That's what happened."

"But you used to believe. Now you talk about drowning like it's a joke. It's like your faith got tested and you just gave up."

"At least I've faced that test. If I challenge you, you ignore me."

"You're not challenging me, Fran. You're just arguing for the sake of it."

"Let me get this straight: If you disagree with me, we're debating. If I disagree with you, I'm playing devil's advocate. How is that fair?"

"If you like debate so much, why did you leave the team?"

She slaps the water. "I didn't leave. I was kicked off."

"You left. You had a choice of sticking to the dress code or leaving. You made your choice."

"There wasn't a dress code until I showed up!"

She's raising her voice, so I lower mine. "They have standards."

"Yes, they do," she says, mimicking my tone. "Their standards of debate are inversely proportional to their dress code. How'd it go without me this year?"

The words may be quiet, but her message is fierce

and self-righteous. It makes me want to scream. "If you thought they were wrong, why didn't you fight them?"

"Why should I have to?"

"Oh, right, I get it. It's not your fault. Nothing's your fault."

"Don't be so naive," she snaps.

"Personal attack."

"Screw you!"

"Vulgarity. Automatic disqualification."

She snorts. "If you'd seen what I've seen this year, you'd have a crisis of faith too. I kept waiting for something to change . . . or some*one*. I just needed a sign, that's all. Is that really too much to ask?"

I shrug. "Blessed are those who have not seen, yet still believe."

"Like you used to believe in me?" she asks quietly.

Fran is half-naked, and it's a challenge for me not to look away in shame. If this is her sport, I'm unprepared to play. "Yes," I say finally. "Just like that."

"But not anymore, huh?"

I don't want to lie, so I say nothing at all.

Fran takes off her vest and steps to the water's edge. I can see her bra.

Then she turns around.

Instinctively I look away. But as the seconds tick by in silence, my eyes gravitate back to her. Frances

Embree stands before me, a figure from my dreams with a body to give me nightmares. Her purple hair touches her shoulders, metal earrings catching the sun, too many to count. But more horrifying than any of that, I see the same black lines that are etched into her forearms are scarring her stomach too.

We're alone in our very own Eden, and all I want to do is cry. In the face of all this perfection, Fran has turned against herself, hell-bent on destruction. It's a path I can't follow.

I turn and leave. Behind me I hear the gentlest of splashes as she slides into the crystal-clear water, uninhibited, unashamed.

I wonder if I really ever knew her at all.

6:10 P.M.
Havasupai Lodge, Supai, Arizona

The water trickles down my body, rust-colored rivulets that puddle at my feet. I'm halfway through washing my hair when I hear someone coughing next to me. I practically tear down the shower curtain in surprise, and the shampoo runs across my face. "Who is it?"

"It's me," says Matt. "What other guys join you in the bathroom?"

"But I'm showering."

"No kidding."

I try to rinse the shampoo from my hair and face, but it spills into my mouth and nostrils and my eyes. I start whimpering.

"Man up, bro. It's only soap."

I swipe at my face, slapping at anything that feels soapy or filmy. It doesn't help at all.

Matt doesn't speak until the whole embarrassing performance is over and I'm collapsed on the floor. "Luke, the Bible gives us several examples of true suffering. Not to sound judgmental or anything, but I'd have say that on a scale of one to biblical, soap in the eyes barely even counts."

He tosses me a towel. I wrap it around my waist and join him in front of the mirror. Side by side, we're like before-and-after photos for a bodybuilding program, with me on the wrong side of the illustration. My eyes are red and puffy too.

"Why are you here?" I ask. "Shouldn't you be making out with Alex or something?"

"Actually, yes. But I promised Mom you'd have clean clothes for all your events, so I'm hand-washing your shirts from the weekend."

I look at the sink—sure enough, he's cleaning my

white shirts. I can't believe it. It makes me especially glad I decided to bring my whole backpack. "Thanks, Matt. That's really . . . wow. Can I have a word with Mom and Dad too?"

"Uh-uh. Phone's recharging. But they send their love. Told me to make sure you're not late again."

"Oh. What about Colin? Has he called?"

"No. Were you expecting a call?"

"I guess not."

Matt rinses the first shirt and wrings it out. "Look, I know you probably don't want to talk about this, but I really need you to try harder with Fran."

All the goodwill between us evaporates immediately. "But she shouldn't be here!"

"But she *is* here. And I've read enough of *Hallelujah* to know that the boy in that book—the boy I saw on *The Pastor Mike Show*—would do everything possible to make her experience positive. Right?"

To be honest, I don't remember much of the Pastor Mike interview. I recall hanging out in the greenroom, but as soon as I walked onto the set, everything was overwhelming. My voice found some kind of zone where words came out, but my mind was flitting around like a moth distracted by the countless studio lights. But I see what Matt's getting at: The boy in *Hallelujah* wouldn't stop trying to make a difference, no matter how exhausting that might be.

"Please, Luke," he says, filling the silence. "Underneath it all, she's still Fran."

"Okay," I say, because really—what other answer can I give? "In return, can you promise me there'll be no more detours like this?"

Matt rinses and wrings out my other shirt, and hangs both of them up to dry. "Sure. I can absolutely promise you there won't be any more detours like *this*," he says, putting so much emphasis on the last word that I almost wish I hadn't asked. "Hey, this is going to be a trip to remember. You might want to consider enjoying it."

As Matt ambles off, I wonder if maybe he's right for once. Maybe the worst is behind me. Maybe all I need is a good night's sleep.

At least that's something I can control.

11:20 P.M.
Havasupai Lodge, Supai, Arizona

I'm fast asleep when the banging starts. I stumble out of bed, open the door, and guard my eyes from the flashlight aimed directly at my face.

"She with you, man?"

I can't see the guy who's speaking, but I can smell him just fine. I can also make out Fran's stooped figure beside him, and nod before I think better of it.

"Better keep an eye on her then," he says. "She's wasted, man. Totally wasted."

He's clearly telling the truth. Fran will hit the ground the moment he lets go of her.

"Is she going to be sick?" I ask.

"Not sure. Depends, you know? She blew chunks all over the cactus over there, so she might be running on empty." He lifts her arm off his shoulder and lets it fall over mine. "Another thing: I'd try to get away early tomorrow, if I were you. People around here are pissed, man. Dudes love that cactus like a brother."

The guy shakes his head and walks away, and it's just me and Fran and the stench of barf-breath hanging between us.

"Bathroom," mutters Fran.

I drag her inside, shut the door, and direct her to the toilet. As I turn the light on, she wraps her arms around the bowl and liberates some more of her half-digested dinner. She wipes her mouth with a piece of toilet paper and leans back as she flushes it away.

"Sorry," she says. "I drank too much."

I don't know what to say. It's a confession, not a question.

"I said I'm sorry."

"Why did you do it?"

"Don't know. I didn't mean to get drunk. We were just having fun, you know?"

"This is fun?"

She shakes her head, and a few purple strands of hair slip over the seat and into the toilet bowl. She doesn't even notice.

"Remember Thanksgiving dinner?" she asks suddenly, words slurred. "When you picked up those metal tongs . . . pretended to defibrillate the turkey?" Her eyes are closed, but she's smiling.

I remember it, all right. Fran and me standing side by side, serving dinner at the downtown homeless shelter. She snorted so loud when I did it—made me do it again too, until everyone in line cried tears of laughter. How could I forget the way she looked at me in that moment?

That was our last Thanksgiving dinner together.

"Never mind," she says. "It was a long time ago."

"Yes, Fran, I remember! What's your point?"

"You used to laugh a lot. But not anymore."

"Am I supposed to be laughing now?"

Fran shakes her head; it causes a fresh round of vomiting, although there's nothing but bile left. She shudders.

I put a washcloth under the tap and wring it out.

When I place it against her forehead she sighs, a sound I recognize from a former life when we were friends, and sharing the same air with her was enough to complete me. Of course I used to laugh. Of course I seemed happier back then. How could I not?

Fran places her hand over mine and guides the washcloth back and forth across her forehead. Her black fingernail polish has chipped, and when she pulls the cloth away and looks up at me she can't even focus. Will she remember this in the morning?

"I should get back to bed," I say.

She reaches for my hand. Misses. "I'm sorry, Luke."

I turn to leave.

"I said I'm *sorry*."

I stop in the doorway, but I don't turn around. "No, you're not. Nobody's making you do this, Fran. Nobody wants to see you mess up your life. Especially not me."

Her breath catches. "Why do you hate me?"

"I don't hate you. I just don't know who you are anymore."

I glance at the mirror above the sink and see her reflection. She's on her knees, eyes closed. Tears stream down her cheeks.

"Do you need anything before I go to bed?" I ask.

She shakes her head. "I'm sorry."

I want to scream at her—*If you're so sorry, why are you doing this? Why don't you come to church anymore? Why did you give up debate? Why do you ignore me? What have you done with Fran?*—but instead I take a deep breath and swallow my questions. I mustn't judge her, no matter who she used to be. No one is perfect, certainly not me. Even though people seem to think I am.

I climb into bed and pull the covers tight around me. I want to go back to sleep, but I can still hear her—the rush of water and the clatter of objects falling to the floor.

Then she gasps.

I jump out of bed and run to the bathroom. Fran is leaning over a sink full of water, staring at her reflection in the mirror as she drives a needle through her left earlobe. Dripping blood forms pink clouds in the water. She's choking on her tears.

"Oh, my—" I struggle to catch my breath. "What have you done?"

"Go away."

"I'll get help."

I turn to leave, but she grabs my sleeve. There's blood on her fingers.

"This isn't happening," I say.

She releases my arm and extracts the needle from

her ear, wincing in pain. Blood falls freely, and she's having trouble staunching the flow with the cloth. The water in the sink is uniformly pink. Eventually she gives up on the washcloth and reaches for a hoop she has placed beside her. She lifts it to her ear, but she's nowhere near sober enough to find the hole.

She's not the only one crying now. "Why are you doing this?" I ask.

She prods around her ear, but she can't find the hole because of all the earrings around it. It's brutal, sickening. "Because I can. Because it's *my* body, and I can do whatever the hell I like with it."

"You need help."

"Then help me."

"Not my help. Professional help. A doctor or something."

She almost smiles at that, but the pain is too much. "Go away, Luke."

She tries to find the hole again, and the blood keeps flowing. The water has shifted from pink to red. I don't know how much blood it's safe to lose; I'm afraid we're going to find out.

I pick up her toiletries bag and rummage around. There's a tube of antiseptic ointment in there, a pack of Q-tips, even a bottle of rubbing alcohol. I unscrew the lid and pour some over a Q-tip. My hands are shaking so hard that most of the liquid ends up in the sink.

"You need this." I hold out the Q-tip, but Fran shakes her head. "It'll get infected," I say.

"So?"

"Don't you want it to heal?"

"No, I don't!"

She grits her teeth and this time she finds the hole. She drives in the hoop and screws it in place with a tiny metal ball. Her ear looks mangled.

I'm still holding the Q-tip. "Please, Fran. Please use this."

"Stop pretending you care."

"I do care."

She stares at my reflection in the mirror. "No, you don't," she says, but softly. Maybe seeing me cry is making her unsure. Finally she takes the Q-tip and attempts to clean her ear with it. Then she takes a cotton ball from her bag and douses that in rubbing alcohol. Repeats the process with shaking hands. Finally she looks at what she has done, and bursts into sobs that rack every part of her body.

I reach out, but I can't touch her. "You need help," I whisper.

"Screw you, Luke Dorsey! Screw you and screw your moralizing and screw you for pretending to give a crap about me."

This is one of those moments when Christians prove themselves. It's my chance to be a Good Samaritan. So I open my mouth, trusting that the right words will come just because I need them to. I can always conjure words. I wrote a book full of them.

But when our eyes meet in the mirror, blood is seeping from her ear again. I try to cast aside the image of the Fran I used to know—the one who bubbled with energy and undiluted joy—but I can't. If she were a stranger I could offer a kind word, or simply listen. But I've seen what she was, and I'm seeing what she is, and though it kills me to admit it, I don't believe she'll ever be the person she used to be.

So I say nothing. I just cast my eyes down, retreat to my bed, and pray for her: that she'll get help; that she'll find God again somewhere, somehow.

When I'm done I wait for a feeling of calm to overtake me—the way it used to—but instead there's just emptiness and a bunch of unanswered questions: Why won't God help Fran? Why did He allow this to happen in the first place? Why has my life felt wrong for the past year?

I should feel ashamed. I'm more popular than ever before. I can't get through a day without someone telling me I've inspired them. I know I ought to be happy. But somehow none of it matters. I don't want to inspire others; I want to feel inspired myself. I don't want other people to tell me that humor has a place in *Hallelujah*; I want to know what it feels like to laugh again.

I'm afraid I never will.

TUESDAY, JUNE 17

Mishaps 3: 4-9

4. *Four days did the boy suffer. And lo, on the fifth day, he stood his ground and asked the bully, "Why do you bully me, bully?" And the bully spake thus: "I don't know. It's what bullies do, right?"* 5. *And the boy heard these words, and was much troubled by them. "But would it not profiteth you to sow love, not hate?" he asked. "To salve, not hurt?"* 6. *And the bully thought about this. And thought about this. And thus did several seconds elapse.* 7. *And the boy knew that his words had been received by the bully's open heart, and said: "For disagreement is sadness. And accord is joy. Therefore let us help one another, that we may all be joyful."* 8. *And the bully bowed his head, and left the boy alone.* 9. *Until Monday.*

8:40 A.M.
Supai Café, Supai, Arizona

I down my cup of coffee in a single gulp, but it can't undo a sleepless night. Across the table, Matt and Alex look rejuvenated.

When Fran finally joins us, Alex stares at her, head tilted to the side. Then she shifts her attention to me. It's intense, that expression of hers.

"Come on, Fran," says Alex gently. "Let's go sort it out."

"Sort what out?" asks Matt.

"It's fine," says Fran.

Alex huffs. "It's not fine. It might already be infected, and I really don't want you losing your ear while you're in my care." She forces her lips together in a tight smile. "I can be selfish like that."

"Sort what out?" repeats Matt stubbornly.

Fran sighs, but follows when Alex heads to the restroom.

Matt waits until they're out of sight. "Okay, what the hell was that about?"

"Fran got drunk last night and stuck a needle through her ear."

aits for me to catch up, he bounces up and
is toes like he's afraid his legs will cool off
ety-degree heat.

I thought we'd lost you," he says. "You try-
d us?"

my backpack on the ground. "Why didn't
e we'd be hiking on this trip?"

came up."

— I'm not stupid, Matt! Colin told me he'd
day free, and I never asked him to do that.
lodge was completely full. Are you telling
t happened to grab the last two rooms?"

tes his cheek. "Okay. I was afraid you'd say
dn't mention it."

I've said no. This is a book tour, not a camp-
ou dork."

ly, it's a combination book tour and road
ou really just call me a dork?"

nd will you please stop bouncing on your
'cause you're wearing appropriate footwear
ean you have to rub it in."

ks at my feet and stops bouncing. "Oh," he

akers are wet. A strip of fabric trails from
shoe like a decorative ribbon. Tiny stones
creeping into the hole left behind, and I

Matt rests his elbows on the table. His head sinks into his hands. "What did you say to her?"

"Nothing! She showed up drunk in the middle of the night. She couldn't even walk." The words come out fast, like an alibi that even I'm not buying. Matt seems unimpressed. "Are you listening to me?"

"Yes, Luke, I'm listening."

"I never wanted to share a room with her in the first place."

"No, you didn't. It's just . . ." Matt's fist connects with his arm, and he inhales sharply. "I'm so freakin' stupid."

"Are you crazy?" I grab his hand before he can hit himself again. "What's going on?"

"I told Alex that Fran would be okay with you. I said you'd have time for her, listen to her. If the author of *Halle*-freakin'-*lujah* can't be there for her, then who the hell can, huh?"

"She was *drunk!* Anyway, why did you tell her that?"

"So she'd actually stop worrying for one millisec- ond!" Matt takes a deep breath. "They were insepa- rable, remember? Alex blames herself for what's hap- pened to Fran."

"Huh? What did she do?"

"It's not what she did; it's what she didn't do. Alex wasn't around last summer, so she didn't know how bad it had gotten. Fran wasn't telling her half of what was going on. Problem is, I don't think Alex really asked either. She'd finally gotten away from her parents, she was in L.A., and everything was great. It wasn't until she heard about the tattoos that she realized how messed up everything was."

I almost wish he were right—that Alex is responsible for Fran's transformation—but I don't believe it for a moment. "I can't look after her, Matt."

Matt rubs the red spot on his arm in slow circles. "I don't want you to look after her. I just want you to get along."

"Why?"

He looks directly at me. "For disagreement is sadness. And accord is joy." He waits a moment to let my own words sink in. "But I guess that depends on the situation, right? Or maybe who you're disagreeing with."

Fran and Alex reappear before I can reply. When Fran sits beside me I catch a glimpse of a Band-Aid wrapped around her left ear. Suddenly I have no appetite at all.

11:10 A.M.
The Havasupai trail, Sup

The hike back is torture. M
remember the final mile of
switchbacks that slope upv
ahead, holding hands. Righ
feeling pretty smart that c
school club she didn't ditch

Meanwhile, Matt boun
goat. He shuttles between t
out rock formations and t
crosses our path from time
eight miles with an ascent
much of a workout for hir

We're halfway back w
the others and me grows
them. I'm not really worri
ous, but it makes me thir
whether I'll make it on ti

Right on cue, Matt
shouts. His voice echoes
I don't answer. It's a st

As h
down o
in the r
"Dud
ing to a
I dro
you tell
"It ju
"Oh,
kept Mc
Plus, th
me we j
Matt
no, so I
"I wo
ing trip,
"Actu
trip. Did
"Yes.
toes? Ju
doesn't
He lo
says.
My sr
my right
have bee

know when I look at my foot later I'll find raw skin. Or maybe no skin at all.

"Sorry, bro. But you have to admit, the waterfall was beautiful."

"That's irrelevant."

"No, it's not. See, that's the thing about you—you're always so freakin' intense. This whole trip is stressing you out; I can see it is. But a hike like this forces you to slow down and look around. I watched you when you saw the falls, and I swear, it was the most relaxed you've been since I met you at the airport." He glances over his shoulder, but there's no one else around. "You'll remember that moment forever. And whenever you think of it, you'll imagine yourself back there. Which is a good thing, right?"

Maybe it is a good thing. But Matt knows me well enough to realize how uncomfortable I am with this detour. "You should've told me."

He still doesn't apologize—just picks up my backpack and walks away.

"I can carry my own stuff," I say.

"Yeah, you can. But you also want to get to your next book signing. And you won't look so good onstage if you can't stand up straight." He waits for me to join him. "Speaking of which, you should start lifting. You're like a stick insect."

I pretend to be annoyed that he's taking my bag, but I don't think he's fooled. He simply adjusts it on his shoulders and forges ahead as though it were empty.

3:15 P.M.
Route 66, west of Seligman, Arizona

We're back on Route 66 when Matt's cell phone breaks the silence with "We Will Rock You." He taps the steering wheel in time with the song's incessant clapping and stomping. We're halfway through the verse when he stops. "Don't worry," he says. "It'll go to voicemail."

The song continues as the desert moonscape grinds by.

"It might be Colin," I say. "I'll get it."

"Don't bother." He grabs the phone and the car veers to the side of the road, kicking up dust. "Yo, this is Matt."

I detect a New York accent on the other end, and I only know one person with that accent.

"Is it Colin?" I ask.

Matt waves off my question with a flap of his hand, which means that neither of his hands is on the steering wheel. I try to relax by picturing one of those posters showing a field of corn blowing gently in the breeze, with the word *stillness* underneath.

Matt contributes an occasional "yeah" or "sure" or "great," but otherwise the conversation is one-sided. I'd swear that Colin is in mid-sentence when Matt announces: "Absolutely. Good idea. We'll talk later."

He hangs up and slides the phone into his pocket.

"Did you just hang up on my publicist?" I ask.

"Huh? No!"

"What did he want?"

"Oh, just stuff. You know."

"No, I don't. Was he annoyed? He sounded kind of loud."

Matt doesn't speak for a while, but he takes his foot off the gas and for the first time we're going at the posted speed limit. "Okay, if you must know—did you tell him you slept badly on Saturday night?"

"Uh, I guess so."

Matt exhales loudly. "Bad move."

"Why?"

"Well, let's see—this little jaunt of yours is costing a fortune, and what do you do? You complain. It wouldn't hurt for you to be grateful, you know."

I hadn't thought of that. "Here, give me the phone. I'll call him and apologize."

"No way. Give him time to simmer down, bro. Apologies can wait."

There's an ominous silence after that. I'm actually grateful when Matt accelerates, and the engine drowns out my thoughts.

7:25 P.M.
The Good Samaritan Bookstore, Flagstaff, Arizona

I'm dressed in a white shirt and creased khaki pants. I'm sleep-deprived, and my freshly bandaged feet are killing me. My calves, butt, and even my shoulders ache. I want to lie down and sleep until the weekend.

Meanwhile, the questioner awaits my response, and the rest of the audience waits with him. He's small—maybe six years old—and I'm sure he should be in bed already. Instead he's here, tormenting me with curveball questions.

"What about Santa Claus?" he asks.

No one is going to interrupt this kid. He's cute, funny—in a *what-the-heck-is-he-talking-about?* kind of way—and he's on a roll. Plus he has a lisp that's reducing the grandmothers in the audience to tears.

I throw the question back at him to see if I can get

a clue where he's going with all this. "What about Santa?" I ask.

"You tell me."

"Well . . . Santa Claus isn't really part of Christian mythology. You know that, right?"

"He's not?" This is clearly news to the kid.

"No. Neither are Christmas trees. Those are a pagan tradition."

"Pagan?"

"Yes. It means not-Christian. Sort of."

"So . . . but . . . Santa puts presents by the Christmas tree. And God sent Santa, right?"

Deep breath. This could take a while. "Not exactly, no. Actually, the history of Santa Claus is kind of interesting. Earliest references link him to Saint Nicholas, but it wasn't until the late nineteenth century that he was depicted with red robes and a white beard, and then Coca-Cola used his image in advertising and . . ."

The kid is crying.

THE KID IS CRYING.

His mother wraps an arm around him. "Luke doesn't mean that Santa isn't real, love. Any more than God isn't real. Right, Luke?"

She peers up expectantly. She's given me an opportunity to redeem myself. Only, I'm kind of confused about what she just said.

"Um, I . . ." I look around for help, but don't get any. Reluctantly I lock eyes with the kid again. "Sure, your mom is right," I tell him, because honestly, I don't care. "Listen to her."

I figure that will be the end of it, but a lady in the middle of the room coughs ostentatiously. "So you're saying God doesn't exist?"

"Wha—? No, I . . . I . . ."

This is going horribly wrong. Smiles are still pasted on everyone's faces, but the eyes are narrowed. They're waiting for me to join the dots of this crazy dialogue, to tie everything up with a nice, neat bow. Surely I wouldn't be saying these insane things unless I had an endgame in mind. But there's no endgame. I just have a head clogged so full of thoughts that I can't get out of my own way.

Christmas trees and paganism! Santa Claus and Coca-Cola! There's a laundry list running through my mind, loud and invasive like a stock market ticker. I'm tempted to press my hands against my ears to block out the whole mad world.

"What did you do on your day off?" somebody calls out.

It's Teresa. And though she looks different again, I'm so pleased to see a friendly face that I could almost cry.

"I hiked to Havasu Falls," I mumble.

"Wow. That's a busy day off. Can you tell us about it?"

I can't be sure, but I get the feeling she understands what I'm going through—that I'm floundering in a strong current and need a lifeline.

"It's beautiful," I say. "There's a long hike through a valley with the reddest rock you'll ever see, and then another hike to the falls. It's as close to paradise as any place I've ever seen. Just thinking about it takes me back there, you know?"

The audience murmurs in agreement. I hope Matt doesn't find out what I just said, or I'll never hear the end of it.

"It's like the story in Realizations six, verses five to nine: the boy who finds silence inside himself," I continue. "I think I've brought some of that peacefulness with me. That's probably why I'm so slow and incoherent." There's a ripple of nervous laughter. "I don't know . . . maybe the point of all this is to show that I don't have all the answers. Actually, I don't think I have any answers at all. But I do know that when I stood looking at those falls last night, there was a moment when everything seemed to make perfect sense."

Some members of the audience applaud, and I breathe a little easier. I turn my attention back to the kid as his mother dabs his eyes with a handkerchief.

"So, hey, it's okay for you to believe in Santa Claus,"
I tell him. "If that's your *place* where things make
sense, then go with it. Believe me, I remember what
it was like, back when I was your age—you know,
until my brother ruined it by telling me Santa doesn't
exist."

"And that's a good time to break for signing," says
the bookstore owner, his words drowned out by the
wailing of a six-year-old boy.

8:30 P.M.
The never-ending signing line at the
Good Samaritan Bookstore, Flagstaff, Arizona

Everyone has questions, and for once I'm determined
to answer them—or try to, anyway. After the embar-
rassment of the event itself, it's the least I can do. I can't
promise complete sentences or intelligent responses,
but it doesn't matter; everyone's expectations have
been lowered so much that a grunt sends them off
happy. What would my debate coach say about this?

The line drags on and on, and after a while I realize
I'm waiting for one person in particular: Teresa—who

understands me, doesn't judge me, and saves me. I need to thank her.

She's at the end of the line, as always. I'm so pleased to see her that I even manage not to stare at her form-fitting pink T-shirt, and the braids all piled up on her head like a medieval warrior princess. The supersized crucifix is back again too.

"My two favorite lovebirds!" exclaims Fran, appearing as if from nowhere. I didn't even know she was here.

"Not now, Fran," I say, trying to stay calm.

"Ooh, that's an impressive piece of body armor you got there, Teresa." Fran points to the cross. "I've seen Kevlar vests that offer less protection."

Teresa pouts. "It's a sign of my allegiance to the Holy One."

"To the *Holy One,* huh? Well, I'm sure the Dalai Lama can see it all the way from Tibet."

"I don't mean the Dalai Lama. I mean God."

"Really? Then why don't you visit a church, instead of haunting Luke's events?"

"Why? Luke speaks more eloquently than any pastor I've heard. I sometimes wonder if God is speaking straight through him."

I open my mouth, but I can't think of a sensible thing to say to that.

Teresa studies me. "Don't say it hasn't occurred to you. Why do you think all these people come to see you?"

"Oh, whatever," groans Fran.

Teresa turns to face her. "Don't dismiss something just because it seems miraculous. The list of holy miracles is endless: walking on water; water into wine—"

"The list of delusional disciples is endless too, you know."

Teresa's mouth hangs open; a single tear glides down her cheek.

"Why are you crying?" asks Fran.

"Ask not why I cry. Only wonder what thou might do to salve me."

Fran snorts. "You've got to be kidding."

I tug at my shirt collar, feeling suddenly hot. "Teresa is quoting from *Hallelujah*."

"Yeah, I picked up on that, thanks," she says, like I'm the stupidest person in the world.

"Why are you being so obnoxious?" I whisper.

"Huh?" Fran's mouth remains caught in the shape of a smile, but it quickly disappears. "Oh, don't be an idiot, Luke." She stares at me with an expression I remember so well. It says: *My logic is irrefutable. Surrender now.* Only she hasn't offered any argument at all. "Okay, you know what? I'm outta here. You two are, quite literally, made for each other."

Fran turns on her heel and strides away, chunky black boots clomping on the hardwood floors so loudly they drown out conversations across the store.

Beside me, Teresa shivers. "Why does she say those awful things? Why would she want me to question my faith?"

"I know exactly what you mean."

"Everywhere I go, people like her . . ." She looks away.

"What?"

"Hurt me." She shakes her head. "I should go."

"Do you want to talk about it?"

"No, it's okay. I know you're busy."

"I can make time."

Teresa smiles at last. "Okay, then. I'd like that very much. More than you can imagine."

8:50 P.M.
A coffee shop, Flagstaff, Arizona

We cross the street to a coffee shop. I hold the door open for Teresa and her braids brush against me as she slides by. All eyes turn toward us, though I'm fairly certain no one is looking at me.

The store has large windows and muted lighting. Soft jazz plays in the background. It seems like the kind of place you'd bring a date, which sets my heart racing.

Before the door has closed behind us, a man at a nearby window table grabs his newspaper and leaves. Teresa hops onto his vacated stool and pats the one beside her. "Good timing," she says.

I nod, and my reflection nods back at me from the window. Teresa glances at the window and catches my eye, the corners of her mouth twisting toward a smile.

"Thank you," she says.

"For what?"

"For speaking to me. You're so popular and, well . . . I got the feeling you didn't have time for someone like me."

"Why?"

"Because I'm not popular." She pulls a tissue from her bag, so I guess more tears are on the way. "The kids at school make fun of me because of my beliefs. Even the way I look. They say I'm . . . *conservative*."

"Really? I mean, I don't think that hairstyle would count as conservative at my high school."

"Oh." She sinks a little on her stool.

"So, uh, you want coffee?"

"Yes, please. Whatever you're getting will be great."

The place is full and the line is long—at least five couples before me. When I glance over my shoulder, Teresa has left her seat, but her bag is still there. I hope I didn't offend her by saying that stuff about her hair.

By the time I've paid for the coffees, Teresa has returned. The braids, however, have gone, replaced by cascading waves of hair that extend past her shoulders.

"I didn't like that style either," she says, watching my face. "I just figured I needed a change."

"Why? You look amazing."

As soon as the words are out, I want to take them back; not because I didn't mean them—I just don't want her to think that I think this is a date.

Teresa lowers her eyes. "How much do I owe you?"

"Uh-uh. My treat."

"Thank you." She takes a sip. "I wish you went to my school. I'd give anything for someone to talk to. It's terrible to feel like an outsider all the time."

"You?"

"Yes, me. You know that passage you wrote about the bullies? Mishaps, three: verses four to nine?"

I nod.

"That's my life, Luke. Every day. The last week of school I did a book report on *Hallelujah,* and the teacher told me to pick something else. But I wouldn't, so she told me not to read it aloud 'cause everyone would laugh at me." Her face has a faraway look now, her voice barely a whisper. "But I read it anyway, and she was right: Everyone laughed, and cast stones at me—"

"They *stoned* you?"

She blinks. "Oh. Well, sort of. Metaphorically."

"In *school*?"

She bites her lip. "They were actually balled-up pieces of paper. But they felt like stones."

"And your teacher let them do it?"

"I know. Horrible, right? But now I'm wondering if it was all part of some grand design to bring us together. Just talking with you really helps me. I hate the thought that it might never happen again."

The air feels charged. I take a sip of coffee, just for something to do, but Teresa's eyes never leave me.

"Don't move," she says. She reaches across my right shoulder and around my neck and lifts the back of my shirt collar. "What's that?" she asks, craning her neck over my left shoulder.

"I-I don't know."

I tilt my head toward her and try to see what she's seeing. Her fingers brush the tiny hairs on the back of my neck, and I forget to breathe.

She's so close to me.

Her fingers brush my neck again.

I lock in on her almond eyes and sense her lips parting by the smallest degree. Her lips are full, accented with a delicate pink gloss. I can feel her breath, practically taste the scent of coffee and mint. I don't know whether this moment has anything to do with God, but I don't really care either. I just want her to kiss me.

Suddenly there's shouting outside: a nonstop stream of obscenities that carries through the plate-glass window. Teresa pulls back. On the opposite side of the street, beside the bookstore entrance, a man is dragging himself up from the sidewalk. Standing over him like a victorious boxer is Fran.

Fran?

I jump off my stool and run outside in time to see her disappear around the corner. I zip through traffic and try to help the guy to stand, but when he takes my hand he practically pulls me over with him.

"Don't bother," he says. "I'll do it myself."

Teresa appears beside us. "Are you okay? What happened?"

"That girl assaulted me," he says, pointing in the direction that Fran just ran. "I'm standing here minding my own business and the next thing I know she's kneed me in the nuts and grabbed my camera."

"She *what?*" cries Teresa.

"She took my camera," he repeats, slower this time.

I can't believe this is happening. If Fran's goal is to derail this book tour, I'd have to say she has just succeeded. I'm about to go after her when I see a camera sitting on top of a mailbox a few yards away.

"Is this yours?" I ask, bringing it to him.

"Yes!" He practically hugs it. I'm not surprised. It looks really expensive.

"Well, thank goodness," says Teresa. "Are you sure you're okay?"

"Yeah." He inspects every part of the camera, his face brightening. Then, just as suddenly, he sighs. "Oh, crap."

"What?"

"She took the memory card."

Teresa looks as furious as I feel. "You're kidding."

"I'll sort it out," I say. "I know who did this."

"It was that girl, wasn't it?" she says. "Your *friend* Fran."

"She's not my friend."

Teresa takes my hand. "Just let it go, Luke. Fran is really mixed up right now. She obviously wants you to follow her. Anyway, I'm sure this man has backups of his photos." She looks for confirmation, but the guy shakes his head. "You don't?"

"No. Why would I? In case I get *assaulted*?"

"I'll take care of it," I say.

"Uh-uh. He'll have other memory cards." Teresa

turns to him. "You have other cards, right?" She doesn't sound as sympathetic anymore.

The guy's jawline bulges. "Yes, I have other memory cards, thank you," he says.

"Well, thank goodness. Come on, Luke. Our coffee's getting cold."

She's halfway across the street when she notices I'm not following. She glides back. "What's the matter?"

"Fran just attacked this guy. We can't stand idly by. We have a duty as Christians."

"But he seems fine now."

"Sure, but what if she'd hurt him badly?"

The guy grunts. "She kneed me in the nuts, man. Trust me, it was plenty painful—"

"We'll sort it out later," says Teresa. "I promise."

She holds out her hand. It still looks like porcelain, even under the amber streetlight. I'm about to take it when I see the guy grimacing.

"We can't make him wait, Teresa. I have to get that memory card back."

I turn to leave, but she grips my arm. "Please don't go. Don't you see? She's only doing this to make you come after her. She's jealous because you chose to talk to me. You can't let her win."

I know that Teresa's right, but when I see the guy again, eyes narrowed in pain, I realize that Fran has already won. Someone needs to hold her accountable, and while I wish it didn't have to be me, it's clear that no one else is going to do it.

"Come on," I tell them both. "Let's straighten this out once and for all."

I leave quickly—long, determined strides that psych me up for what I have to say to Fran. She's made it personal now, and I mustn't back down.

It's only a couple hundred yards to our hotel. By the time I get there, I'm alone.

9:35 P.M.
Crater Hotel, Flagstaff, Arizona

Fran is sitting on the bed, staring at Alex's laptop computer, a couple of pillows propped up behind her. In spite of all the vomiting last night, she's holding another miniature bottle. It's almost empty.

"I don't know what to say to you, Fran."

She doesn't look up. "That's all right. I'll wait."

"This isn't funny."

"No, it's not." She presses a couple of keys. "My bag strap got frayed when I hit that guy. I've had it since fifth grade. It's an antique, and he ruined it."

"You need to go back and apologize."

Now she looks up. "You're kidding."

"What you did was terrible. You're lucky he didn't call the police."

She furrows her brows. "Hmm. I wonder why not."

"Maybe because he didn't want you to get in trouble."

"Yeah, I'm sure that's it. You've got to check out these photos, by the way."

"No. They're not mine. Or yours. You need to return that memory card right now."

She shakes her head. "Or not."

"I'm warning you, Fran—"

"No, Luke, I'm warning *you*. Come and look at these *now*. Because if you don't, I swear . . . I might just do what you say."

"That'd be nice for a change."

"Screw you!" She ejects the memory card and grasps it between her fingers so tightly they make a fist. "You think you're so wise, don't you? Well, fine. You deserve what's coming."

She places the laptop on the bed and heads straight out of the room. I brace for the sound of the door slamming behind her, but it doesn't come. Instead she stands in the hallway, completely still, eyes closed.

"I can't do it," she whispers. "Even though I really want to hurt you right now . . . I just can't."

"Can't *what?*"

She turns around. The memory card rests in her upturned palm. "Look at the photos, Luke. Don't argue with me. Don't fight. For once, just do it. *Please.*"

Something in her voice breaks me down, tells me I have no choice. It's a tone I haven't heard since the tour began; a tone I haven't heard in a year. I take the card and slide it into the laptop.

A grid of photos is arrayed on the screen. When I lean in for a closer look I see they're all the same: me and Teresa in the coffee shop, my face crystal clear even in the soft lighting. The first dozen or so are of us chatting, but then she's leaning toward me, reaching around me, her hair draped across my face. Our lips don't just seem close; they seem locked together, as though we're sharing an intimate kiss. Judging by these photos, I'm the star of a steamy seduction scene.

I bring a finger to my lips, wondering if we actually kissed and I just forgot about it somehow. "I don't get it," I say.

"I can see that." Fran sighs. "The photographer was paparazzi, Luke."

"I didn't know Teresa was famous."

"She's not. It's *you* he was shooting."

It takes a while for those words to seep in. "But I'm not famous either."

Fran runs a hand through her hair, purple streaks heightened by the light from her bedside lamp. "You appeared on nationally syndicated TV. Journalists show up to your signings. That's pretty much the definition of famous."

"But how did he know we were at the coffee shop? Do you think he followed us?"

She groans. "Wake up, Luke. He works with Teresa. She's paparazzi too."

"No. She can't be. She's just—"

"What? A disciple? Auditioning to be the fifth member of the *Hallelujah* posse? Come on! She's been at every event. She asks you out. She keeps changing her appearance. The way I see it, she's either a stalker or paparazzi. Either way, she's bad news."

I don't know what to say. Maybe I'm naive, but having lost faith in everything else, I wanted to believe in someone again. "I just thought . . ."

Fran sits on the other bed, elbows on her knees, chin resting in her hands. "Luke, before this book you were just another geeky high school kid. Did you really think girls like her would throw themselves at you just because you wrote . . ." Her voice trails off and she reddens. "I'm sorry. I didn't mean that. The last bit, anyway." She smiles. "But you are a geek, you know."

"Takes one to know one."

She laughs. Actually *laughs*. "That's the lamest comeback I've ever heard."

"Well, yeah. I'm not good at the whole retaliation thing."

"No, you're not. At least, you didn't used to be. It was one of things I liked so much about you." She reaches over and closes the laptop. "So . . . something you want to say to me?"

"Like what?"

She purses her lips. "Come on, Luke. You can do this."

"Do what?"

"Say thank you!" She waits. "Or maybe you can't. Such easy words, but it'd mean accepting you were wrong about something . . . about someone."

There's silence now, and the air feels heavy. Fran fingers the Band-Aid on her left ear.

"Thought so," she says, turning away from me.

I head to the bathroom. It's late, I'm tired, and I need to brush my teeth, to get rid of the sticky coffee taste in my mouth. It reminds me of Teresa as we sat side by side, knees bumping, her breath hot against my cheek. Which reminds me of Fran beside me at the Thanksgiving dinner, laughing together, her bright eyes and easy smile.

I step back into the room. "I'm sorry," I say, just loud enough that she hears me as she turns off her lamp. "You were right. Absolutely right. Thank you."

Fran doesn't say a word, but in the darkness I hear her breath catch.

WEDNESDAY, JUNE 18

Lessons 12: 17–21

17. For there was evil in that town. 18. And the boy saw the evil and spake thus: "There is evil in this town." 19. And the people heard him and said, "This we know, but what can we do?" 20. Yet, the boy was undeterred. "We will keep our distance from the evil, and call it by its proper name, that others may be inspired by our example and henceforth follow our lead." 21. And the people kept their distance, and called the evil "evil," until finally the evil retreated, and almost ceased to exist at all.

9:20 A.M.
Somewhere east of Flagstaff, Arizona

We hit the road and leave the snow-capped San Francisco Peaks behind us, heading east on I-40. The speed limit is seventy-five miles per hour, so Matt keeps us going at a steady eighty. Going at or below the limit is simply not in his DNA.

We've been driving through the orange-brown landscape for about half an hour when I see a sign for the Meteor Crater exit. I've actually heard of it—the best-preserved meteor crater in the world. Alex spots the sign as well and flips through her guidebook until she finds the entry.

"The Meteor Crater," she recites, "was formed approximately fifty thousand years ago. The meteor collision displaced up to four hundred million tons of rock, forming a crater four thousand one hundred feet across, and five hundred and seventy feet deep."

The exit is only a couple hundred yards away. I'm really looking forward to seeing this.

"Today, visitors can tour the rim, study interactive exhibits, and watch a movie re-creating the meteor's path through the earth's atmosphere." Alex pauses as the exit signs approaches . . .

And disappears behind us.

"Uh, Matt, I think you just missed the exit," I say.

"Oh, come on," he groans. "It's got a movie and interactive displays. There's probably some dude in a meteorite outfit selling hot dogs. Anyway, you should be focused on your interview."

"What interview?"

Matt turns to Alex. "Didn't you tell him?"

"Why would *I* tell him? Colin left the message on *your* phone," she says.

"Tell me what?" I'm practically shouting.

Matt sighs. "You have an interview on the Christian Radio Network at noon."

"Where's the station?"

"You'll do it by phone. They'll call my cell just before noon."

"And you were planning to tell me about this when?"

"Chill out. I only got the message this morning." He pulls out his cell phone and studies the screen. The Hummer drifts into the neighboring lane. "Just be grateful I charged up before we left."

"Are you sure we'll get reception?"

"Shoot. I hadn't thought about that." He slides the phone into his shorts pocket. "Hey, we've still got two hours to find somewhere with reception," he says brightly.

As I stare at the wilderness stretching before us, I wonder if we'll see another town all day.

11:50 A.M.
Continental Divide, New Mexico

Matt insists we'll see signs for a restaurant or gas station soon—somewhere populated, where cell phone reception and a comfortable chair come standard. But Matt is wrong. He's been wrong for several miles now, and my interview starts in ten minutes. I'd pray, only I'm coming to the conclusion that Matt acts as a spiritual black hole, extinguishing positive energy. The more I pray, the more powerful he seems to become.

At 11:52 he pulls off at Exit 47, and stops the car by a sign announcing that we've reached the Continental Divide, elevation 7,245 feet. The air feels thin, the sun especially strong.

"Here you are," says Matt, handing me the phone. "And look at that: one whole bar!"

I step away and wait for the call. At 11:56 the phone starts playing "We Will Rock You." I flip it open.

"Hello. This is Luke."

"It is?" I can't decide whether the guy sounds delighted or surprised. "Luke Dorsey?"

"Yes."

"Coooooool." The word takes several seconds. "Okay, well, I'm Orkle's, uh . . . producer. Orkle's wrapping up the previous segment, but after a commercial break he'll get right back to you, 'kay?"

"Um, sure."

"Great. Now don't hang up or anything, Luke, 'kay? That'd really screw with his head, and Orkle's an ornery sonofabitch, if you know what I'm saying."

"Uh—"

"Yeah. So you just hold tight."

Twenty yards away Fran is fiddling with the car stereo. Matt and Alex appear to have left for some alone time. Fran leans out the driver's door and shouts, "What's the station ID?"

I relay the question, but the producer isn't answering. Then there's a faint beeping sound: call waiting, I think. No way I'm taking that. I wouldn't even know how.

The producer rejoins me. "You still there, Luke?"

"Uh-huh. What's the station ID, by the way?"

"Oh. Um . . . ninety-nine-point-three." Either the reception is terrible, or his voice is flaking out. "You're still here!" he adds, like he can't quite believe it.

"Indeed, still here." I shout out the station ID to Fran, who turns her attention to the stereo.

"Okay, I'm passing you to Orkle on three, two, one—"

I'm deafened by the whine of electric guitar. Then Orkle takes over, his hyperactive spiel dotted with scatological sound effects. It's the opposite of the Continental Divide's soundtrack: the gentle hum of the interstate, the ever-present wind, and the occasional shriek of a hawk gliding overhead.

"Iiiiiiiiiit's Orkle!" he screams, to a background of clapping that morphs into farting. "And today I have a special guest. A *very* special guest. Welcome to the show, Luke Dorsey."

"Hi," I say, still trying to purge the memory of the farting.

"So, you and the legendary Pastor Mike, eh?" says Orkle, sounding eerily similar to his producer. "Kind of a big fish, isn't he."

"Yeah, he's a great guy."

"Sure is. I read a poll where Midwesterners like your good self were asked which of four adjectives best described him, and sixty-two percent chose *angelic*. What do you think of that?"

"*Angelic?* Really? What were the other adjectives?"

"Damned if I know, Luke, but that's hardly relevant, is it?"

"Well, I—"

"So where do you stand?" he asks, as if I haven't spoken. "Is Pastor Mike a direct descendant of the deity?"

"Um, I suppose so . . . because we're all children of God."

"Indeed, we're all descended from the big guy in the sky. Which leads me to the night of the naughty nookie."

"The *what*?"

"Sex, Luke. Rumpy-pumpy. Amorous apples. The old heave-ho, the—"

"Oh!"

"Yeah. So are you a spokesman for procrastinating procreators?"

"Sorry?"

"Celibacy, Luke." He sighs like a teacher forced to explain the same simple question over and over. "Do you advocate the monastic method for today's motivated minors?"

"Um, if you mean abstinence, then, uh . . ." Actually, I really don't care what other kids do, but I'm also fairly certain that the author of *Hallelujah* ought to care, or at least have an answer. And I think I know what that answer should be. "Yes."

"But research shows that preaching the awful absence of amorous application is ultimately useless."

"Are we still talking about abstinence?"

"Yeah."

I'm already exhausted and we've only been speaking for a minute. "Well, the weakness of today's youth should not be taken as an implicit failure of the principle itself," I say, a line that I may have stolen from someone else, but sounds pretty airtight.

"But it's not just *today's* youth. And if the principle, as you put it, is perennially pointless, then perhaps it's the principle that requires revision."

"Have you got a better idea?" I try to sound calm—we're on familiar debate territory here, after all—but actually, I'm annoyed. I wish we could change topics.

"Sure I do. Follow Uncle Orkle. Practice safe sex. Fewer unwanted pregnancies, fewer STDs—"

"In your opinion."

"No, Luke. In the opinion of numerous professional associations in the fields of medicine, health, psychology . . . You want me to go on?"

"Hey, if that's your bandwagon, then so be it. I'll stick to abstinence."

"Judging by your author photo, that shouldn't be too difficult." He adds another sound effect that I can't place. "But don't you have a social duty to educate and enlighten? Or at least to discuss this dangerously detailed data."

"What data?"

For a beat, the line is silent, and I wonder if we've finally lost our connection. But then he's back. "Let me get this straight. The St. Louis high school debate champion holds an immutable position on teen sex without being aware of most of the evidence."

It's not an immutable position; it's just *a* position— one he's forced me to take because he refuses to talk about anything else. It's pretty clear he's not on Team Luke. Unfortunately, with every passing second it becomes more obvious that he's got me cornered.

"Okay," he says finally. "So no nookie for you. But what about the beckoning of the boss below? I know I'd suffer if I suppressed the mojo man for more than a day or two."

"Are you really talking about what I think you're talking about?"

"Oh, come on. Surely you choke the bishop every now and then?"

"Which bishop?"

"Um, yours, Luke. Unless you choke someone else's. Which is totally cool, by the way. Uncle Orkle's an open-minded dude."

I wish I knew how to end this interview. "I-I haven't choked anyone."

"Riiiiiiight," says Orkle, and for the first time, he seems lost for words. "I gotta tell you, Luke, I've heard that Midwesterners are a mellow breed, but the fact that you've survived high school so far is a testament to that." Another sound effect: someone being punched in the gut, I think. "And with that, I'll let you go. Good luck, Luke, with the tour and in life. You're gonna need it."

The line goes dead. I return to the car in a daze. I can replay the interview at will, but can't begin to explain why Orkle would be so fascinated by my views on sex. Or why every comment had to be accompanied by a sound effect. Unless . . .

Fran is leaning against the Hummer. She looks as anxious as I feel.

"Did you hear that?" I ask.

"Some of it. Once I found the *real* station ID, instead of the one they gave you."

My heart is pounding. "You don't suppose that wasn't actually the Christian Radio Network, do you?"

Fran busies herself wiping dust off the wing mirror. "Well, something wasn't right, that's for sure."

"I *knew* it! Those questions were so weird."

"Then why didn't you hang up?"

"I couldn't. It was an interview."

"So?"

I guess she has a point. "Pastor Mike says it's our Christian duty—"

"To spread God's word and engage with everyone. Yeah, I know. But that doesn't mean making yourself an easy target for paparazzi and pranksters, right?"

"I didn't know he was a prankster. I just try to be nice to everyone, that's all—no matter how much I disagree with them."

Fran winces, but recovers with a deep breath. "You're not going to be able to make everyone like you, Luke."

"It's not about being liked."

"Isn't it?" She stops cleaning the wing mirror. "I'm just saying, it's okay to let people down once in a while. Sometimes it's what you have to do if you want to stay you."

She turns away, and the conversation is over. That's when I realize she wasn't talking about me at all.

12:15 P.M.
Continental Divide, New Mexico

Before we set off, Matt checks his cell phone for messages. He turns the screen away from us all like he's afraid we're copying his answers on a quiz. I hear his sharp intake of breath clearly above the roar of the a/c.

"Eight?" he mutters. "What the—" He jams the

phone against his ear. Barely five seconds later he looks over his shoulder, eyes trained on me. "It's a voicemail from Colin. He wants to know why you're not doing the interview?"

"What?"

"Hold on." He returns his attention to the phone, and promptly turns white. "Luke, exactly who did you just speak to?"

"Whom."

"What?"

"It's *whom,* not *who.*"

Matt groans.

"He said his name was Orkle."

"Orkle. Right." Matt bites his lip. "And just who the heck is Orkle?"

"The interviewer."

"Wake up, Luke! How many interviewers on the Christian Radio Network have names like Orkle? What did you talk about?"

"Sex," says Fran. "Orkle asked him if he chokes the bishop."

Matt snorts. "Luke, my sources"—he waves his cell phone in the air—"suggest there's an above-average possibility that your interview with the Christian Radio Network just got—what's the word I'm looking for?—*hijacked.*"

I try to act surprised, but fail. Meanwhile, Matt listens to another message. Apparently, this one brings everything into focus for him.

"Yup, your interview got hijacked," he says, like everything is okay now that the mystery has been solved. "Orkle's a student at the University of New Mexico; broadcasts out of a frat house. He's quite notorious: hijacks interviews, then reproduces them as podcasts on his website. Makes his money from donations. Bummer for you, but you've got to admire his ingenuity."

"How did he get our number?"

"Wait a second." Matt listens to the rest of the message. "Wow, that's clever. His frat brothers apply for internships at media outlets, and send him the contact information of the interviewees. Seems like he has fans in the computer science department too, and they just do it the traditional way—hacking into the media outlet's computer systems." Matt furrows his brows. "You okay?"

I try to answer. Fail.

"Hey, it's not so bad," he says. "At least Colin hasn't had a chance to hear—"

The phone interrupts us with "We Will Rock You." I really hate that song.

Matt glances at the number. "Then again . . ."

"I need to speak to him, Matt. Explain what happened."

"Oh, no, you don't. Why don't you let poor Colin cool off? No need to add insult to injury."

"But he can't be mad at me. I didn't know!"

"I hear you, Luke. But I can also appreciate his predicament. Somehow, he has to explain to everyone why you didn't hang up on a prank call."

"I didn't know." It comes out sounding like a question.

"Oh, come on. Procrastinating procreators? Beckoning of the boss below?"

I just stare at my lap.

"I'm sorry," says Matt, not sounding sorry at all. "On the bright side, you're about to become a cult figure for frat boys everywhere, and that's a wealthy demographic."

A cult figure. Sure. I can already hear them laughing at me as they listen to the podcast on endless repeat.

7:00 P.M.
Converted Bookstore, Albuquerque, New Mexico

My spiel is getting better. Slicker. I cover the bullet points in five minutes, so I can get to the signing part of the evening a little quicker. Unfortunately, there are questions first, and this audience is *prepared*. I don't know if someone—a teacher, a pastor, a state senator—made *Hallelujah* required reading or something, but they know it inside-out. And while I'd always hoped that people would discuss *Hallelujah*—spreading God's word is the duty of every Christian, after all—I guess I hadn't imagined there'd be several hundred of them in a single room, talking about my book like it really matters. Why not talk about the Bible instead?

Before long, they start discussing amongst themselves, like a well-trained class of overachieving students. I sit back and wonder if I'll actually be required to speak again, or if I can just coast to the finish line, sign a couple hundred books, and phone Colin with the good news.

Every now and then I glance at Fran. It's weird to see her here—she definitely stands out—and even weirder that she's listening attentively. I wonder what she's thinking—whether she's impressed by the discussion, amazed by the turnout, or simply bored.

"I'm sorry to bring this up, Luke," says a girl, interrupting my thoughts, "but I've heard parts of your interview from this afternoon and . . . well, I think what that student did was evil."

Predictably, I turn bright red. Honestly, I change color quicker than a chameleon. "It wasn't ideal," I admit.

"No," she says. "It was *evil*. Do you understand?"

This girl is younger than me, with a robotic voice and unreadable expression. As I nod in agreement, she doesn't even blink.

"Good," she says. "As you taught us in Lessons twelve, verse twenty: Evil is real. It is a living, breathing, destructive force. We must call it by its proper name."

It's true—I did write something like that—but hearing her say it, I wonder what the heck I was thinking. I'm clearly not the only one who's freaked out either. Half the audience is gawking at the girl, and the other half seems to be checking for exit signs.

"Uh, I guess I'm pretty naive when it comes to this stuff," I say. "Maybe a little too trusting as well. Still," I add with fake enthusiasm, "I learned a valuable lesson today."

"Do not blame yourself, Luke. Do not be ashamed of having pride, and faith, and values. If the man who interviewed you had any of these, we wouldn't be having this conversation."

Conversation seems a bit of a stretch. This girl is monologuing. I'm starting to think she's older than she looks—maybe thirteen or fourteen—but the asymmetrical braids in her hair and young-girl clothes make it hard to be sure. In any case, she's like a snake charmer, commanding silence so her whispered words carry across the room, forcing us to listen and obey.

Sure enough, the audience's enthusiastic hum has died down to an awed quiet. When the girl unexpectedly stands and begins clapping, almost everyone else seems compelled to follow her lead, as though she's holding them at gunpoint. She has a future as a military dictator, this one.

Fran has morphed from attentive to uncomfortable.

When everyone is seated again, I wait for the next question, but all I get is blank expressions. No one knows what to say. Or perhaps no one dares to speak at all. None of the audience wants their sincerity doubted by this girl. To be found *spiritually lacking*.

Except Fran. She raises her bare arm, the only person brave enough to break the silence. I admire her for that, and nod encouragingly.

She produces a goofy grin, large eyes twinkling behind curtains of untamed purple hair. "So what exactly *is* choking the bishop, anyway?" she asks.

I can't believe she said that. Even more amazing, I don't much mind. Because I *recognize* this girl: She's the old Fran, the one with a wicked sense of humor. She wants to defuse the atmosphere. And to be honest, so do I.

"Well," I begin, daring to play along, "it's like this—"

"Don't answer that," interrupts alpha girl. Not content with her cameo role, she's staking her claim for top billing in tonight's entertainment.

"Luke's a big boy," says Fran. "He can decide for himself whether he wants to answer." Her voice is still teasing, but her expression has shifted: She's sporting her *I'm-about-to-win-the-debate* look.

"You seem to assume these *good* people want to hear your question answered," the girl replies.

"Is that how I should decide what to ask?"

"I think any Christian would take into account the sensibilities of those around her, yes. You disagree?"

Somehow Fran is still smiling. "Is that what you were doing when you decided to dominate the discussion?"

The girl's eyebrows twitch, but otherwise she remains perfectly still. I wonder if she has a pulse. "I sense that you are angry with me, and I want you to know I mean you no ill will. If I have offended anyone here with *my* comments, I beg forgiveness."

She looks around as if she's waiting for someone to confirm her worst fear. There are two hundred people who'd probably like to do just that; but no one will, and she knows it.

"Well," says Fran. "Your comments have offended *me*."

The girl looks Fran up and down. "And you are in a minority of one. Yet you seem to believe you have the right to ignore everyone else. Perhaps you'd prefer that we all left."

The bookstore owner steps forward with much hand-wringing. "Please don't make a scene," he begs Fran.

Fran laughs, but it's anxious now. "I'm not making a scene."

"Please don't," he tries again, as though she has pulled a knife.

"I'm not. *She* is."

The girl shakes her head slowly—a gesture adults reserve for petulant toddlers.

"Well, you are!" Fran insists. "Everyone was into this until you made a big deal about that radio interview. Now everyone's too scared to talk."

She's right, of course, but she's just accused two hundred people of being cowardly, and it's clear they don't appreciate it. What's more, they've decided now is the time to prove her wrong.

"Haven't you said enough?" asks the man sitting beside Fran.

"Exactly," echoes another.

Fran looks around for support, but finds none. She's made them all choose sides—small, idealistic girl or outspoken, tattooed, purple-haired teen—and is only now realizing she's an island. Aside from Fran, I might be the only person in the room who believes they all chose wrong.

"Any other questions?" I ask, my voice unsteady. "Anything?"

"Why do some people feel the need to sabotage your good work?" demands android girl, overriding the ten people whose hands are raised. "To insult you, hurt you . . ."

For the first time, she pauses—hardly an emotional gesture, but after her earlier weirdness, it's the equivalent of anyone else breaking down in racking sobs. And the audience waits for her, supports her.

She takes a deep breath. "First the radio interviewer, now . . . *this*." She raises an eyebrow in Fran's direction.

But Fran's not there. She's being escorted away by a pathetic-looking guy in round glasses and a checked shirt.

When Fran reaches the door she looks over her shoulder and smiles bravely, but I'm not fooled. I can see her tears from across the room.

8:05 P.M.
Converted Bookstore, Albuquerque, New Mexico

Every signing line seems longer than the last. I'd never considered that even the most basic motor skills—smiling, nodding—take a toll after several days. I hear people's names and I write them down, but the words mean nothing to me, and from my glazed expression I think they know it too.

A book slides in front of me, with a note asking me to inscribe it to "Teresa." When I look up, she's standing there, the gigantic cross bouncing off her chest.

"What are you doing here?" I ask.

She looks surprised. "I'm sorry?"

"You have some nerve, you know that?"

Teresa shares a shrug with the other people in line. "I think you must be mistaking me for someone else."

"I'm not signing your book, Teresa." I lower my voice. "That thing last night—the whole seduction routine—you probably thought it was really clever."

She gasps. "Did you just say . . . *seduction?*" Her voice is loud. There are tears too, summoned so quickly that I wonder if she practices.

The conversations around us stop. Teresa has drawn them into our personal soap opera; belatedly, it occurs to me that she's probably more experienced at this game than I am.

"I'm a sophomore in high school," she cries. "I've never even met you before. And . . ."—her voice rises until she's almost screaming—"and you accuse me of *seducing* you?"

There's complete silence now, nothing but my breathing and the imaginary sound of crickets.

"Is there a problem here?" the owner asks.

Teresa grips the table for support. "He accused me of . . ." She shakes her head. "I can't say it. It's too horrible."

"I don't understand," says the owner, staring at me wide-eyed, waiting for some sort of explanation.

"She's a reporter." The words dribble out of my mouth.

The owner stares at me like I must be crazy.

"I-I'm *sixteen,*" blubs Teresa, both hands wrapped around her cross.

I consider pleading my case, but the last thing I want to do is tell a couple hundred of my closest acquaintances that Fran—exiled villain of tonight's event—has shocking photos of Teresa and me on the verge of making out. Since I have no other line of defense, I settle for turning bright red instead. I may as well hang a *guilty* sign around my neck.

"I've never been so humiliated," says Teresa, filling the silence. She chokes on her tears. "If my daddy was here, he'd . . ."

On that note she flees for the door, the sounds of her wailing drifting through the store long after she should have exited. I figure she's probably standing just outside the room. She's a pro, I'll give her that.

Unfortunately, she's not the only one who leaves, much to the chagrin of the checked-shirted guy selling copies of *Hallelujah*. He implores them not to forget to buy a copy, but they're not forgetting anything—they have no interest in reading my book anymore.

To be honest, I don't blame them.

8:50 P.M.
Hotel Lobo, Albuquerque, New Mexico

Fran is on her bed, typing on Alex's laptop while listening to a complicated piece of classical music. She turns it down as I enter, but she doesn't look up.

"You're back early," she says.

It's true, but I haven't felt so tired since the tour began. "Don't ask."

"Okay. I won't." She turns the music back up.

I didn't mean it to come out like that, so I walk over and turn the volume down again. Our hands are practically touching on the laptop keyboard. "I'm sorry," I say.

"It's okay."

"No. I mean, I'm sorry for what happened at the event."

She takes a swig from her bottle. This one's brown. The sight and smell of it makes me pull back. I sit on the other bed, facing her.

"It wasn't your fault," she says.

"Still, I'm sorry. I should've . . ." Should've *what?* Offended two hundred people by supporting a girl whose favorite evening activity is getting wasted? Yes. Yes, I should have. "I'm just . . . sorry."

Fran doesn't take her eyes off the laptop. There are several photos onscreen, but none of them involve paparazzi, thank goodness.

"Teresa showed up again," I tell her.

"Wow. She's persistent. So, you two make out this time?"

That hurts, but not as much as being thrown out of a bookstore, I guess. "What did you do with the memory card?"

She huffs. "I stuck it underwater and stomped on it."

"Thanks."

Another grid of photos appears onscreen: Fran and Alex kayaking together, swimming together, running together.

"You must've missed her this year," I say.

She closes the computer, but her eyes remain locked on the same spot, as though she can still see every photo. "Yeah. I always thought I was running interference for Al—especially when she started applying to colleges as far away from St. Louis as possible. But last summer I realized we'd kind of been protecting each other really. And when she was gone . . ." Fran closes her eyes. When she opens them again, she turns to me. "This has got to stop. Right now. You've got five minutes, okay?"

"For what?"

"To ask me all the stuff that's on your mind." She finishes the bottle. "I promise to answer truthfully. I just can't have this . . . *thing* between us anymore."

My mind isn't ready for this, but the look in her eyes tells me this is the moment that has been brewing for a year. I have to dive in.

"Four minutes, forty seconds," she says.

"Okay. Why do you drink?"

"I don't drink. I'm drink*ing*."

"Semantics. Fifteen—love."

"Wrong. I haven't touched alcohol all year. Just on this trip. Replay the point."

"Why are you drinking now?"

"Because I can. Because whether I do or don't, Alex will still love me, and apparently you'll still hate me. What have I got to lose?"

I don't agree with her logic, but then, I'm not convinced she does either. She just unscrews the cap on yet another bottle and takes a big gulp.

"Where did you get it from anyway?"

"There was a minibar in our first hotel room."

"There was? I didn't see it."

She rolls her eyes. "Well, duh! You wouldn't, would you."

I guess she means that someone as straight and narrow as me wouldn't even look for such temptations. I can't tell whether she means it to be insulting or complimentary. Doesn't really matter—I'm okay with being that person.

"Why are you rude?" I ask.

"Why shouldn't I be?"

"You didn't used to be."

She flares her nostrils. "So?"

"What about blasphemy?"

"I wasn't aware blasphemy is the same as being rude. Love–fifteen."

She's right: They're not the same thing. I don't even know where I was going with that one. I only asked it because I haven't gotten up the nerve to ask her what I really want to know. And I still can't.

"You always seem angry now," I say. "Is it because you don't believe in God?"

She looks confused. "I *do* believe in God. It's everyone else I lost faith in."

"But you don't go to church."

"Love–thirty for thinking those are the same thing."

"Okay. But why don't you go anymore?"

Fran looks away. "I have my reasons."

"You promised to answer my questions truthfully."

She fingers her hair, takes refuge in another long gulp from her bottle. "My parents prefer not to be seen with me."

"Oh." Somehow this has never occurred to me before. "I didn't know."

"You do now."

"But your parents aren't to blame for everything else."

"*Naaaa*. That's an opinion, not a question. Love–forty. Break point. And you still have two minutes, fifty seconds left to ask *questions*."

"Okay, okay." I try not to smile as I spot a loophole in her rules. "*Why* did you give up on everything else as well?"

She shakes her head and exhales loudly. "Whatever. Just forget it."

She stands as if she's going to leave. Instinctively I reach out and take her hand. It's warm. For years I dreamed of holding her hand; and here I am, doing it. I let go suddenly as my face turns red.

"I'm not contagious," she says.

"I know. I'm sorry. I shouldn't have said that about you giving up. Please don't go."

She hesitates a moment before sitting back down. Our knees are so close they almost touch. "You've got two minutes, twenty-five seconds," she says, holding up her scratched plastic watch so I can see she's playing fair.

"Why did you stop joining in with church events?"

"Because I wasn't welcome."

"But they were important to us. To me," I add.

"And they're still important."

"So come help out again. Do the Thanksgiving dinner this year."

"And ruin all the photos?" She bats her eyelids.

"Can you stop playing the victim for a moment?"

Fran stiffens. "Who said I'm a victim? Not me. I'm just aware that for one day every year the shelter belongs to your congregation, so I stay away. I do Sundays instead. Turns out, homeless people like to eat then as well."

"Every Sunday?"

"Almost, yeah. At least since my dad made it clear he wouldn't be seen with me at church."

"But why?"

Fran stares at her forearms. "Why do you think? Please don't pretend to be shocked. Even you're secretly grateful I haven't been there this past year, right?"

I can't answer that question, but my silence shames me.

"Whatever," she continues. "It's why I help at the shelter. It's funny how easily people with no money, no home, no food can overlook stuff like that."

I can't think of the right thing to say, so I just shrug.

"Okay, well . . . I guess that counts as breaking serve. How does it feel?" I'm trying to be light.

Fran doesn't play along; she just taps her watch. "You've got thirty seconds left. Why don't you just ask me?"

"Ask you what?"

"The biggest question of all."

"What are you talking about?" I croak.

She sighs. "Fine. Have it your—"

"Why do you look like that?" I ask, the words tumbling out.

She has a smile prepared, but still her eyes betray the hurt. Or is it surprise? Was she expecting me to ask something else? "Because I want to remind people how bitter disappointment feels," she says.

Her words hang in the air for several seconds. I replay them over and over, trying to make sense of them. And then, finally, I think I understand. "Including me?" I whisper. "Do you want me to know that too?"

She looks away and breaks the connection. Her eyes drift across the room, as though she's trying to find something steady to latch on to. Eventually she gives up and looks at her watch again.

"Sorry," she says, almost too softly for me to hear. "Time's up."

THURSDAY, JUNE 19

Lessons 25: 13–15

*13. And though the boy was lonely and con-
fused, yet he knew that patience was good.
And so he knelt down and prayed, even as
the children around him played. 14. The
next day his faith remained strong, and
he cast out all evil thoughts and prayed
again that he might yet understand. Even
as the children around him played. 15. The
next day, still lonely and confused, the boy
gnashed his teeth and cried out, "Why am
I forsaken? Why am I alone? Why is my
world undone?" And only the sight of children playing reassured him there was any
joy left in the world.*

8:20 A.M.
Albuquerque, New Mexico

Matt starts today's journey by announcing a detour to Santa Fe. He says it matter-of-factly, as though no one will mind. I can't tell whether it's a calculated move, or if he's simply clueless. I'm guessing the former.

Before I can complain, Alex rubs her hands together and opens the guidebook: "Santa Fe, Spanish for 'Holy faith,' is the state capital of New Mexico." She continues with a list of invasions and occupations that blend into one massive bloody mess covering several centuries. Despite the catastrophic loss of life that stains Santa Fe's history, Alex's narration never once loses steam.

"That's all?" Matt says, when she's finally done. "What about it being the Healing Stone capital of America?" he teases. "What about artist studios for rent at Manhattan prices?"

Alex doesn't reply.

"Doesn't your book even mention the phrase 'upmarket kitsch'?" he continues.

Alex closes the guidebook with a loud snap.

"I'm just joking, Al."

No reply.

The sign over the highway announces the turn for Santa Fe. If we skip the detour, we'll be in Texas by lunchtime, and I'll have time for a nap at the hotel, and a shower. I'll be able to get my head straight, and after last night, that's my top priority.

"Can we just keep going, Matt?" I ask.

No response.

"Please? I could really do with an easy day."

"I'm sorry," he says quietly. It's weird, but he sounds like he means it too. "We need to . . ."

Need to what? I want to ask. But Matt glides toward the turn and we're on our way to Santa Fe. A sign shows we have sixty miles to go.

"I didn't mean that stuff, Al," he says. "I was just being silly."

"I know," says Alex. "I think I'd prefer to look around by myself, though."

Now it's Matt's turn to be silent. Alex responds by leaning over and pecking him on the cheek. He doesn't react at all.

"Good idea," agrees Fran. "It's bound to be a long ride this afternoon. We could all use some alone time."

It suits me, suits Alex, suits Fran. But Matt sinks deep into his leather seat, his shoulders slumped.

Turns out, the person responsible for the detour is the least happy that it's happening.

Calculated? Clueless?

Definitely the latter.

10:10 A.M.
Santa Fe, New Mexico

There aren't enough synonyms for *sand-colored* to describe Santa Fe. Old and new buildings creep up the hills like a haphazard stack of LEGO bricks. And though we're at 7,000 feet and the air feels paper thin, mountains dominate the horizon, peaks still capped with snow.

I'm aware of the beauty of this place, and the energy generated by the bustling crowds. But it's the first time I've been by myself since the trip began, and although I ought to enjoy the solitude, instead I just feel lost and lonely.

I'm tired too, so I start looking for a coffee shop— somewhere to sit and rest. I stop a passerby, but before I can ask for directions I'm distracted by something in the window of the store across the street: a life-sized cardboard cutout of someone I recognize very well.

Me.

"You okay?" asks the man, mustache twitching. "Look like you've seen a ghost."

I cross the street in a daze and stare at the smiling cardboard version of myself. Only it's not exactly me. Gone is the mole on my chin, and my skin is flawless. My teeth look a thousand times brighter than they'll ever be in real life, and even my eyes have an unsettling vibrancy, like I've consumed a dozen shots of espresso. In short, I've been Photoshopped. Me, given the cover model treatment, as though my appearance has anything to do with what I wrote. I'd be appalled if I weren't so jealous of my cardboard alter ego.

I wander inside the store—a bookstore, it turns out—where an entire table has been covered with copies of *Hallelujah*. For a moment I just stand there, gawking at the artful way they've been stacked. Then three kids my age approach—two boys and a girl— and instinctively I walk away and hide behind a book- shelf. I don't want them to see I'm not *that person*. It's bad enough that I feel like a fraud for claiming to believe all the things I wrote; now I'm suddenly ashamed of my tiny mole and my less-than-perfect teeth as well.

Through a gap in the shelf I watch them flipping through the pages of my book, stopping every now and again to read something aloud. They laugh, which ought to be a good thing, but every quote ends with an insult. I'm a "dork" and a "moron" and a "loser," apparently. The abuse continues until an employee drifts by. Then they lower their voices and bow their heads and produce heartfelt *ma'am*s, laughing again only when the coast is clear.

Outside the store, Fran's purple hair catches my eye. She stands statue still, blindsided by the cutout, her upper lip curled. When she shakes her head in disgust I want to tell her it's not my fault. I wish she'd never seen it at all.

The main door swings open and Fran approaches the table of books slowly, almost reverentially. She picks up a copy and turns to the back, the flap with my biography and the black-and-white passport photo.

"Can you believe this crap?" one of the boys asks her.

Fran doesn't respond.

"You're not going to buy it, are you?" asks the girl.

Fran looks up now, tilts her head.

"It's just . . . have you *heard* this kid?"

"Yeah," says Fran. "I have."

"He's a freakin' mutant, right?" This from the other boy, desperate to have his say. "There was this interview yesterday—the guy *grilled* him. Total humiliation."

Fran smiles, but it's cold, almost lethal. "How inspiring."

"Yeah, right?"

"Takes a lot of intelligence to ambush someone in an interview. Very mature behavior too."

The boy narrows his eyes. "Wha—?"

"Have you actually read this book?"

"Hell no."

Fran grips her copy tightly. "Check out page seventy-seven. There's a passage on bullying, and how to keep your faith and rise above it. It's funny, and it's some of the truest stuff I've read. Believe me, with all the jerks at my school, I'm a freakin' expert."

She hands the book over to the shell-shocked boy, turns on her heel, and strides out of the store. I half expect the trio to break into laughter, but they don't. Instead they remain rooted to the spot.

I take a deep breath and emerge from behind the shelves. They all look at me, but it takes a moment before they make the connection. Even then, no one speaks.

"Here," I say, reaching for their books. "I'll sign them for you." I pull out my trusty Sharpie and autograph the first two, but as I'm finishing the last, someone tackles me.

"That's it!" my attacker shouts. "I've had it with you kids defacing my stock."

The three kids are already slipping away, but the woman isn't interested in them. I'm the one in her sights, and she doesn't look as though she's in a sympathetic frame of mind.

"Being rude, mis-shelving books, and now *graffiti*. I'm calling the police," she says.

"I was only signing copies for them," I explain.

The woman leans closer, inspects my face and compares it to the photo on the flap of my book. "Oh," she says. She releases my arm. "Well, then, keep going. And let me know when you're done. I have another five boxes out back."

My arm hurts. It feels as though the tendons have petrified. "I'd love to, but—"

"Great. Hurry up, then."

"I'm sorry, but my arm hurts. And my hand."

"Your hand hurts." She mulls each word. "Forty days and forty nights did our Lord sojourn in the wilderness with wild animals—*wild animals,* you hear?—but your *hand hurts.*"

"Mark, chapter one, verse thirteen," I say.

She fixes me with an icy stare. "Exactly."

"But I have to meet my brother soon."

"Then you'd better get started."

"I'd really like to help, honestly I would, but . . ."

She rubs her chin rhythmically. "I understand. Just wait here while I call the police, okay?"

"*What?*"

"You defaced my property."

"I *autographed* it. It's my book."

"No, Luke. It's *my* book. You just wrote it."

Her look of triumph makes me want to scream. I would have signed her stock if she'd just asked nicely, but not now. If I do, it'll be because I'm weak and scared. But Fran wasn't weak when she stood up to those kids and spoke her mind. She said that what I'd written actually meant something to her. I don't know how to process that right now, but I do know that if Fran is willing to stand up for me, the least I can do is stand up for myself.

I re-cap my Sharpie, carry the three books to the checkout, and hand over a hundred-dollar bill to the timid-looking man standing behind the counter. By the time the woman realizes what I'm doing he's already rung me up and handed over the receipt.

"I want those back," she shouts.

I put the books under my arm and head for the door. By the time it closes behind me I can't even hear her whining anymore.

12:55 P.M.
Parking lot, Santa Fe, New Mexico

I get back to the car just a few steps behind Fran. She leans against it and rests her hand above her eyes, blocking out the sun.

"So," she says, "see anything interesting?"

"Sort of. How about you?"

"Not unless you count overpriced boutique stores as high culture."

It's so unbelievably hot, but she isn't even perspiring. Perhaps I should join the cross-country team next year.

"So what rocked your world?" she asks.

"A life-size cardboard cutout of yours truly in a bookstore window."

I tilt my head slightly so that I can watch her response, but she doesn't even blink. "Of *you*?"

"Yeah."

"Huh. Sorry I missed it."

She's completely unreadable. If I hadn't seen her at the store I'd honestly believe she'd never been there. I want to talk about what she said to those kids. I want to ask her why she didn't tell me she'd read *Hallelujah*—liked it, even. But I don't know how to begin.

Matt and Alex head toward us, arm in arm, reconciled once more. When Matt sees me, he gives a thumbs-up. "Dude, there's a cardboard cutout of you in a bookstore!" he says.

"I know."

"If it wasn't so freaky, it'd be kind of cool." He unlocks the doors. "So what's next? Luke Dorsey: the mini-series? Luke Dorsey: the IMAX experience?"

Fran pauses at her door. "Luke Dorsey: the IMAX experience," she repeats in a movie-trailer voice. "Hey, I can think of worse things."

She gets into the car, while I wonder exactly what that means.

5:15 P.M.
The MidPoint Café, Adrian, Texas

Matt points a finger at the upcoming mileage sign for a town called Adrian. "Guess we'll be making today's signing in plenty of time. Now, repeat after me: Detours are good."

I'm not sure which of us he's speaking to, but no one says a word.

We pull off I-40 at the next intersection and join Route 66. I guess this is how we'll make our triumphant entry into Adrian. I'm sure the crowds will be lining the streets for us.

Or not. Turns out, Adrian is a small town. *Really* small. But at the side of the road, like an oasis in the desert, is a giant sign pointing to the MidPoint Café. The number of cars in the parking lot suggests that things are looking up.

"Mecca," cries Matt, and Alex and Fran nod in agreement. I think it might be the first time today we've all agreed on something.

We order quickly—burgers and fries, followed by a slice of the tantalizingly named "ugly crust pie"—and wallow in our good fortune.

A lady at the next table leans over and waves a too-tanned arm. "You kids passin' through?" she asks.

"Sure are," says Matt.

"Paying homage to the Mother Road." She smiles, which seems to activate a hacking cough she can barely control. "Know why this is the MidPoint Café?"

"Presumably because it's the midpoint of Route 66," says Alex.

The woman raises her penciled eyebrows. "Well,

ain't you smart as a whip. Yep, this place is one thousand one hundred and thirty-nine miles from Chicago. Care to guess how far we are from Los Angeles?"

We all exchange glances.

"I'm just foolin' with ya," she says, laughing and coughing again. "But it's good to know you're halfway, ain't it?"

"We're stopping in St. Louis," says Alex.

"You ain't gonna make it all the way to Chicago?"

"No."

This news sends the lady into a funk so deep that she turns away and downs her coffee in a single gulp.

The food arrives and we tuck in. It's sublime, and the headache that's been building since my run-in at the bookstore finally disappears.

No one speaks until pie time. Then we all lean back as if to make a little more room for the impending caloric onslaught.

"So where exactly is this bookstore?" I ask Matt, fork poised to attack the pie.

"Sixth Ave. Which, I seem to recall, is also Old Route 66."

Suddenly the lady rejoins our conversation as though she'd never left. "Sixth Ave., you say?" She runs her tongue across her teeth. "Hmm. Ain't no Sixth Ave. here, hon. You mean Sixth Street, not half a mile away. Tell me what you're looking for."

Matt frowns. "Some Christian bookstore. Can't remember the name. I just remember noticing that it's on Old Route 66."

"Sixth Street ain't on Route 66, hon. Now, Sixth Ave. in Amarillo—*that's* on Old Route 66. You sure you're in the right town?"

"Yeah, we're sure," I say. "Aren't we, Matt?"

Matt frowns. "Shh. I'm thinking."

"What about?"

"Shh."

"I'll be back in a minute," says Fran. The look on her face makes me to drop my fork and follow.

She stops beside a guy who is typing on his laptop. "Hi," she says, waving. "Sorry to bother you, but we really need to use the Internet. Would you mind?"

The guy seems mesmerized by her hair. "Uh, sure," he says.

Fingers flying across the keys, Fran pulls up my publisher's website. It claims that my signing is at The Goodly Shepherd in Amarillo, not Adrian, which is really strange.

"Check the bookstore website," I say.

Fran does a quick Google search for The Goodly Shepherd. Their homepage loads in breathtakingly slow motion. At the top, in big red letters, is a flashing announcement: "One night in Amarillo: Luke Dorsey!"

I sprint back to the table. "Maaaaaatt!"

All the diners turn to face us.

"Dude, you seriously cannot shout my name," Matt hisses.

"Dude, I seriously am. Why does my publisher's website say tonight's signing is in Amarillo?"

He clicks his tongue. "Ah, dang it. I was afraid you were going to say that."

"You were *afraid*? When were you planning to mention it?"

Matt stands, but his mouth is too full of pie for him to answer.

"Now, calm yourself, hon," says our neighborly lady. "Amarillo's practically the next town over. Just a straight shot on I-40."

"Oh." I offer a silent prayer of thanks.

"Yeah, that's cool." Matt sits back down and gobbles more pie.

"So how far is it?" I ask.

"About sixty miles," she says cheerfully. "Dead on an hour."

For a moment we all freeze. Then Matt slaps a wad of cash on the table and we're out the door, piling into the Hummer. He fires up the engine as Alex pulls out the map and spreads it across her lap.

"It's five fifty-three," I wail. "How the hell did this happen?"

"Chill. Alex is doing her best."

"Hey, Luke, did you just say *hell*?" mumbles Fran.

"Yes, Fran, I said *hell*. And if I ever doubted its existence before, I'm pretty confident I've found it now!"

Matt spins around in his seat. "Get off Alex's case. It's not like she meant to screw up."

"What?" explodes Alex. "Don't blame me, you prick."

"But you're in charge of the itinerary."

"No, Matt. *You're* in charge. I just said I'd stay on top of things too. And I've tried. It's not my fault that page is missing."

"What?" I scream.

"Why didn't you say so?" asks Matt.

Alex smacks her fist against the map, slicing it down the middle. "I figured you knew, since you're obviously the one who lost it. Anyway, you told me the next signing was at the town in Texas that begins with an A, and when I opened the map you pointed at Adrian."

"No, I didn't."

"Did too."

"Did not. I was driving, not looking at the map." He wiggles the steering wheel as if we need an illustration of what driving involves. "I wasn't pointing to Adrian, I was trying to show you where Texas is."

"Oh, thanks. I'd never have found Texas without

you. Especially not on a MAP OF TEXAS! Geez, it's only the biggest state in the country."

"Second-biggest. Alaska's biggest."

"Biggest of the forty-eight contiguous states, you pedant."

"What did you call me?"

"Pedant. *P-E-D-A-N-T*," she drawls. "If you don't know what it means, ask Luke."

"I know what it means, thanks."

"I highly doubt that."

"Enough!" shouts Fran. "Grow up, the pair of you. Either of you could've checked the publisher's website to make sure."

"And how would we do that?" asks Alex. "We haven't had Wi-Fi in days. We haven't even had cell phone connection for ninety percent of this trip. And even if we had, it wouldn't have mattered, because Matt never answers his phone."

"Why not?" I ask.

"Yes, Matt," says Alex. "Why not?"

Matt doesn't answer.

"She's kidding, right, Matt? You have been checking your messages, really. Haven't you?"

Matt still doesn't answer. He just puts the car in gear and gets us back on Route 66. Two minutes later we're on I-40 heading east, and I know I won't be able to get him to talk again for the rest of the journey.

I lean back in my seat as we move to the far left lane and accelerate.

And accelerate.

It's 5:58, and I'm feeling carsick. I'm about to be late for yet another signing, and I didn't even get any pie. And because that's not enough, my brother is behaving strangely. It's all too much.

But then Fran reaches across the seat and takes my hand. I don't know if it's because she's scared or wants to reassure me, but I hope it's the latter.

In any case, I don't pull away.

6:58 P.M.
The Goodly Shepherd Bookstore, Amarillo, Texas

Matt pulls up to the bookstore and dares to point out that we're two minutes early. Somehow I manage not to smack him with Alex's guidebook.

Fran and I jump out together. "You okay?" she asks, elbows resting on the roof.

I nod, although we both know it's a lie. I haven't showered. Haven't *peed*. Haven't changed clothes, except to throw on a creased white shirt over my filthy yellow T-shirt.

"Hey, good luck," she says. "Knock 'em dead. . . . But not literally."

"Better keep Matt away then," I say, and Fran laughs. Her white teeth glisten in the streetlight, and yet again it feels like we've turned the clock back a year. I guess she knows that's what I'm thinking too, because she closes her mouth, lips pulled tight in a thin line. "I'd better go," I say. This time she just nods.

A woman with Clark Kent glasses and a business-like ponytail is waiting for me inside. "Oh, thank goodness you're here." She pumps my hand once and guides me through the store like an excited sheepdog. "I've heard you like dramatic last-minute arrivals, but I couldn't help wondering if you'd forgotten us altogether! I swear, I wasn't looking forward to telling all these people you'd bailed on us. It's the biggest crowd we've ever had."

"Really? How many?"

"Three hundred or so, last time I looked. Could be four hundred by now."

"Whoa."

"Yes, whoa. Anyway, sorry if you get an earful from your publicist, but when you weren't here at six fifty-five, I felt I had to call him."

Oh, great. So Colin knows I'm late. *Again.*

"And here we are," she says.

It's the largest room I've seen so far. You could hold a rock concert in here.

A few people recognize me, and there's a kind of staggered standing ovation as I wind my way toward the podium. The walk feels longer than usual, the eyes more weighted with expectation. I'm not in the right frame of mind to be doing this.

There's a bottle of water by the podium and I drink the whole thing. By the time I'm done, the applause has stopped. As one by one they sit down, I stare at this ocean of people and wonder what on earth I'm doing here.

I give my spiel and everyone laughs, though the words feel dull and empty. I talk about the tour, but it's so heavily edited I wonder if I'm just making it all up. If it weren't for the breathless anticipation that awaits my every word, I honestly think I'd bring things to a close right now.

Clark Kent lady seems delighted with my paltry effort, and opens the floor to questions. The first comes from a guy near the door—like me, a late arrival.

"I saw you arrive in a Hummer," he says. "Do you really think that goes hand in hand with your message of self-sacrifice, modesty, and charity?"

He's got me there. The debate champion in me is scouring for a rebuttal, but the real me just doesn't have the energy. So I do something unusual: I tell the truth.

"Well, I can't drive yet, so my brother is driving me around. He also chose the car. I didn't have any say in it, but if he'd asked me, I'd have begged him not to get a Hummer. You're absolutely right, it feels inappropriate and . . . wrong."

The guy nods. "So your brother's driving. What about the girl you were talking to?"

My heartbeat quickens, and debate champion Luke receives a sudden influx of adrenaline. "What girl?"

"The one with the purple hair. Weird markings on her arms. She was waving to you as you walked into the store. Kept waving even after you were inside."

"She did?"

"Uh-huh."

"Oh. Well, she's, uh . . . a cousin. Her parents wanted her to come along on the tour."

"I get it," he says, nodding sagely. "And has it worked?"

"Excuse me?"

"You know . . . has she changed? Gotten better?"

"Uh . . . I think the trip has had a positive effect on her, yeah."

Everyone seems to accept my answer, though I already know I shouldn't have said that Fran is my cousin. It just slipped out. Although, come to think of it, I didn't say that she was *my* cousin—just *a* cousin; which I'm pretty sure she is. And nothing else I said is wrong—conveniently vague, maybe, but not *wrong*.

A tall, frail lady stands and crosses herself. "God bless you, Luke Dorsey," she says. "Anyone would think you have enough going on already, what with all your death-defying experiences. But you also find time to help lost souls."

These book signings haven't always gone smoothly, but with the exception of the past hour on I-40, I'd hardly call them "death-defying." I'd ask her what she means, but I'm stuck on the fact that she just called Fran a *lost soul*. Two days ago, I might have agreed; now it makes me uncomfortable.

"Well," she continues, "as the good Lord says, 'Suffer little children, and forbid them not, to come to me.'"

I can guess how Fran would react to being called a *little child*. "Matthew, chapter nineteen, verse fourteen," I reply, reverting to autopilot.

She nods, and the old man beside her stands too. He clears his throat and recites: "'Verily I say unto you, inasmuch as ye have done it unto one of the least of these my brethren, ye have done it unto me.'"

So now Fran has been demoted to *the least of these my brethren*. "Matthew, chapter twenty-five, verse forty," I reply.

Another satisfied customer takes his seat. I haven't even expressed an opinion yet, but I can feel that the audience is behind me—more than at any event so far. It would be almost perfect if I deserved this support, but I don't. I feel tired and cranky. I feel like a fraud.

"Okay, uh . . . look, there's something I need to say." I pick up the bottle of water, but it's empty. "I'm not who you think I am. I'm really happy if *Hallelujah* speaks to you, but all I did was write it. That's all. It doesn't mean I'm special."

"You don't think being Luke Dorsey—doing all these amazing things—makes you special?" asks Clark Kent lady, standing not ten feet away.

"No, I don't." I turn to face the audience, large enough to burst the seams of the room. "Look, when I started writing it, everything in my life seemed perfect, and I was psyched about sharing that feeling with the kids at Sunday school. But then everything changed, and I started having doubts. I still have doubts—lots of them. The book's published now, so I can't do anything about it; but whenever I read it, I don't think I should be promising those kids anything at all."

Some people are hanging on every word, but others have taken on a vaguely freaked-out look, like spectators forced to watch someone spontaneously combust.

The old guy raises his hand again. "You know," he

says, "being modest and self-critical doesn't make you any less inspiring. On the contrary, I think I speak for all of us when I say that's why we're here tonight. To see someone—just a kid—who's already done so much and is still trying to make a difference; who is human enough to admit he has doubts, but committed to exploring what faith and understanding and steadfastness mean and writing about them in a new way. A way that resonates with the young folk. Don't underestimate the power of your words and actions, Luke."

Soliloquy complete, he bows his head. Murmurs of agreement hum like an electrical current. And the smiling faces of everyone here are proof of their unwavering support. I'm practically witnessing a ticker tape parade in my honor. I should be elated.

But I'm not. I figured my only problem was that I had doubts about what I'd written, but it's clear I've got another issue too: What these people see isn't the boy who wrote *Hallelujah,* but the boy *in* the book; the one who never puts a foot wrong, spiritually speaking, because an army of editors have made sure he doesn't. I tried to tell them who I was, but it's clear they don't believe me. So what do I do now?

I could let them all down and reveal the truth: how the darkest passages were written at the church retreat, when I felt alone and confused; how my editor alternated the funny and serious passages; how I begged him to remove all traces of humor and fantasy, once I realized it was all just crap; how I haven't looked forward to church in a year, but I'm too afraid of what that means to stop going.

But I won't say any of these things. Because these people have given up an evening to show me that at my very best—my most idealistic—I have something to say. So I'll try be my very best again, even though my best has very little to do with me.

9:10 P.M.
Panhandle Hotel, Amarillo, Texas

Fran is sitting on the toilet seat, painting her toenails purple so they match her hair.

"How'd it go?" she asks.

"Okay, I guess."

"Good." She narrows her eyes as the tiny brush glides across her nail.

"No, that's not true." I lean against the sink. "Actually, it was strange."

The brush stops moving and Fran peers up. Her eyes are rimmed with black eyeliner. It's the first time since Sunday that she has worn makeup. "Strange how?" she asks.

She's looking at me intently, searchingly. I recognize that look; it used to make me clam up, and it's having the same effect now. "It's nothing," I say.

She won't look away. "Strange how, Luke?" The way she says my name sounds odd: gentle, caring. She really wants to know what's eating me.

"Are you going out?" I ask instead.

She knows I'm blowing her off, but to her credit she doesn't get angry. "Why would you think that?"

"You're all dressed up."

"You like, huh?" She laughs quickly, before I can respond. "I wasn't planning on it, but it's a good idea. A little fresh air would be nice." She returns her attention to the remaining toenail, but the brush doesn't move. "You want to come?"

"Yeah. I guess I could do with some fresh air too."

She exhales, and the brush begins moving again.

My bag has been placed on one of the beds, so I rummage through and find a polo shirt. It's not exactly clean, but at least it doesn't smell. I'm setting the bar low tonight.

Fran appears in the doorway, hair loose around her shoulders. "All right, then," she says.

"All right, then."

Outside the air-conditioned hotel, the night is

sticky. The air is thick with bugs. Fran and I walk side by side, but I'm not sure which of us is supposed to speak first. We pass the first two blocks in silence.

At the curb, we wait for the lights to turn. I wish they'd hurry up so we can start walking again and our footsteps will cover the sound of my breathing—too fast, too loud.

"So the nail polish is dry, then?" I ask.

Fran begins to laugh. "Good. Now you've broken the silence, we can actually talk again."

I smile at that. It's so *Fran*.

"I'm ready to talk," she says. "About what happened last year." Her voice sounds brittle. "Lights have changed."

"Huh? Oh."

We cross the street and keep going straight. We're not heading anywhere, I realize. We're walking because it's a distraction, and that's what Fran needs if she's ever going to open up.

"Remember the day we won the debate championship?" she asks.

"Are you kidding? Best day of my life."

"Yeah, mine too. Just the intensity of the whole thing, and then finding out we'd won. I was on such a high. Everyone wanted to shake my hand, and then my dad came up and said he'd never been prouder. It was like . . . I don't know . . . the stars aligning, or something." She breathes in the memory. "I remember my mom taking photos, and telling us to get closer. I wrapped my arm around your waist, but it took you forever to put your arm around mine. And I was laughing, but when I looked at you, you looked kind of scared. I didn't understand at first, but then I got it . . . that maybe you liked me. I swear it was the first time I knew how you felt. It was also the moment I realized I really liked you too. So I kissed you."

Actually, it more like a peck on the cheek, but it was still the most amazing moment of my life.

"I remember thinking that the church retreat was in ten days, and that maybe you and me . . ." She trails off, and her footsteps slow down. "Never mind."

"No, keep going," I say, needing to hear her say these things. Needing to remember the time when Frances Embree—the *real* Fran—had shared my feelings for her.

"Well, then that reporter came along, and Dad muscled in on the picture, as usual. He stars in his own commercials, you know, so it's not like he was going to miss out on a chance to get his face in the paper. Anyway, I was feeling kind of strange, and elated, and I just needed to let it out."

"You mean the rabbit fingers behind his head?"

"Yeah. I wasn't trying to embarrass him or anything. And I swear I only did it on one of the photos, but that was the one they chose." She's practically slowed to a standstill. "Can we sit down?"

"Sure."

There's a café nearby with outdoor tables. We choose one on the perimeter and keep quiet as the waiter approaches. "Can I interest you in a drink this evening?" he asks.

"A Long Island iced tea," says Fran.

He cocks an eyebrow. "Do you have ID?"

"I've got a library card that says I'm sixteen. Will that do?"

The waiter plants his hands on his waist, but he seems amused. "Tell you what, I'll make you one without the gin, rum, tequila, vodka, and triple sec, okay?"

"What does that leave?" she asks.

"Coke."

"Perfect. Make it diet, please."

"Same," I say. Which is when I realize that Fran hasn't been drinking this evening. I can tell in her face and her speech and her attitude. I like her better this way.

"So, my father . . ." Fran selects a fingernail and picks at it. "After the competition, my parents took me out for dinner. Dad said he was proud of me for being so clever and hardworking. And Mom said I was by far the prettiest girl in the competition; which wasn't relevant, by the way, but she almost never said anything nice like that. She told me she'd made an appointment for me to see her hair stylist the next day, so I could get the highlights I'd been asking for. I was so excited, it took me two hours to go to sleep that night, and I spent every minute of it giving thanks to God."

The drinks arrive. Fran takes several small sips, and I know right away the feel-good part of her story is over.

"Mom woke me early the next morning—hit me with the newspaper. She said Dad had left the house to cool off and by the time he got back I'd better have an explanation." Another sip. "I didn't know what she was talking about. I mean, I could see the photo, but who cares about my stupid little fingers behind his head, right?"

"Right. My parents thought it was funny."

"Well, Dad didn't. He said I'd humiliated him. Said he was pulling the new TV commercials, 'cause I'd ruined his reputation. Said he was embarrassed by me, and how could I be so stupid? And every time I thought he'd run out of steam, he'd come up with something else. Even when I started crying."

I still remember the photo. It was tiny, black-and-white, and stuffed in the middle of the "local interest" section, which no one ever reads. "I'm sorry, Fran. That's awful."

"Yeah. Worst of all, he went back on everything he'd said the day before. I wasn't smart; I was stupid. I wasn't hardworking; I just had a well-prepared partner. I was rude. I was a brat." Fran takes a steadying breath. "After he left, Mom said he shouldn't have been so hard on me. She was trying to be nice, but I told her to tell *him* that, not me, which made her mad too. After that, I didn't even want to go to the salon anymore, but she practically dragged me there. So I decided to do something to piss them off." She touches her hair. "I skipped the highlights and went with purple."

I'm swigging my Coke every few seconds, but I can't taste it.

"Mom picked me up afterward and completely freaked. She made the stylist promise to undo it all at another appointment the next day. And to be honest, I was *glad* she was angry. I wanted to have it out with her and Dad—tell them my life wasn't just about making them proud. I didn't want to be like Alex, counting down the days until college, and never looking back. I even practiced everything I wanted to say, like it was a debate competition. But when we got home, Dad just took one look at me and walked away. Then he told Mom not to talk to me either."

I know Fran's father, which is why I'm not surprised. Matt used to call him the iron fist in a velvet glove, but that's being kind; the glove is almost nonexistent. Still, Fran must have known how he'd react.

"Mom took me back to the salon the next day— gave me a hundred dollars to 'fix things.'" Fran uses air quotes to make her point. "But when she drove off, I just left. There was a tattoo parlor a few doors down, so I went in and got the cartilage at the top of my ears pierced—one for each parent."

Her fingers drift up to her right ear, and she fingers the top hoop. There have been a lot of additions since that day.

"When Mom saw what I'd done, she stormed off. I waited an hour, but she never came back. So I walked home—six miles. They were both waiting for me. Said I'd made a decision and there were consequences. When I was ready to apologize and stop the nonsense, they were ready to forgive me."

I'm so engrossed in her story that I just nod.

"Did you hear me?" demands Fran. "They said *they* would forgive *me*." She downs the rest of her Coke.

"I'm sorry."

"Are you?" She closes her eyes. "Don't answer that. I'm just . . . they hurt me that day, you know? I thought nothing in the world could hurt so bad. I was wrong, but that's what I thought. See, all I wanted was for them to talk to me again. Instead, they cut me off."

When she opens her eyes, she's looking right at me. "Everything went wrong after that. On Sunday, Dad said he wouldn't give me a ride to church, so I missed the service. Later in the week, I turned up to the church retreat and . . . I just couldn't do it." A tear appears suddenly, and she wipes it away. "I kind of lost it after that. I wanted to get away, but there was nowhere to go. Alex had already left for Caltech and my friends were at camp, so there was no one to talk to. When they got back from camp, they weren't in the mood to listen. And when school started, it was like the teachers took a step back too. Coach Penny was the only one who said she wanted me."

So the mystery of Frances Embree's transformation has finally been solved. Or has it? After all, the Fran who showed up on the first day of sophomore year had tattoos on her arms and a whole lot more than one hoop in each ear. She practically dared the teachers to exclude her.

"Why didn't you just go back to how you were?" I ask.

"What?" She seems puzzled by the question, though it must have occurred to her a million times. "How could I?"

"Just change your appearance."

"Even my arms?"

"You could've covered them up."

"Yeah. That would've made it easier for everyone, wouldn't it? They could've welcomed me back, shown me I'm nothing but the sum of my looks." She swirls the ice around her glass. "Remember the time in freshman year when we were trying to start a Christian fellowship at school, and those seniors made fun of us?"

"Yeah."

"Remember what you told me?"

No, I don't. All I remember is that I was standing beside Frances Embree, and she wore a soft rose-colored sweater, and she'd just had her hair cut in a bob, and her hair was lighter than usual because she'd spent so much of the summer outdoors. I remember being paralyzed by want.

I shake my head.

"You told me we couldn't let them change us, or the things we stood for. You told me it's what's on the inside that matters, that being teased by seniors couldn't touch who we really were. You said I was *godly*, which meant so much to me. I mean, it was the beginning of freshman year. I was so afraid people would think I was a freak. But you reminded me I wasn't alone."

She's paying me a compliment, but I can see where this is going now, and it's killing me.

"Even now, I haven't changed on the *inside,* Luke. I'm still the same Fran; have been all year. Only, no one wants to know this version of me. And, well, if that's how little everyone thinks of me, I guess I don't really need them on my side anyway."

I want to believe she's playing devil's advocate, but I can tell she means every word of this. And I'm the one who gave her the argument.

But she misunderstood me that day. I know what I said, but it wasn't what I *meant.* What I meant was that no one could be allowed to change her, because she was already perfect. Perfectly beautiful. And the thought that someone might change a single thing about her was more than I could bear.

"I'm sorry, Fran." I want to hit myself. I want to go back in time and tell the freshman me that every self-ish word has consequences. "I'm so sorry."

"Really? You mean that?" She's not asking, she's begging me to say it again, to assure her that it's true. Behind the armor of jewelry and hair dye, Fran is as fragile as she was that day in freshman year. Perhaps even more so. I can't be the one to let her down.

"Yes," I say. "I mean it. I wish I'd known how you felt."

She takes my hand then as a tear rolls down her face. In this moment, she's beautiful again. She doesn't even ask me why I never bothered to find out.

FRIDAY, JUNE 20

Mishaps 11: 3-7

3. Although the Mississippi was wide, yet the boy's will was strong. And he cried, "I will cross thee, O Mississippi!" 4. But the Mississippi said nothing. 5. Again the boy cried, "Your currents will not deter me, nor your pollution ail me. For I am strong of will. And though I cannot swim, and wear a personal flotation device, nevertheless I will conquer thee, for I am—as I have already mentioned—strong of will." 6. Still the Mississippi said nothing. 7. And so the boy stared down the barges and the flotsam and crossed the river, and with every stroke overcame the Mississippi's silence.

9:00 A.M.
Just outside Amarillo, Texas

We park beside a wheat field and follow a dirt path. A hundred yards ahead of us is a line of large, multicolored cars, all planted nose-first into the ground.

"Cadillac Ranch," announces Matt. "Memorial to Route 66."

I swallow a yawn. "Why on earth are we here, Matt?"

Matt keeps his eyes fixed ahead. "If you were one of those ancient pilgrims on the way to some big, important pilgrimage place, would you hurry to get there, or stop at the churches along the way?"

"I'd stop at the churches to get food and water."

"But if you didn't need food and water?"

"How would I not need food and water?"

"Just work with me here."

"Okay." I puff out my cheeks. "I guess it'd depend on whether I had a book signing that evening at the big, important pilgrimage place."

Matt doesn't respond to that, but picks up his pace toward this automobile Stonehenge.

The half-buried cars seem bigger because they're sticking straight up. Well, not *straight* up, but leaning slightly. They're perfectly spaced too, all ten of them. There's no doubt that someone went to a lot of trouble to make this.

"Cadillac Ranch," says Alex, flicking to the appropriate page in her ever-present guidebook. "Created in 1974. Moved to the present location in 1997."

"Someone *moved* it?" I ask.

"That's what it says here."

"Who moves a bunch of half-sunken car wrecks?"

Matt huffs. "Just hurry up and add your graffiti."

"What? Why would I want to do that?"

"Because this is a living, breathing installation. And you can give it life." He stuffs a Sharpie into my hand. "Write. Now."

The car in front of me looks as though it has been painted and repainted a thousand times. There's only a tiny area of white where the pen would even show up, and there's some rust there too. I could cut myself on that and get an infection—tetanus, or gangrene, or one of those flesh-eating ones that have Latin names. "I'd prefer not to."

Fran steps forward. "It's okay, Luke. You don't have to do anything that makes you uncomfortable."

"Thanks."

"You're welcome. Although I must say, if adding a

line of graffiti to a car in the middle of a wheat field gets you all freaked out, you could really do with loosening up. I mean, look at it—it's already a wreck."

She tilts her head and tries to hide a smile. This is a dare, I can tell. It's peer pressure. Fran is trying to lure me to the Dark Side. So I uncap the pen and scrawl: *Luke was here*. I even add an exclamation point.

The others stare at what I've written.

"Luke was here," Matt repeats slowly. "You graffiti the headstones of Route 66, and the best you can do is 'Luke was here'?"

Fran and Alex don't stop laughing all the way back to the car. I guess my initiation to the Dark Side has been put on hold.

1:55 P.M.
I-40, somewhere in Oklahoma

We pass the world-famous leaning water tower of Groom; Texas's first Phillips 66 service station in McLean; the U-Drop Inn in Shamrock. Roadside curiosities drift by to the accompaniment of Alex's monologue, like illustrations from a coffee-table book come to life.

We stop at each one and take photos. Time passes, but the landscape changes less and less. It makes me long for the interstate and dangerously high speed limits.

We cross the border into Oklahoma, and though it's nothing but a line on a map, it feels like progress. Oklahoma borders Missouri, and I live in Missouri. It's a step closer to home.

Luckily, Route 66 has been consumed by I-40, so we move fast through dust bowl territory. Looking out at the sandblasted, sun-scorched land, it's hard to imagine how anyone ever survived here.

Eventually the landscape includes some greenery. Matt pulls into the right lane and signals.

"Why are we getting off?" I ask.

"Because it's lunchtime and I'm hungry. Plus I'm suffering Route 66 withdrawal."

Sure enough, he's found an old alignment of Route 66.

"Why do you keep doing this?" Alex groans. "Are you allergic to keeping things simple?"

"It's not a big detour, Al. And we've got ages. I bet Oklahoma City's only an hour or so away."

"You don't know that!" I snap. "Just for once, can we please stay on the interstate?"

The road veers left and the interstate disappears from view. My heart sinks. I-40 has become my security blanket: Five seconds of separation and I want it back.

We cross an impossibly long iron bridge with more arches than I can count. Below us, the Canadian River meanders through a suddenly fertile area.

"You don't get stuff like this on I-40," says Matt quietly.

"That's not the point," I tell him. "Some of us have seen enough of Route 66 already."

Matt shakes his head and turns on the radio. It's just static.

Alex turns it off.

As Matt turns it back on, there's a resounding *thunk,* followed immediately by an equally ominous *thud.*

Alex screams. Fran makes a grab for my hand and misses. Even Matt flinches. I'm guessing it was a possum, although it could have been almost any small animal. It's not like we'll be stopping to identify the carcass.

"Oh. My. God." Alex is hyperventilating. "You just killed a . . . a . . . *something.*"

Matt rubs his chin. "I'm not certain."

"I saw it, Matt."

"Really? I thought you were messing with the stereo."

"It *bounced.*" She presses her palms against her eyes as though she's trying to erase the image. "Oh God. I saw its fur, and its legs. I think it was a skunk. It was looking at us. It was trying to tell us something."

"To slow down, maybe?"

"This is not funny!"

Matt sits up a little straighter and resumes his normal speed. "Look, stuff like that's going to happen. It's the circle of life. Darwinism. Still, no harm, no foul, right?"

"What do you mean, no harm?"

"To the car. That's the advantage of driving a Hummer."

She spins around to face him, teeth clenched. "All hail, harbinger of road rage," she cries, stretching her arms and bowing. "Glory to you, all-powerful Hummer driver."

Matt bites his lip. "Are you being sarcastic?"

"God, Matt. You can be such a dick."

Matt grips the steering wheel tightly. We veer to the left and cross the lines in the middle of the road. Forty miles per hour suddenly feels very fast indeed. "Why are you so angry?"

"Why do you think? You just killed an animal. And instead of feeling bad, you congratulate yourself for driving a military assault vehicle. Why didn't you just go all out and get us a freakin' Sherman tank? We can't even go a hundred miles without stopping. You're spending a hundred bucks a day on gas."

"I wanted us to ride in comfort. Is that so bad? Geez, Alex, I thought you might actually like it."

I'm bracing for Alex's expletive-filled comeback, but she looks at Matt very steadily and asks, "Is that true?"

"Yes," says Matt, perhaps sensing a breakdown in her resistance.

Alex leans back into her seat and runs her hands through her hair. "Why would you think that? After three years together, how could you believe I'd like a Hummer, of all things? Please, tell me you know me better than that. Just tell me you know me at all."

Matt doesn't answer, but a moment later he pulls to the side of the road and skids to a halt.

Alex responds with a bitter laugh. "Oh, so *now* you stop."

"I don't have much choice."

"Why? Because I'm pissed as hell, or because you've grown a conscience?"

"Because the temperature gauge is rising and there's steam coming from the hood."

No offense to the roadkill we left a mile back, but this is by far the worst news of the day. Even when Matt turns the engine off the steam thickens. It looks like the car is on fire. The air-conditioning is off too, and the temperature rapidly heads toward intolerable.

"The engine will cool down in a minute, right?" I try not to sound desperate.

"Chill out," says Matt. "There's a reason I got us AAA." He takes the cell phone from his pocket. "Oh, no," he mutters.

"What?"

"No reception again. Bad timing, bro. Seriously bad timing."

2:20 P.M.
Somewhere strikingly hot, Oklahoma

"You don't think Matt's suicidal, do you?" asks Fran.

Fran, Alex, and I are crouching beside the Hummer. The sun is almost directly overhead, so there's only about three square feet of shade. We have to crush up together to savor it, which kind of defeats the purpose.

"I'm just saying, it's been ten minutes," she continues. "Plus, Alex was pretty harsh."

"Hello, I'm right here," says Alex. "And I don't think it's unreasonable to be upset when your boyfriend of three years doesn't know the first thing about you."

Right on cue, Matt joins us. "AAA's on the way," he says.

"Thank God!" cries Fran. "How long?"

He rubs his foot across the ground, kicking up dust. "An hour or so."

"An *hour*?" I glance at my watch. "How long is it going to take to get to Oklahoma City from here?"

Matt puffs out his cheeks. "That kind of depends on where *here* is."

"Have you looked at the map?"

"Our map collection seems to have an unfortunate gap."

Fran pats my arm. "So how did you describe where we are?" she asks Matt.

"I said we're stuck on Route 66 west of Oklahoma City. The woman sounded cool about it. She told me there's a truck out on Route 66 anyway, so we should just flag it down."

"And how did she know that would take an hour?" I ask.

Matt sighs. "I don't know, Luke. For all I know, she may have been blowing smoke up my ass."

"So what do I do now?"

Matt kicks at the ground. "I don't know, okay?" He turns away from me. "I'm sorry, though. I'm really sorry."

I believe him, but it doesn't change anything. "Please, Matt. Tell me what to do."

"The only thing I can think of is hitching a ride. I'll wait here, get this thing towed to Oklahoma City, and join you all at the hotel. Just . . . don't tell Mom and Dad, okay? If they know you're hitchhiking, they'll kill me."

"No, they won't," says Alex quietly. "They'll tell you they're disappointed, and you'll make up some BS about how it wasn't your fault, and they'll believe you. Because that's how ridiculously nice they are." She flares her nostrils. "Sometimes I wish we could switch parents. Just for a day. Just long enough for you to realize how easy you've always had it."

She grabs her bags from the back of the Hummer and walks to an open stretch of road about twenty yards away. A few minutes later a car approaches: an ancient Cadillac with tinted glass. She raises her thumb, and the driver slows down and pulls to the side. Fran and I grab our bags and run to join her.

The passenger window opens. "You got a problem?" The driver is a woman, at least sixty. She has a freshly lit cigarette in her right hand.

"Yes, ma'am," says Alex. "Car broke down and we need a ride to Oklahoma City."

"Well, I can get you partway there. Who's *we*?"

Alex steps back and allows the woman a clear view of Fran and me. As she studies Fran, the corners of the woman's mouth tilt down disapprovingly. "I'll take him and you, but I ain't taking her."

"What?" cries Alex.

"You heard me. Far as I'm concerned, if kids has got the right to look however the hell they want, I've got the right to say they ain't welcome in my car. You understand?"

Fran sighs. "I understand perfectly."

"Please, ma'am," I say, leaning forward. "My name is Luke Dorsey. I wrote *Hallelujah*. And this is my friend Fran."

The woman does a double take. "I heard about you on the radio. Your book too. Which is why I'll gladly give y'all a ride. But I ain't taking the chance of getting home without my wallet 'cause this one"—she stabs her cigarette in Fran's direction—"decided to filch it."

"Fran's not a thief," I protest.

I look to Fran to argue her case, but she just laughs. "Well, there was the vodka," she says.

"No, Matt paid for that," says Alex, playing along.

The woman purses her lips. "I'll take *you*," she says to me. "But *only* you."

She opens the passenger door and dribbles ash onto the seat. Maybe it's the heat, but as I contemplate my next move I feel as though time has slowed down around me.

"Go ahead, Luke," says Alex. "We'll come along with Matt."

I shake my head. "I'm staying."

"No," says Fran. She takes my hand and squeezes it. "Please. Missing your signing because of me won't help either of us."

I feel so hot, so tired as I grab hold of the door-frame. "Thanks for stopping, ma'am," I say. "You have a safe journey now."

Slamming that door is the most satisfying thing I've done all week.

3:30 P.M.
Somewhere astoundingly hot, Oklahoma

None of us expect the eighteen-wheeler to stop. Alex barely bothers to raise her hand. But when it pulls up a hundred yards away, we don't waste any time.

Alex opens the door, and the truck driver tugs the rim of his baseball cap in greeting. "Need a ride?" he asks.

"Could sure do with one," says Alex.

"Okay, but three'll be a squeeze."

"That's okay. It'll just be these two."

Fran and I turn at once. "What?"

"You go ahead. Matt and I need to talk."

"I'll stay with you," says Fran.

"No." Alex bites the inside of her mouth. "I've got a lot to say, and it'll be easier without an audience."

Fran and I climb in, me first, and Alex tosses our bags to us. As we pull away I can see her in the side mirror; she keeps waving until she disappears behind a cloud of dust.

"You kids in trouble, by any chance?" the driver asks.

Beside me, Fran tenses. I wish I could stop this from happening to her. I bet Teresa has never had to answer that question, even though she's the definition of *trouble*.

"I guess that's a yes, then," he says, when neither of us replies.

Fran sighs. "This kid knocked me up."

I just about have a heart attack.

"Dear Lord," he says.

"Actually, I'm kidding. But if you really want to hear my troubles, well, let's see: I'm not speaking to my parents, my left ear's infected 'cause I stuck a needle through it when I got drunk, and worst of all, I'm clean out of booze." She huffs. "Speaking of which, you got any spare? I'm not picky."

The guy takes a deep breath. "Sorry. I-I wasn't prying or nothing." He lifts his cap and pulls it down again, fingers shaking. "I just thought . . . well, maybe you needed some help. Only seemed right to offer."

Fran turns bright red. "Oh, no, *I'm* sorry," she says. "I don't know why I said that. And it's kind of you to ask. But we're fine. Really."

I can see how much she wants to take the words back. It makes me wonder why she said them in the first place. Maybe she thinks that's what people expect her to say, but so what?

Fran is Teresa's opposite in many ways, but it occurs to me they have one thing in common: Their appearances mask who they really are. Teresa's good-girl persona had me fooled; but so did Fran's bad-girl, don't-mess-with-me act, and she's been hiding behind it all year. How did it take me until now to realize it?

The silence lingers as the guy adjusts his cap yet again. Then he clears his throat. "I haven't seen my daughter in two months. She's eighteen. Pregnant. Ran away from rehab without telling her mom and me. Now no one knows where she is."

I can feel Fran melting into the seat in shame. But only for a moment, and then she reaches across me and places her hand on the man's arm. "I'm so sorry. I hope she contacts you soon."

He blinks back tears. "Yeah, well . . . we'll see, you know? Not much I can do now 'cept keep looking for her." He turns his attention to me. "What about you? Everything right in your world?"

I look at my lap, and Fran's outstretched arm. She's still holding on to the guy, reminding him that he's not alone, her thoughtless words already a distant memory. And the tattoos and purple nail polish can't disguise the fact that *this* is the Fran I remember—the one who *cared,* and wasn't afraid to show it. It ought to be me doing that, I realize. Everyone thinks *I'm* that person. But what do I have to say to this man? How can I possibly understand what he's going through?

Still Fran holds on tight, turning back the clock until she's the girl I adored, with a heart big enough for everyone.

"Yes," I say finally. "Everything in my world is perfect."

The Divine Depot, Oklahoma City, Oklahoma

This is the youngest crowd yet—maybe because it's a Friday night, or because my interview with Orkle is gaining notoriety. Either way, they seem to have a lot more energy than me. By the time I've completed my introduction I'm pretty much pooped.

"Are you okay?" asks a boy my age when I tug at my shirt collar for the twentieth time.

"Yes, fine."

But I'm not fine. I spent twenty minutes showering, and when I emerged I turned the white hotel towel brown with Route 66 dust. I can still feel it in my pores, under the freshly ironed shirt and black pants. I wonder if I'll ever feel clean again.

"What's it like being on tour?" asks the girl beside him.

"Exhausting." I can tell from her face that this is not the uplifting reply she's looking for. "And . . . enlightening." Now she seems happier. "Just this afternoon, I got a ride in a truck. And the driver is looking for his pregnant teen daughter who just ran away from rehab."

Now there's silence. The girl seems flustered. "Oh," she says, her voice about an octave higher than before. "And, uh . . . were you able to comfort him?"

I imagine I'm back in the truck cab, but I can't picture the guy at all. All I can see is Fran's hand resting on his arm, her face a picture of empathy.

"I guess that when I got out, he was more optimistic than before. But it had nothing to do with me."

"You're just being modest," she says. "What were you doing in a truck, anyway?"

"We broke down on Route 66. So we left my brother with the car and hitched a ride."

There's an unusually long silence before a woman raises her hand. "Who's *we*?" she asks.

Oh, crap. "Uh . . . my brother and me."

"But you said he stayed with the car."

"Yes, I did." I try to think of a reasonable—and non-incriminating—response, but instead my brain returns to the cab again. Fran was touching the driver, not *me*, but her arm rested against my leg for almost a minute. Perhaps it means nothing; or perhaps it means she's comfortable around me. I so want her to feel comfortable around me.

"So who was with you?" the woman asks again.

I can't think straight. My brain has latched on to

Fran and refuses to let go. I'm like a dog with a bone: single-minded and relentless.

"Fran," my mouth announces, before I can stop it.

"Who's Fran?"

Think, Luke. *Think.* "A cousin."

"Is that the same cousin as in Amarillo yesterday?" shouts a girl at the back of the room.

"Uh . . ." How does she know about yesterday's signing? "Yes."

"Oh, good. My friend e-mailed me about that. It's so sweet that you're helping with her recovery."

I almost flinch, but turn it into a shrug at the last moment. "Well, it's not that big a deal."

"Not for you, maybe. Because everything you do is so . . . extraordinary. Like that passage in *Hallelujah* about swimming across the Mississippi River—I read it, and I was like, *seriously?*"

Thank goodness we're changing topics. "Yeah, that's what my editor said too."

"It must've been so hard." The girl's eyes are practically bugging out. "I read that the Mississippi has really strong currents. Polluted too."

"True. But I really wanted to get across this idea of putting your doubts aside and going for it, you know? Because every now and then, you get lucky, and something wonderful happens."

"I guess." She puffs out her cheeks. "Still, I can't imagine doing something that crazy."

A young boy raises his hand now. "That's how I felt about the part in the desert."

"Realizations, chapter four," I say. Another section my editor told me I wasn't allowed to ditch.

He nods. "That bit where the animals attacked, I practically peed myself."

His mother tilts her head and *tsks* loud enough for all of us to hear. Stifled laughter ripples around the room.

"So which desert was it?" he asks.

"Sorry?"

"In *Hallelujah*—which desert are you talking about?"

"Just a desert. Any desert," I say. "It really doesn't matter which."

The boy's smile looks frozen in place. All around him, people exchange glances. I've clearly said something wrong, though I can't figure out what.

"Any other questions?" I ask.

A stony silence has descended on the audience. When people speak, it's to each other, mutterings I can't decipher.

Normally I'd be pleased to end things early, but something about the silence is really unsettling. "Anybody got a question? Seriously. Anything at all. Please?"

Two boys about my age are elbowing each other

in the ribs. Finally the taller one raises his arm. He's chewing so much gum it takes him a moment to prepare his mouth for speaking.

"Hey, man," he says. "So, like, I just read this rumor online that you might've, you know, been emptying hotel minibars. Is that true?"

I can literally feel the blood rushing to my face. Who would make up something so ridiculous? How could anyone possibly think . . .

Oh. My. God.

I picture Fran opening one after another miniature bottle. Sure, I haven't taken anything from a minibar. But what about her?

"I don't know what you're talking about," I say. "I'm pretty sure most of the hotels haven't even had minibars." I think I sound persuasive, but the silence that greets my defense is anything but reassuring.

"So you notice that sort of thing, then?" the boy asks.

"Oh, no. No!"

"But you don't deny taking alcohol."

"Of course."

Gasps resonate throughout the hall, followed quickly by desperate whispers that leave me feeling weak-kneed and nauseous.

"I mean, of course I deny taking alcohol. I'm on a book tour for *Hallelujah*. I'd be crazy to drink."

"But if you weren't on tour?"

"No! I still wouldn't drink. Don't drink. Honestly. I promise."

There's a collective exhalation. They seem reassured.

But I'm not. Because whoever leaked this information in the first place may be able to prove that Fran took something from a minibar. And if they do, I'll be forced to explain why I've been sharing a room with a female "cousin" instead of my brother.

These events aren't getting any easier, that's for sure. The question is whether I can survive two more of them.

9:10 P.M.
The Divine Depot, Oklahoma City, Oklahoma

Matt's standing by the main door of the bookstore as I leave, but I'm in such a daze it takes me a moment to notice him. I think it was Pastor Mike who told me to be ready for anything; or maybe it was someone else. Anyway, what does that even mean? Who can be ready for sleep-deprivation and hunger and several hundred people asking completely irrelevant questions? Seriously, who can do that?

"Follow me," says Matt.

"Where are we going?"

"Out to eat. You look like you're starving, and I think it's affecting . . ." His words trail off.

"Go on—say it."

"Okay. I caught the end of your performance, and it wasn't exactly . . . inspirational."

I know he's right, but I hate hearing him say it.

"Did you hear the question about the minibars?" I ask him.

"Yeah. That one's got ugly written all over it."

He ushers me outside and around the corner. It's no quieter here, but at least we won't be overheard. Still, I can't help scanning the streets in case Teresa and her photographer are nearby. I've become paranoid.

"Listen, I know this is going to sound weird," I say, "but can we stay radio silent until we get to St. Louis? It's only two days. Then I'll call Colin and explain everything."

"Sure. No problem. What about Mom and Dad?"

"Shoot. I didn't think of them. Geez, I haven't spoken to them all week."

"Don't worry about it. I called them this afternoon—explained the car problem. I figured Al would probably tell them eventually, so I should just fess up."

"And?"

"And they *definitely* didn't see the funny side." He smiles, but it seems like hard work. "Anyway, they're fine, and they know you're busy. So you want a complete blackout on communications, right?"

"Yeah. That'd probably be best."

"I'm all over it." He takes out his cell phone and turns it off. "Now, about these events . . . I'm no expert, but it seems that as long as you're smiling and saying stuff they want to hear, almost everyone is happy."

I haven't got the energy to talk about this right now.

"I get it," he says. "Less talkie, more eatie."

We stop at an all-day-breakfast diner that claims to be the home of "The Coronary." Matt selects a booth at the back and a waitress joins us almost immediately.

"Coffee, please," says Matt. "And my brother will have a Coronary."

She looks me up and down. "Indeed he will."

"So where's the car?" I ask, once she has gone.

"At the hotel. AAA towed us to a dealership, and the mechanics rodded out the radiator—said something about a blockage in a tube—and after that, it was fine. They also said it had nothing to do with hitting the possum, if you can believe it. I think Alex was disappointed. She figured it was divine retribution for the roadkill."

Hearing Alex's name reminds me of what's so wrong about this scene. "Hold on. Why are you here? And where's Fran? She said she was coming tonight."

Matt nods. "Yeah, well . . . I think they wanted some girl-bonding time, you know? At least, *Alex* did. I can't speak for Fran, but they went out together anyhow."

"Oh."

The Coronary takes barely a minute to arrive, which is pretty disturbing. Matt hands over Colin's credit card without a thought. He catches me watching. "It's a legitimate expense," he says.

There are five strips of bacon on the plate, and another three on a saucer beside me. There's also a mound of scrambled egg, four pieces of toast, three sausages, and something that's either a burger or a sausage patty. Guess I'll find out which.

"Have we really been spending a hundred bucks a day on gas?" I ask.

"Alex exaggerates." Matt scratches his stubble. "It's more like eighty."

"And I'm guessing this isn't coming out of your pocket."

"It's a legitimate—"

"Tour expense. Yeah, I know." I'm getting tired of that word: *legitimate*. "But a rental car was never part of the plan. Especially not an expensive one."

"Hey, it's a whole lot cheaper than flying you from city to city. Which, by the way, is what Colin's doing with that other author."

"Oh." I didn't know that. "Even so, he never would've let us get a Hummer."

"It was Sunday morning. I tried three rental places before I found one that was open." He huffs. "We did what we had to."

"No, Matt, we did what *you* wanted to do. It's not the same thing."

"Why are you getting mad at me? I'm trying to be nice."

I clatter the knife and fork onto the plate. "Why do you think? Because I barely make it to my events. I stink half the time 'cause I didn't get to shower. I'm so tired, I say dumb stuff, and half the audience leaves before buying the book. But all you care about is Route 66 and stupid detours to the armpits of America. Haven't you noticed? No one else gives a crap."

Matt brings his hands together as though he's praying. "You don't really believe that, do you?" He pauses. "Oh, come on, bro. This is Alex's tour, not mine. Do you hear me reciting entire chapters from the guidebook?"

"You can't. You're driving."

"Oh, man." He shakes his head. "I'm doing this for her, okay?"

I stab a strip of bacon. "Why?"

"Because I'm freakin' desperate, you idiot. That's why."

My fork hangs in midair. "What do you mean—desperate?"

"I've lost her. Can't you see that? I've been losing her all year. I don't know if there's someone else, or if she just doesn't feel the same way about me anymore. But ever since high school she's talked about driving along Route 66—always said we'd do it the summer after freshman year. So I made plans: not just Havasu Falls, but a bunch of other stops too." He watches my expression. "Yeah, this has been planned since forever. Mom and Dad knew about it too. When Colin bailed on you, they asked if I could change things so they wouldn't have to take off work. I didn't want to do it, but they practically begged me—said Colin would cover expenses. So I canceled all the motel reservations except Havasupai Lodge, and made new ones to fit *your* stupid itinerary."

I swallow hard. "Mom and Dad never told me."

"Because they didn't want you to feel bad about it. Didn't want you to have any distractions. Never mind what Alex and I wanted. No, we just have to keep to a ridiculous schedule that means we miss every freakin' stop I had planned. I have to check my cell phone for messages every two hours. And when I can't get a signal, I get chewed out—like it's my fault!"

"I'm sorry, Matt. I . . ."

"What? You *what*?" He leans back and rubs his eyes. "It's okay, bro. This isn't really your fault. I kind of knew things would be crazy. I just never figured on having to woo Alex all over again too."

I'm not used to seeing Matt's vulnerable side. I'm not sure I even knew he had one. Since I don't know how to respond, I say the first thing that pops into my head: "Did you just say *woo*?"

The server returns and Matt signs the credit card receipt. He leaves a *really* generous tip on Colin's behalf. "I'll see you back at the hotel."

"Don't go. Please."

Matt helps himself to a strip of bacon. "I need some alone time, okay? Anyway, you can counsel me back in our room."

"*Our* room?"

"Yeah. Alex didn't want to . . ." He shrugs. "I'm sorry."

He walks away then, and though I feel sorry for

him, I also feel sorry for me. I know I shouldn't—it's really selfish—but it kills me that I won't see Fran until the morning.

Tomorrow morning feels like an impossibly long way away.

9:50 P.M.
Hotel Okie, Oklahoma City, Oklahoma

Matt is lying on his bed. His eyes are closed and he's wearing noise-canceling headphones. He may as well hang a neon sign saying: DO NOT DISTURB.

Suits me. I'm tired too. Although . . .

I step out of the room and wait for the door to latch behind me. I need to go for a walk, get some fresh air. Just for a few minutes.

It's quiet outside, except for the occasional sounds of traffic. There's no fresh air, just the stale heat of a humid summer evening. Still, it's peaceful, so I close my eyes and try to shut out the nagging doubts from tonight's event.

"Oh, hi." Fran appears beside me. "I didn't know you were out here."

My heart leaps, and for some reason I wave. "Yeah. I, uh, just came out for a walk."

"Me too." She narrows her eyes. "You didn't get very far."

"No. I decided to take a break."

"Lucky me."

We sit side by side on a concrete wall, feet dangling beneath us. Fireflies gather just beyond arm's reach.

"Sorry I couldn't make it this evening," she says. "How'd it go?"

"Oh, you know . . . terrible. People asked me all these weird questions about the book. It's like they want every word to be so meaningful. Truth is, I don't think it means anything at all."

Fran exhales. "Whoa. You know, this is *not* a good time to have a crisis of faith."

"It's a little late for that."

"What do you mean?"

Deep breath. "Look, I wrote most of *Hallelujah* in the days after we won the debate competition. Andy read a couple pages at the church retreat and said I should keep going, but I couldn't write the same way anymore."

Fran must realize this has something to do with her, but she doesn't interrupt.

"Anyway, when I finished it, Andy sent it to Pastor Mike. And Pastor Mike sent it to an editor he knew.

Everything happened so quickly after that. It wasn't until we were halfway through editing that I realized how much of it meant nothing to me. I asked if we could cut stuff, but my editor said no way. Now it doesn't even feel like my book."

"Why not? You still wrote it."

"Did I? Sure, I wrote the first version, but then I gave it to Andy and he suggested a gazillion changes—all of which I made. And then my editor made more, and my copyeditor corrected all the little mistakes, and by the time it came out, it wasn't anything like the book I wrote."

"So?"

"So—it's like the teachers did my homework, and now everyone's congratulating me for getting an A on a topic I know nothing about."

She laughs, and knocks her feet against mine playfully. "It's not like that at all. Anyway, Andy's suggestions were so small: Change this word, cut this section, explain something better."

"How do you know?"

"Because he showed me your first draft. Let me read it too." She watches my reaction. "We've stayed in touch, Andy and me."

I can't believe she read it. I wish she hadn't. Why did Andy even show it to her? Surely he realized how much it had to do with her? And what did she make of the sudden change in tone in the second part, when I couldn't crack a smile, let alone a joke? Did she know she was the cause of it?

"Look, you want to go for a walk?" she asks. "It's why you came out here, right?"

She jumps off the wall, and holds out her hand as though I might need help. Her hair falls across her face, giving her an air of mystery. In the dark I can't tell that it's purple at all.

I take her hand and jump down. There's almost no space between us. I figure she'll let go of my hand now, but she doesn't.

We wander around the back of the hotel, where a security light casts an amber glow across a bank of grass no bigger than a tennis court. Beyond it, I can see the outline of a pond.

We stop walking—both of us, at the same time. I'm not sure what has led to this understanding that we've already reached our destination, but barely a second passes before Fran reaches across and takes my other hand in hers. I stare into her wide eyes. Then, as if it's the most natural thing in the world, I lean forward and kiss her.

With our lips gently touching, the stress of the evening melts away. I can't imagine what a crisis of faith might be. It's like I've been transported back in time, and I'm standing beside her after the debate competition. I'm in paradise again, and when my lips begin to open, it's the other Luke making it happen.

Fran pulls back a few inches, enough to break the spell. Our hands loosen.

I turn away from the light, ashamed at myself. "I'm sorry," I say.

"For what?"

"For doing that."

"Why? I want to kiss you too. I just need a moment, that's all." She looks at her nails. In the light I can see she's been picking at them again, and the polish is speckled and ugly. She's hiding behind her hair too, unmistakably purple now. "Hey, lighten up, okay? It's just a kiss."

"Yeah, I know. No big deal, right?"

She stares at me with eyes full of hurt. "You know that's not what I mean."

Oh crap. She's going to leave now—I just know it. "I'm sorry. I shouldn't have said that."

Now she looks confused. "So why did you?"

"I don't know."

"Not good enough. Try harder."

"Okay, it's . . . it's because I'm afraid you're going to break my heart."

"Oh." She raises her eyebrows. "Why would you think that?"

"Because you're *Fran*." I take a couple deep breaths. "Under it all . . . you're still Fran."

I expect her to ask me what the heck *that* means too, but she just waits.

"I was ten years old the first time you came to church," I tell her. "I remember the date, and the weather, and the dress you wore. And for the next five years, I never heard a word of Andy's sermon because I was too busy thinking about you. When your mom told me you were going to join the debate team, I got to school early and said I wanted in. I knew I'd never have the guts to sign up if you joined before me—you know, in case everyone guessed why I was really doing it. You were so out of my league. So popular. Outside the church crowd, no one even knew who I was."

"They do now."

"Yeah, because they think it's cool that I have a book. Before that, I wasn't even friends with the church crowd—not really. They were your friends, not mine. You just shared them with me."

"Not this year, I didn't." She shoves her hands in her pockets. "What's your point, Luke?"

"I don't know. I just feel like everything's changed. Like, I don't even know why I go to church anymore. I pray to God all the time, but it's just a habit. I watch the younger kids getting excited, so I pretend to be excited too, but it's an act. When I look around me, I see this big, happy club. I want to be part of it, but I'm not. It's like my membership expired a year ago."

"When I changed."

"Yeah."

I sit cross-legged on the grass; not because I'm tired, but because I'm afraid I'll run away if I don't. Fran joins me, pulling at the grass beside her.

"I liked you so much the way you were, Fran. Loved you, even. I've spent this whole year hating that you changed."

"Only on the outside. If you'd talked to me, you'd have known that."

"But the outside was part of what I loved. Maybe that's wrong, but it's the way I felt. And just now, when I kissed you, I closed my eyes and pictured you the way you used to be."

"If this is supposed to be an apology, it's not going well."

"I know. I'm just trying to tell the truth for once. When I think of you that way, I still feel like I'm not good enough for you." I bite my lip. "So I push you away first, say dumb things, just trying to put off that moment."

I can't believe I just said that. I guess I'm not the only one either; Fran stares at the pond, head nodding gently. "That's the most honest you've ever been," she says finally.

"Yeah. It is."

"You've been so weird all year. I'd see you at school, and you just looked pissed the whole time. I thought when the book came out you'd be happy, but you weren't. But now you're finding yourself again, I think."

"Doesn't excuse me for being an idiot."

She leans across and kisses me on the lips, just once. "Thank you for admitting that," she says. "So, come on. Since we're having this heart-to-heart, you got anything else you need to confess?"

"Well, I may have told someone at the signing that you're my cousin."

"Your *what*?"

"Yeah, and—"

"What do you mean *and*? There's more?"

"Yeah. Somehow people have the impression you're along for the ride because I'm trying to, uh, help you."

I can tell she was steeling herself not to react, but she flinches anyway.

"I'm sorry, Fran! I know it's wrong. Please forgive me."

"It's a lie, Luke! Forget about offending me. You *lied*. Is it really that easy for you?"

Actually, it *was* really easy. And it shouldn't have been.

Fran doesn't allow the silence to linger. She's probably no more eager to hear the truth than I am to tell it. "Well," she says, "if we're cousins, I guess we can forget about making out in future."

"Huh?"

"It wouldn't be right," she insists. "The thought of kissing my cousin grosses me out. So no more of this"—she takes my hand and brings it to her lips, kisses it gently—"or this"—she turns my hand over and brushes her lips across my palm—"and absolutely none of this"—her lips glide along my index finger. When she reaches my fingertip, she opens her mouth and places it inside, runs her tongue around it.

It's so intense, so beautiful I can barely stand it.

She sits back suddenly, her face a giant question mark. "Unless, you know . . . we're not really cousins at all."

I swallow hard. "Does that mean we're . . ."

"What do you think?"

She puts my index finger in her mouth again and peers up at me with those irresistible eyes.

"I-I don't know." My voice sounds odd, breathy and unreliable. "I guess I'd kind of like it if, well . . . you know."

She returns my finger with a butterfly kiss.

"I think it means whatever we want it to mean, Luke. And I think we both want it to mean the same thing."

I could agree with her, but my hand is already reaching behind her head and pulling her toward me. And as we fall onto the ground and I feel her body beneath me, I realize there's nothing more to say.

SATURDAY, JUNE 21

Realizations 4: 22–25

22. That was the night the boy gave up, and wept cruel tears, and gnashed his teeth, and pounded his fists, and did lots of other things that signified the extraordinary degree to which he was giving up. 23. And, yea, it was not merely because of the heat—though the desert was hot—or the dryness—though the desert was dry— or the insects (well, actually the insects were a pretty big deal)—but because in his heart he felt abandoned. 24. But as a mirage holds the promise of water, so his dreams assured him that he had not been abandoned. 25. And when, finally, he emerged, he recognized at last the presence that had been within him all along. And it filled him with joy.

6:00 A.M.
Behind the Hotel Okie,
Oklahoma City, Oklahoma

The sun is already rising when I wake up. Fran is folded into me, her purple hair draped across my arm. My entire left side has cramped up from being on the hard ground, but I don't move a muscle. If I wake Fran, she might leave. At this moment nothing in the world is more important than being beside her.

I can see our campsite at last. It's a regular dumping ground—entire trash bags tossed into the tall, brown grass. Even the pond is inky, and the stench of waste wafts up on the morning breeze. The whole place is a pit, and yet, as I turn my attention to Fran, I realize that it's just as romantic now as it was before. With Fran beside me, everywhere becomes Eden.

"You planning to wake me anytime soon?" she asks, eyes still closed. She's been reading my thoughts again.

"Uh-uh."

A smile blossoms on her face. "So no more kissing for you, huh?"

"That's not what I meant."

She opens her eyes, takes in the sunrise. "Today is June twenty-first. Summer solstice."

"Yeah, I suppose it is."

She shifts position so that her head rests on my outstretched arm. "This event—this sunrise—was a holy time for ancient civilizations. It was a time for worshipping the earth, and getting married, and celebrating the plants and crops. I get it too. It makes sense to me."

I pull her close. "Do you ever find yourself wishing our faith had moments as . . . *definitive* as this?" I ask. "Something you can feel and see. Something so obviously real."

Fran tilts her head toward me, a serious expression on her face. "Yesterday, I did. But today I woke up next to you. If that isn't a miracle, I don't know what is."

The sun is already above the horizon, a reminder that just as the solstice is temporary, so our time here is fleeting too. Which is why I kiss her, knowing I'll never forget this moment as long as I live.

7:50 A.M.
Parking lot, Hotel Okie,
Oklahoma City, Oklahoma

Matt is standing beside the Hummer. "I've already put your bags in," he says without looking at us.

Alex arrives bearing doughnuts and coffee. She hands one to each of us. She even remembered that my favorites are jelly-filled.

"This is cream-filled," says Matt, spitting out a hunk of doughnut.

"I thought you liked them," she replies, her face a picture of innocence.

Matt pops the half-eaten doughnut back in the bag and climbs into the driver's seat. "Bus leaves in twenty seconds. You snooze, you lose."

"Excellent use of a tired cliché," says Alex, reaching for the back door handle at the same time as me. "No, Luke. You ride shotgun today."

"Actually I'd prefer to—"

"Just get in the front seat!"

I do as I'm told, but it doesn't feel right. I haven't even finished adjusting the seat before I'm aware of the emptiness of not having Fran beside me. I lower the sun visor and adjust it so I can glimpse her in the mirror, but it's not enough. I close my eyes and picture her lying beside me, the gentle smile teasing her lips, the delicate curve of her body.

"Stop groaning, dude," says Matt.

"What?"

"I'm just saying: A sound like that shouldn't be public."

Fran reaches around the seat to hug me. "Something on your mind?" she whispers. "Maybe some*one*?" She laughs softly, which sends a rush of air that jolts every fiber of my body. She leans closer, so that her lips brush my left ear. "Dream on, Luke Dorsey. Just make sure it's about me."

I'm bright red now, but since she said it's okay, I close my eyes again and dream sweet dreams as the purring engine lulls me to sleep.

9:55 A.M.
Route 66, somewhere in Oklahoma (I think)

I'm woken by a crash of thunder. Drool dribbles down my chin. I turn to face Fran, see the same bleary-eyed expression on her face that I know must be on mine. We smile guiltily, mirror images of each other, impossibly in tune.

Fran opens her window just enough to squeeze her hand through, and I do the same. Rain lashes down, cool and refreshing, but I never take my eyes off Fran. I can't. She's a vision of open smile, high cheekbones, delicately arched eyebrows, and feather-soft hair. Nothing exists but her and the rain running down my hand and along my arm.

"I love the rain," I say finally.

Fran beams. "It feels so fresh, so cleansing."

"Praise be!" cries Alex. "Oklahoma's getting an enema!"

Having shattered the mood, Alex flounces back against her seat and stares blankly out the window. Fran blows me a kiss, and I know it's my cue to turn around, to hide what we're really feeling—what we've become.

"Where are we?" I ask no one in particular.

Matt grunts. "Don't know. Somewhere past Tulsa."

"Do you know where we are, Alex?"

"No, Luke. How the hell would I?"

I gulp. "I don't know. I thought maybe it says something in your guidebook."

"Would that be the guidebook in the glove compartment in front of you?"

"Oh. Yeah, I guess so."

"Great." She claps her hands together. "Now here's an idea: Why don't you look yourself?"

"Enough!" shouts Fran. "We've got one more day together, and I will *not* let you screw it up. Pull over, Matt. We need to talk."

Alex leans forward and growls in Matt's ear: "You pull over, you lose a testicle."

"Oh, yeah?" says Fran. "The way you two are behaving, I don't think you'll get close enough to do that."

Alex inhales sharply. Then she busts out laughing.

"Just do it, Matt," says Fran gently. "Your testicles are safe with me."

Matt glances at me and turns bright red. "That doesn't mean what you think it means, bro. Honest."

10:05 A.M.
Catoosa, Oklahoma

Matt pulls into a parking lot and jams on the brakes.

"Well, would you look at that," he says.

Alex undoes her seat belt and leans against the two front seats. "I guess we know where we are now."

Actually, I have no idea where we are. I just know that in front of us is a larger-than-life painted blue whale stuck in a pond.

"The Blue Whale of Catoosa," announces Matt, like we've stumbled on the eighth wonder of the world. "Incredible. We just . . . found it."

"No, you didn't," says Fran. "I told you to stop the car so you two can make up before I have to kill you. But hey, I'm glad this place is meaningful for you."

As Matt and Alex turn and glare at her, she playfully winds her hair around a finger. She has the cute younger sister role down cold; well, except for the purple hair, piercings, and tattoos.

"What's the Blue Whale of Catoosa?" I ask.

The guidebook is sitting in my lap, but no one reaches for it.

"The Blue Whale of Catoosa," begins Fran, pretend narrating, "was built to celebrate the Year of the Whale. Legend has it that the whale comes to life every leap year, and that the pond water was once clean enough to swim in."

"Is that true?" I ask.

"No, silly. You're the one with the guidebook. I'm just filling the awkward silence."

I get out of the car and begin sweating immediately. Still, it's not like I've showered yet today, so no great loss. Fran doesn't seem to mind either—she holds my hand and we practically skip toward the whale. Matt and Alex follow us, arms by their sides, not a finger touching. How have we changed roles so quickly? Did Fran and I shift the balance of the universe?

When we reach the whale Fran turns around. "Okay," she says, "you two have five minutes to take photos or kiss the whale or whatever it is you're supposed to do with freaky roadside attractions. Then we talk. Got it?"

She pulls me into the hollow belly of the whale and pushes me against the metal wall. My hands grip her waist as our lips come together, tongues gently touching. No matter how close we are, I need us to be closer. I want us to be one. I want—

I pull back suddenly.

"What is it?" asks Fran.

"I . . . I just had an impure thought."

Fran's mouth crinkles into a smile. "And what would that be?"

"I can't say."

"What can't he say?" asks Alex, rounding the corner. Matt is a step behind her.

"What can't you say?" parrots Fran.

"I-I can't say."

Fran is enjoying this way too much. "Hmm, the witness is not being forthcoming, Your Honor." She paces in tiny circles before me like a lawyer contemplating her next move. "Though, from his behavior, we may surmise that it is a combination of many things: a desire to express his affection physically, perhaps; the need to apologize for once having lost sight of that; a hope that our years of friendship are sufficient to overcome any minor obstacles between us."

"Minor?" cries Alex.

"Yes, *minor*," replies Fran, no less forcefully. "And most of all, I imagine, Luke is looking forward, considering what he wants for us both in the future. And discovering that the depth of his feeling is surprising to him."

Alex stares at me now, and I have to look away. I feel like the frog dissected in freshman biology: my innermost everything revealed. I can't believe Fran has seen it all so clearly. I don't know if I should feel ashamed, or apologetic, or—what? Meanwhile, Alex continues to watch me, a tear running down her cheek.

"Are you okay?" I ask her.

She nods. "I'm okay."

As if a spell has been cast, she steps back into Matt's waiting arms.

I want to know how Fran does it, but she grasps my hand as if the case is closed and it's time to leave. I throw our siblings a final glance as we leave, and quickly wish

I hadn't. They're back together again, yes, but something isn't right. Matt holds on to Alex as though his life depends on it; but she's just a rag doll in his arms.

That's how I know Fran wasn't really talking about me. And whatever spell she has cast already seems to be wearing off.

I squeeze her hand once, and don't relax until I feel her squeeze back.

2:50 P.M.
Route 66 Hotel, Springfield, Missouri

The Kansas section of Route 66 is so short I almost miss it. We arrive in Springfield, Missouri, with two hours to spare before tonight's event, but I'm not exactly relaxed. In the back of my mind I keep replaying last night's debacle. What if people ask about the minibars again? What if they have *proof* that something was taken? If I blame Matt, will he get into trouble since he's under twenty-one?

Matt pulls up at the hotel, and Fran and I enter together. The receptionist narrows his eyes as we approach the front desk. "Can I help you?" he asks.

"Two rooms under Dorsey, Luke."

"Ah, yes. Luke Dorsey. Rooms twenty-one and twenty-two." He hands me two keycards. "I'll let your publicist know you're here."

"C-Colin is here?"

"Indeed." The guy dials a number and purses his lips as he awaits a response. "Yes, sir. Mr. Dorsey is here. Uh-huh. No problem." He hangs up and looks me square in the eye. "He's on his way."

My heart is pounding. I have a pretty good idea that if he could have, Colin would've preferred to chew me out over the phone. Since I've made that impossible, he's flown out from New York City—or wherever the heck he was—to do it in person. No one flies a thousand miles or more to say "Well done!"

Fran studies my expression and acts quickly. "Well, come on, *Matt*," she says, tugging my arm. "We'd better go get your brother."

It takes me a moment to catch on. I hadn't realized she could lie smoothly too. "Oh, right. I'm sure he's just outside."

"You're not Luke Dorsey?" asks the receptionist.

"I'm his brother," I say as we shuffle toward the exit.

We're almost to the door when I have to stop. I'm hyperventilating, and now would be an inconvenient time to pass out. "What am I going to do, Fran?"

She scans the foyer, all business. "You're going to take the stairs to room twenty-two. Don't take the elevator in case you meet Colin. I'll wait outside for five minutes, then come back and tell him you've gone to the bookstore. By the time he realizes something's up, you'll be showered, dressed, and out of the room."

"How will you know what he looks like?"

"I figure he'll be the one screaming obscenities."

I feel the blood drain from my face.

"Kidding!" She laughs. "Look, you double back and head for the stairs. Just give me the keycard for room twenty-one so Matt and Alex can start repairing their relationship."

"What do you— Oh! You mean . . ."

"Yes, Luke, I mean . . ." She wiggles her eyebrows. "Although it's probably better if we don't think about that. Yet."

Now the color returns to my face with a vengeance.

"That's my boy," says Fran, leaning forward and planting a kiss on my lips. "Now, hurry up. I can't exactly help you once you've been caught and dismembered."

I'm back to my pale, wan look again. I don't hang around to see if her prediction comes true.

4:05 P.M.
On the way to Inspiration Bookstore, Springfield, Missouri

I'm ready to go, and there's still an hour until the signing. I take the stairs instead of the elevator, and for good measure exit via the back of the building. I'm behaving like a fugitive, but I have to put off my conversation with Colin until later.

The bookstore is a few blocks away, in a converted redbrick factory with a towering smokestack and the outline of the factory's original name in faded white paint. I head for the entrance.

"You don't want to do that," shouts Fran from an alleyway to my right.

"Hey," I say, jogging over to her.

She meets me halfway. "Colin's waiting for you inside. I said you must've gone back to the hotel, but he's no fool. He's just hanging out—him and his nine millimeter revolver."

"Wha—?"

"Kidding again. But I suggest you find another way to pass a half hour."

"Got something in mind?"

"Haven't you?"

I kiss her then, and if that's not what she had in mind, she's doing a good job of faking it.

She pulls me into the alley, away from prying eyes, and we kiss until things become a little heated.

"Whoa," she says, leaning back. "Let's not forget that someone has a book signing."

"Actually, I'd love to forget it."

Fran laughs as she adjusts my shirt collar and tie. Satisfied with her handiwork, she takes the Sharpie from my shirt pocket and puts it between her teeth. Then she unbuttons the cuff on my right sleeve.

"What are you doing?"

She rolls up my sleeve.

"Fran?"

Still no answer, but the Sharpie is out of her mouth now, and uncapped. She runs her tongue across her teeth. I think I know what she intends to do, and I'm shaking.

"Don't be nervous, silly boy," she says. "You're wearing a long-sleeve shirt, remember? No one'll see."

See *what*? I want to ask. But she's leaning closer, her breath on my arm—warm, electric.

"You have the finest hairs," she says, pressing the pen against my skin. "They're so soft."

She keeps writing, until the whole of my upper

arm has been covered in pretty black cursive. When she's done it reads: *She loves the one who sees her*. It takes me a moment to work out what she means—is the emphasis on *sees* or *her?*—but I get it. I really do. And I'm so overjoyed to be the *one* that I can barely keep myself from proving it to her. But she's holding out the Sharpie, and now my hands are shaking again.

"I can't," I begin.

"You must," she finishes.

I rest my hand on her bare upper arm. The nib hovers just above her smooth, tan skin. What I'm about to do is doing weird things to me—I'm light-headed, breathing fast, sweating, and so completely in the moment that I welcome all of it.

"So thoughtful," she teases. "The furrowed brows. The gritted teeth. A picture of concentration." She's not nervous at all—wants to display this message for the whole world to see.

I bring the nib down. My letters are big and uneven, but Fran doesn't care. It's about the words, not the execution. And I know exactly what the words must be: *His dream come true*.

When I'm done, I blow on the ink—though it's already dry—and Fran shivers.

"Thank you," she says.

"I'm sorry it looks so bad."

"Unlike the rest of my arms, you mean?" She studies her forearms. "I wish I hadn't . . ."

I look too. The lines are so random, it's like she doodled with her eyes closed. But each one must've taken hours, and hurt too. "Why did you do it, Fran?"

She shrugs. "Because no one told me to stop. I figured someone would eventually—someone who cared; someone who was afraid for me. But I was wrong. Everyone was afraid *of* me instead. So I punished myself some more."

I hug her to stop the self-doubt. There'll be time to talk, to mend and heal. Besides, as we kiss again, I realize that I wouldn't change a thing about her. Which maybe, just maybe, is love.

4:40 P.M.
Inspiration Bookstore, Springfield, Missouri

Colin is waiting for me when I enter the bookstore. "Luke, my boy," he bellows. "How are you?"

"Oh, I'm—"

"That's *great!*" He has a crazy man's forced smile, and a voice to match. He places his hand between my shoulder blades and guides me toward the back of the store at a jog. "It's the damndest thing, but somehow I missed you at the hotel."

"Really?" I say. "Oh, I must've been—"

Colin raises a finger to his lips. "How about we step inside this nice empty room first?" he says, pointing to a door marked PRIVATE. "It'd be awfully bad for your image for anyone to overhear the lie you're about to tell."

The room is filled with Luke Dorsey paraphernalia: boxes of books, a stack of posters, even a trio of cardboard cutouts. I can't believe any self-respecting bookseller would actually *ask* for this stuff.

Colin pulls a couple of chairs together and we sit facing each other. He removes his suit jacket and fiddles with his bowtie. "So," he says, "busy week, huh?"

"Yeah."

"And not in a good way."

"Oh."

"To be honest, I'm not exactly thrilled to be here. Nothing against Springfield, you understand—I'm sure it's a lovely city—but today is Saturday. I just got off tour this morning, and I had to cancel my flight to New York so I could join you instead. I won't get back home until tomorrow evening either, which means I miss Sunday morning. And you know what happens on Sunday morning."

I bow my head. "Church."

"Golf, Luke. Golf!" he barks. "So, let's start at the beginning. Mind telling me how you walked into a Pasadena bank armed with nothing but my credit card and convinced a cashier to let you withdraw a thousand bucks?"

"Uh—"

"And while we're at it, just how on God's green earth did you rack up one hundred and seventy-eight dollars of charges at Egghead Kegs?"

"What?"

"My feelings exactly. How do I explain to my boss that America's Golden Boy paid for two kegs of beer despite being underage and in Los Angeles for just one evening? *One evening!* Don't get me wrong—that kind of alcoholic tolerance would be welcomed by any frat house in the country, but in spite of your now-viral interview with Orkle, that's still not our target market."

"I don't know anything about Egghead Kegs."

Colin removes his designer glasses and pinches the bridge of his nose. "Come on now, Luke," he says gently. "I'm on your side. But denial is one of the first signs of alcoholism."

"I'm not an alco—"

"Come on! Everyone knows you raided the minibar in your first hotel room. I've got an itemized list, for Pete's sake. And so does the *National Enquirer*."

"Oh, no."

He puts his glasses back on. "Oh, yes."

"I don't even remember seeing a minibar."

"Really? Because I called the Empress Pasadena myself, and they confirmed the room had one."

"Hold on. Did you just say 'Empress Pasadena'?"

"Yeah. Again, a pretty cheeky move to treat yourself to a hundred-and-fifty-dollar room."

Suddenly the puzzle shifts before my eyes. Alex mentioned the Empress Pasadena, and Fran said that I wouldn't have noticed the minibar in the first hotel. Well, of course I wouldn't—*I wasn't there!* While I was sleeping on a battered mattress, Alex and Fran were living it up in a fancy hotel, and Fran was helping herself to the contents of the minibar. If I didn't adore her, I'd probably want to strangle her. Come to think of it: Why did Matt use Colin's credit card to pay for it anyway?

Colin misreads my silence as a confession. "Listen—and here I'm speaking not just as your publicist, but also your friend—maybe when this tour is over you might want to get some help. I clearly underestimated how stressful this whole experience has been for you. But you have to believe me: Booze is not the answer."

"But I—"

"No, Luke. Don't say anything more. I value honesty in all my relationships, and I'm sure you do too. Obviously there's a lot we need to iron out—like how completely unacceptable it is to go radio silent for practically the entire tour—but for now your main priority is to give these people a good show."

"Show?"

"Event. Signing. Whatever you want to call it." He rubs the crop of fresh stubble on his chin. "Oh, and please tell me you heard about the change of venue tomorrow. I left three voicemails."

I don't even answer—my slumping shoulders speak for me.

"Geez. Your pastor—Andy—arranged with the bookstore to have the event at your church. Sounds like a big place. A thousand seats, he told me."

I swallow hard. "It's huge."

"He reckons we'll fill it too. Said we'd need a thousand copies of *Hallelujah*. Minimum. That's the kind of talk Uncle Colin likes to hear. I've asked all the bookstores in St. Louis to send stock, so we have enough. It's costing a fortune—enough to keep me up at night. And if the *National Enquirer* runs their story on the minibar, we're completely . . ." His voice peters out. "You've gone very pale, Luke."

"Yeah," I croak.

He pats my leg. "Forget it. We'll talk about it tomorrow morning on the way to St. Louis."

"We will?"

"Sure. I'm going to ride with you. It'll give us a few hours to chat."

"But . . . but . . . the car—"

"Is a Hummer, right? By the way, that's another thing we need to talk about." He chuckles, like he's kind of impressed that I'd dare to choose such an expensive vehicle.

"But we don't have any room."

"We'll rearrange your bags. I'm sure you and your brother can squeeze me in. I'll even take the backseat, if that's what you're worried about." He clicks his fingers. "Hey, I've got it: I'll sit beside your *cousin*."

"Oh."

"Yes, *oh!* You know, Luke, we have this thing called the Internet. It allows us to look up what people are saying about you. Including all the references to your *cousin*. Would that by any chance be the purple-haired decoy I met at the hotel?"

I nod apologetically.

"Good grief, Luke. We're supposed to be on the same team!" He shakes his head. "Please tell me she's not your girlfriend."

"Yeah."

"You're touring with your *girlfriend*?" He grimaces. "Wait a minute—when you asked for an extra room . . . oh, no! You haven't been sharing a room, have you?"

When I don't reply, he seems to age ten years.

"You're sixteen! Do your parents know?"

"They don't know we're dating."

"Wow. We *do* have a lot to talk about, don't we?" He glances at the cardboard cutout, and I can tell he's thinking that I have almost nothing in common with that boy. He's right too. "Well, rest assured that I *will* be traveling with you tomorrow morning, no matter what." He forces a chuckle. "It's not like you're saving that fourth seat for a hitchhiker, right?"

I try to laugh too, and fail. I'm pretty sure Alex won't see the funny side either.

5:10 P.M.
Inspiration Bookstore, Springfield, Missouri

The signing should have started ten minutes ago, but apparently people are still fighting their way in, so I wait behind a panel.

I try to forget that my publicist thinks I'm an alcoholic; that no one has told him I'm traveling with not one, but *two* female companions; that tomorrow I'll be doing my shtick in front of a thousand of my closest acquaintances; and that Fran—*persona non grata*—

will be by my side, sporting purple hair, tattoos, and enough stainless-steel earrings to short-circuit a metal detector.

I try to focus. I have to put on a good show.

Whatever that means.

Finally the audience quiets, and a woman in a flowing floral dress introduces me. She uses several superlatives to describe my book. Everyone applauds. By the time she finally calls my name, it's with such an exaggerated tone that I imagine I'm a starter on an NBA team, skipping onto the court as the lights strobe and loud, raucous music rocks my ears. There must be at least four hundred people, all of them ready to witness something special. And for once I'm absolutely determined to give them that. I owe Colin at least that much.

As soon as I'm positioned behind the lectern, I scan the audience for Fran. She isn't hard to find, and when our eyes meet, she turns her arm toward me slightly, showing me my words. I touch my own arm, and take comfort in knowing what's written beneath the shirtsleeve.

I pepper my spiel with jokes, and everyone laughs. I make up anecdotes about what goes on backstage at *The Pastor Mike Show,* and the response is exhilarating. It has taken a week, but I've finally found my groove—what I'm saying matches the tone of what I wrote. I wonder: Is this what I felt during those first few days of writing? Because this feels *real*. At last I glimpse *Hallelujah* as everyone else sees it. And it actually makes me proud.

For the next fifteen minutes I barely pause for breath, and the laughter rarely dies down. Even when I raise my hand and open up to questions, chuckles arise unexpectedly, aftershocks from a comedic earthquake. It's so gratifying that I miss the first question and have to ask the old lady in the pink cardigan to repeat it.

She presses her hands together. "I read a blog that says there's some confusion about which desert you're talking about on page one hundred and twelve. May I ask: To which desert are you referring?"

The question sucks the energy from the room. I want to roll my eyes, but settle for a shrug instead. "It's not any specific desert. It's just . . . a desert," I explain. "So let's not get overheated about which one, okay?" It's a good pun, given the circumstances.

No one laughs.

"I'm not getting overheated, Luke," the lady continues. "I'm a big fan of your book. Bought copies for all my grandchildren. But you were there a month. You must remember which desert it was."

I assume she's kidding, but during the ensuing silence she doesn't even twitch. She truly expects an answer. Even worse, so does everyone else.

"You're not serious, are you?" I ask.

"Yes," she says indignantly. "Why wouldn't I be?"

"Because . . . well, you know." I narrow my eyes. "Obviously I didn't go to any desert."

I still manage a smile, but it's hard work. I'm facing a wall of four hundred blank stares and frigid silence. There's nothing amusing about this scene.

"You didn't go to a desert?" she says, repeating my words slowly.

I try to say no, but my throat is dry. When I grab a cup, it shakes so violently that water spills over the side.

"But in that case your book is . . ."

The old lady's hands cross at her throat. It looks like she's reprising the international sign for choking, but instead her fingers curl around her pearl necklace as though it's a rosary. She might even be praying. She can't bring herself to say *fiction*, even though that's what it is. Of *course* that's what it is. I never claimed otherwise.

"Excuse me, but which desert did you *think* he'd gone to?" The question comes from Fran, and she's looking at the old lady, not at me.

Her faith in me shattered, the old lady seems to be having trouble holding her head up. "I don't know," she mumbles. "I just thought . . . well, maybe Abyssinia. That's biblical."

"Whoa! You figured he spent a month alone in *Abyssinia*?" Fran knits her brows and runs a hand through her crazy messy hair. The overhead lights emphasize the uneven patches of purple dye. "It's not even called that anymore, right? It's Ethiopia. Would you let a high school kid go hang out alone in Ethiopia?"

Fran's trying to be funny, but no one is laughing.

"Come on, people," she continues. "Wake up. This is a parable. The desert is a metaphor for isolation, loneliness. The point is that faith gives you the strength to overcome even the harshest conditions."

As it happens, she's spot on. But the *people* are clearly having a hard time digesting this information.

"So he didn't go *anywhere*?" asks a small boy. He doesn't even bother to address me, just directs his question to Fran, like she's been appointed my official spokesperson.

I'm not sure she's ideally suited for the job.

"No," says Fran.

"So it's just a story. He made it all up."

"It's a *parable*. Remember those? They're really useful teaching tools—totally Jesus-approved." She groans. "Please don't tell me you take everything so literally."

The boy's mother stands up. "Don't talk to my son that way. He's not the one who made stuff up. Luke is. So back off."

But Fran doesn't back off. Instead, she stands too, her baggy army surplus pants unable to hide the smears of Oklahoma dust, her tank top still dotted with dead grass from our make-out session. All the rings in her ears glint in the light, a warning that she's not someone you mess with. Oh yes, and it looks like someone vomited black ink across her arm.

"Is your faith really so weak?" She's addressing everyone now. "Is this all it takes for you to doubt what you believe?"

The sound of several hundred subdued voices rumbles across the room, and Fran smiles anxiously. She's still hopeful, optimistic.

She shouldn't be; wouldn't be, if she could see their faces.

"And who are you?" shouts a man at the end of her row.

Fran locates the culprit and returns his glare with interest. "I'm a friend of Luke's."

I can see where this is heading. I can hear the venom in her voice, the way she's folding her arms across her chest, tattoos facing outward for everyone to see. She wants them to know she's the kind of girl who'll hold her ground—intellectually, sure, but physically too, if it comes to that. But what will that prove?

"You?" The guy snorts. "No way."

"Why the hell not?"

The guy flinches at *hell,* and shakes his head in disgust. "Fine. You're best buds. I really don't care. I'm not staying for this."

He slides out of the row, and when he leaves he's not alone. At least a dozen people exit with him, though it feels like so many more.

"Why shouldn't we be friends, huh?" cries Fran. "Do you see him denying it?"

"You are *not* his friend!" Another woman's voice, launched from the back of the room, high-pitched and desperate.

I crane my neck to see who dares to take on Fran, and my heart just about stops beating.

It's *Teresa.* She's reprising her Amish look, with high frilly collar and supersized cross. She commands the undivided attention of all men and the unconditional respect of all women. No one will interrupt her.

Teresa wallows in the silence, milks it for an eternity. Then she turns back to Fran and detonates her own bomb. "You're his *girlfriend!*" she shouts.

Silence.

I look around, but I can't focus. The audience is blending, merging into a single entity. Their energy converges, and spills out in waves of disapproving whispers that crescendo into something loud and hurt and threatening.

By the time my mind clears, I realize that not one of them is looking at me.

"You've gotta be kidding!" a woman cries.

"Why?" spits Fran, not just standing now, but leaning forward. *"Why?"*

The woman stands too, leans forward too. "Because you're rude."

"Deal with it."

"Just look at you!"

"What about me? What the hell does that mean?"

That word again. It has no place here—Fran must know that—and there's another moment of silence while the crowd digests it. But only a moment, and then they're growling, hurling their discontent at Fran in razor-sharp but oh-so-carefully-inoffensive language. The attacks grow louder and louder, until I can't make out anyone's voice but Fran's as she struggles to hold her ground. They wonder who she is, this force of nature with the foul mouth and the *screw you* hair. They loathe her too—for being confrontational, for intruding when she wasn't invited in the first place. She has gate-crashed the perfect party, and as their eyes shift back to me, I kind of sympathize with them.

I could've handled this situation. I didn't need Fran to swear, to turn a routine event into a riot. It didn't need to be this way.

"Is she really your girlfriend?" asks a small girl

in the front row. She fingers the ends of her blond pigtails, face pulled into an anxious expression she should never have to wear. I swear she's about to cry.

"No." The answer just slips out—even catches me by surprise—but is lost amid the din.

"Really?" she presses, dubious, or perhaps afraid.

I shake my head. "No."

More people hear me this time, and their earnest hushes combine, silencing the room in only a couple of seconds.

"Are you sure about that?" Teresa leans back in her chair, those narrowed eyes like thunderclouds waiting for all hell to break loose.

I can imagine the pleasure she'd get from seeing these people leave in protest—all because Fran couldn't keep her mouth shut. But I won't give Teresa that victory. Not now. Not ever.

"I don't even know her," I say, calm and confident, my eyes never wavering from Teresa.

I expect Teresa to fume—beaten once again—but she doesn't. She tips her head back and brings her hands together like she's offering a prayer of thanks.

That's when I realize what I've done.

I wait for a crash of thunder—something appropriately biblical—but the room simply returns to normal. No one is paying any attention to Fran anymore. My words have confirmed their desire that she is merely an intruder; and now she's history. We've moved on without her, joined together in celebrating the oneness of our lives. Our shared values.

But that's not all. Everybody in the audience—consciously or not—turns away from her too. Having conquered their adversary, they shun her. Worst of all, they're doing it in support of me. I gave them permission to treat her this way, and now I just want to throw up.

Fran doesn't shout or scream, or lash out at them. She simply stares at the words on her arm, reading them over and over. Finally, as tears well in her eyes, she nods just once, like the world that had been off-kilter for the last few days has returned to its proper axis. I can tell it's killing her.

It's killing me too. I need to fill the silence I've created, but what should I say? I feel empty, and now I know for sure what I've suspected all along: My words are empty too. Everything I've written, everything I've said . . . it's all just nothingness.

Fran is already out the door. My legs are shaking so badly that I'd fall over if I weren't leaning against the lectern. I'm so focused on not crying that I have no energy to spare for forming words.

I want to go back in time, before this evening, to the day I started writing *Hallelujah*. I want to tell myself to stop before it's too late. I want to tell myself I don't deserve to own those words. I want to warn myself who I'm destined to become.

But when I recall that day, I know that my younger self would never believe me. Really, how could he?

5:35 P.M.
Inspiration Bookstore, Springfield, Missouri

The signing is over in record time. There's not much to say anymore, nothing to top the drama of what has just unfolded. Floral-dress lady takes the microphone again, but there's no applause. People head for the exits so fast you'd think the room was on fire.

Colin grabs my arm as I walk to the signing table. "Fiction?" he whispers. "This is *fiction*?"

"Yeah. I never said it wasn't."

"It's subtitled: *A Spiritual Chronicle of a Sixteen-Year-Old St. Louisan.*"

"There are lots of sixteen-year-olds in St. Louis."

"You told the audience of *The Pastor Mike Show* that it was one hundred percent truthful!"

"Did I?"

"Don't play innocent."

"I'm not. I just don't remember. I've never watched it."

Colin looks seriously depressed. "*Hallelujah* is about a sixteen-year-old boy from Missouri who bears an uncanny resemblance to you. Nowhere does it state the whole thing is made up."

"Not the whole thing. Just parts. Anyway, I thought you knew. That's why I wrote it in the third person."

Colin has more to say, that's obvious, but a few people still want to buy a book in spite of what they've witnessed. "Go," he says. "Before everyone runs away."

The line moves quickly. People want to ask questions, but they're tongue-tied. I think they're still in a state of shock, unsure what tonight's disaster really means. The only words they exchange concern "that freaky girl," which makes me so tense I can't even conjure a polite smile.

Then someone ups the ante—calls Fran a *freak*—and I accidentally screw up the name of the dedicatee. It's just an accident, but the bookstore owner gives Colin a nudge and I know we'll be paying for that copy ourselves.

The last person in line places a book on the table. "The name is Chastity."

I look up and find myself eye to eye with Teresa. She has a large manila envelope in her right hand; her left rests on *Hallelujah* as though it's the Bible. "What do you want?" I ask.

"I'm a fan. Heck, I'm not even offended that you got angry at me for pretending to be someone I'm not. Although," she adds, frowning, "that was quite hypocritical of you, in retrospect."

"I'm not pretending to be someone else. You know exactly who I am."

"I do now. And so will everyone else. Soon."

"What do you want, Teresa?"

"It's Chastity."

"I know who you are."

"No, Luke. You just think you do. But as I'm last in line, we have time to address that." She holds out her hand. "Chastity Hope."

"Very funny." I don't shake.

She gives up and pulls out her driver's license. There's a picture of her. Her name is Chastity Hope. She's nineteen.

"I'm glad you find my name funny. So did every kid at every school I ever attended. Especially when I showed up in clothes like these every day. Even in summer."

She hesitates, and I realize she's actually telling the truth, giving me a glimpse of who she really is.

"I used to beg my parents for jeans," she continues, "but they wouldn't let me have a pair. Kept talking about modesty and godliness. Well, you know what? I don't think God gives a crap about what I wear. But the kids at school sure did, and they spent all week bullying me for it—even the ones I saw at church every Sunday. When I told my parents, they just reminded me that nothing compares to Jesus' suffering."

"True."

"What do you mean, *true*? It's irrelevant. Saying Jesus had it worse is *not* a justification for bullying. And you know the worst part? I never believed in God in the first place." She stops, allows her words to sink in.

"Then I'm sorry for you."

"No, you're not. You're only sorry for yourself— that's how self-centered you are. Come on, Luke, you just dumped your girlfriend in public to save face. You'll tell anyone what they want to hear—and let them spout whatever crap they want—just so they'll buy your book."

"That's not true."

"Really? Remember our *date*? I told you the other kids at school had stoned me. I kept making up this crazy stuff, waiting for you to call me on it. But you never did. Didn't want to spoil your chances of making out with me over something as minor as a bare-faced lie, did you?"

"I didn't know you were lying."

"Yes, you did! I could see it in your face." She smiles.

"And what about your first signing? Yvonne Bethel—who's a freakin' con artist, by the way, and everyone knows it—says you've performed a miracle, and what do you do? Nothing! And today we discover that your book is a pile of crap, even though you claimed it was all true."

I shouldn't have to explain myself to Teresa, of all people, but I can't help it. "I honestly don't remember saying that."

"Well, isn't that convenient." She shakes her head. "God, Luke, you have no idea how cathartic this whole week has been for me. My editor at the magazine told me not to make it personal. She said I just needed an interview, a couple statements that revealed the *real* Luke Dorsey. But when I saw you on *The Pastor Mike Show,* spouting all this self-righteous crap like the kids at my school used to, I knew this was a once-in-a-lifetime assignment." She's almost tripping over her words now. "Exposing who you really are has been a crusade for me. Bringing you down may not undo all those years of torment, but it's coming pretty damn close."

I push the book back to her, unsigned.

Suddenly she's back in Teresa mode, misty eyed and uncertain. "But *why* won't you sign it?" she whines loudly. *Really* loudly.

I can't risk another scene, so I take the book back.

"My writing may not be legible," I say as I scrawl the name *Chastity* across the top, and follow it with a squiggle that has no connection to my signature.

"I understand. You've signed a lot of books this week. Still, I'm sure you'll look back on this one fondly. After all, it'll be your last."

I hand it over to her.

"No, no. You keep it," she says. "Think of it as a souvenir."

I can think of another, more satisfying use for the book right now. But what would that prove? Years of bullying have brought Chastity here in the first place. Besides, I still want to prove her wrong.

"Blessed are the pure in heart," I say, "for they shall see God."

"Matthew five, verse eight." She nods approvingly. "Well, I guess that rules both of us out. Good-bye, Luke." She hands me the manila envelope. "And good luck."

As she walks away I read the words written across the envelope: *And I only wanted first base.* It takes a moment, but I have a feeling I know what I'm about to find inside. And it breaks my heart.

There are five glossy 8x10 photographs. They're grainy, because they were taken at night, with nothing but the amber glow of a security lamp to reveal the subjects. But it's us, all right—Fran and me—our arms wrapped around each other, faces turned toward the camera. By the third photo, we're kissing. And finally there's the money shot: Fran and me making out, sprawled on the grass, her body under mine as we kiss with open mouths. If I didn't know better, I'd say there's a whole lot more than that going on too.

I'm sure Colin will agree.

6:10 P.M.
The alleyway outside Inspiration Bookstore, Springfield, Missouri

I'm standing in the alleyway where I was kissing Fran just two hours ago. I can still feel her lips, see her large eyes shining at me with nothing but joy and a self-confident glow that had been missing for twelve long months. It'll be missing again now. I wish I had the energy to hate myself more.

Today, my dream finally came true. Tonight, I changed the dream.

"You okay?" It's Matt, hands stuffed deep in his shorts pockets.

I shake my head.

"I know it's hard," he says, "but trust me: You should go and apologize right now. Waiting won't make it any easier." He pauses for me to show I've heard him. "She's your girlfriend, Luke."

"*Was* his girlfriend," says Alex, joining us. "You're a piece of work, you know that?"

Matt touches her arm gently. "Look at him, Al. He knows he messed up."

"No." She shakes off his hand. "Just for once, can we call it like it is? You *lied*, Luke. How could you do that after she'd told you . . ." Alex turns away. She can't even face me. "She loves you. *Loved* you. Do you understand what that means?"

"Give him a break," says Matt. "He's under a lot of stress."

"Don't tell me you're taking his side."

"I'm not taking sides. I'm just saying he's over-whelmed. This has been a pretty intense experience."

She steps back. "Three times did Peter deny Jesus. Three times!"

"*Now* you start quoting the Bible? Come on. Fran isn't Jesus, Alex."

"Well, neither is Luke! Not by a long shot. Doesn't stop everyone from acting like he is."

Matt takes a deep breath. "How about this one: Let he who is without sin cast the first stone."

Alex's shock is quickly swallowed behind a thin-lipped smile. "Egghead Kegs, Matt? Ring a bell?"

Matt's face turns ghostly white. He seems to shrink before my eyes.

"I know you paid the bill," she says. "Just like dear Brianna told me you would."

"Who's Brianna?" I ask.

"Yes, Matt, who's Brianna?"

Matt can't even meet our eyes, let alone reply.

"I didn't believe her at first," Alex continues, "so I called Egghead Kegs to check. One hundred and seventy-eight dollars for two kegs of beer consumed a month ago. Must've been some party."

"I don't really remember," he says.

"Liar. You paid the bill for the entire sorority. Did you honestly believe you could buy their silence for one hundred and seventy-eight dollars?"

Matt grips his hair like he wants to pull it out. "It was one night."

"Apparently it was a pretty special night. I looked Brianna up on Facebook, by the way. I can see the attraction."

"Why didn't you tell me you knew?"

"Why didn't you tell me yourself? Why did you make me find out through an illiterate e-mail from some skanky girl I'd never even heard of?"

Suddenly the bundle of self-confidence known as Matthew Dorsey crumbles entirely. "I was drunk."

Alex winces, and anger gives way to tears. "I wish you hadn't said that. How can you sleep with someone else and expect it to be all right because you were *drunk?*"

"I'm so sorry. Please forgive me."

"I did, you idiot. I never would've come on this trip otherwise. And you know who convinced me to give you a second chance? Fran, that's who. She said three years together means something. Said everyone makes mistakes. Said she was sure you loved me . . . and that I still loved you." Tears stream down her cheeks. She rummages in her pockets for a tissue, but can't find one. "Fran is the reason we're still together, Matt. Not *you.*"

Alex swipes at the tears angrily with the back of her hand. Her eyes flash between Matt and me. "Look at you both. Freakin' peas in a pod!"

"I'm sorry," Matt whispers. "I'm just . . . sorry."

She draws a shuddering breath. "Good-bye, Matthew," she says. "We can find our own way home from here."

"How?"

"What do you care? Train, bus, hitchhiking. It doesn't matter, as long as you're not around."

"What about your stuff?"

"You know where we live. Drop it off tomorrow." She pauses. "Just leave it on the doorstep, though. I don't want to see you."

Alex strides away without a backward glance, and in the silence that follows I feel my heart gouged out and stomped on—not just for what I've done to Fran, but to Alex and Matt too. Everything makes sense now, and maybe I should be angry at Matt for using Colin's credit card to cover up the fact that he cheated on Alex. But I'm not angry. Because I know I've played a role in the final chapter of their relationship too, and it was a terrible one.

Why would anyone buy my book? What pearls of wisdom do I have to share now?

"I'm sorry, Matt."

It takes a while, but Matt turns to face me. He even summons a smile; incredibly, it seems genuine. "Don't be," he says. "I messed up really bad. Tell the truth, I'm kind of glad she knows. It's been killing me."

"But she'd forgiven you."

"No, she hadn't. She hasn't been herself all week. And it's my fault, not yours. You just gave her an excuse to say what's been eating her, is all."

"But—"

"No!" Matt raises his hand. "Save it, okay?"

"But there's things I have to say."

He leans forward and lowers his voice. "I know. But four reporters are heading this way, and there's a lot I don't want to see in print."

I nod once, and we run.

7:50 P.M.
I-44 at St. Robert, Missouri

We outrun reporters hovering beside the bookstore, at the hotel, and in the parking lot. As we drive away from Springfield, they pursue us in cars. On the highway, we're at the head of a convoy with three TV vans. My life—so plodding and predictable—has become a farce. I'm the headliner in my own reality TV show.

I want to know how it ends.

"They're still tailing us," says Matt, after we've been driving for an hour on I-44. He seems surprised, but I'm not. Why would he think they'd give up the chase now? It's not like we're hard to follow. We're in a bright yellow Hummer; we couldn't be any more obvious if we stuck flashing red and blue lights on the roof. "This is really weird," he adds.

"I guess catastrophic book signings are pretty big news."

"Uh-uh." He looks in the mirror again. "There were only four reporters at the bookstore, seven hanging out by the car, and three vans waiting outside the hotel. Now we're up to six TV vans."

"Six?" I crane my neck to get a look. He's right too.

"Yeah. It's weird."

No sooner are the words out than he accelerates, surging forward until we're in the far left lane, passing everyone else on the road.

"Slow down, Matt. We're not going to lose them."

He accelerates again. We're pushing seventy-five miles per hour.

"Please," I say. "I don't care anymore."

Eighty miles per hour. Then eighty-five. I glance at Matt. He's gritting his teeth, and wears a take-no-prisoners expression that assures me he's not listening to a word I say. I wonder what the top speed of a Hummer is. I think I'm about to find out.

Ninety miles per hour. The highway is relatively empty around here, and as I look over my shoulder I notice the TV vans are falling behind. Maybe they can't go this fast. Or maybe they don't want to be implicated in the high-speed accident that finally, tragically takes our lives.

The road curves. Ahead of us is an off-ramp; Matt floors the gas pedal and sends us careening onto it. He slams on the brakes at the end, and we skid to the right and park behind a motel.

"What do we do now?" I ask. I'm whispering. Not sure why.

"We wait."

Seconds pass, but no vans trundle along the off-ramp.

"Just one more minute," he says.

There's a gas station across the road. Some people are filling their cars. Others are just chatting. They don't see us here, and they probably wouldn't care even if they did. And why should they? We're nothing, really. This whole situation is madness. So much energy has been spent discussing what I wrote, and questioning who I really am. But how can anyone hope to know who I am when I don't even know myself? Or am I deluding myself again? Am I actually a fundamentally bad person without realizing it?

Finally, Matt puts the car in gear, and rejoins the country road. We parallel the interstate for a mile—close enough to be seen by passing TV vans—so Matt takes another right turn, and now we're traveling along a long-forgotten stretch of road that makes me feel oddly at home. A sign to the right announces that we're on Historic Route 66.

"I didn't know," says Matt, anticipating my question. "I just wanted to get away, that's all."

He keeps chugging along at a steady thirty miles per hour, though the road is deserted. The only sound is the gentle purr of the engine, and the quiet is exactly what I need.

A mile later Matt pulls to the side of the road at the

approach to a large iron bridge. "Huh. We found it anyway," he says under his breath.

"Found what?"

"Devil's Elbow—a famous stop on old Route 66. I've got a postcard of it at home. They say the view of the river is amazing."

I'm feeling nauseous, so I get out and walk along the bridge. I lean against the railing and stare at the river below as the sun hides behind trees to my right.

"It's funny," says Matt, joining me, "but I was sure this would be our last stop before we got home."

"It is."

He sighs. "Not *ours*. Mine and Alex's."

"Oh, right. Sorry."

"Why? I'm the one who cheated on her. I should've just told her when it happened, but she was already pulling away. I was afraid it'd be the last straw."

"But it wasn't."

Matt hesitates. "No. I guess it wasn't."

"See, it kind of is my fault. If you hadn't stood up for me—"

"I didn't stand up for you. I just told her to cool it a bit, that's all. She wanted retribution, or vengeance, or something. She wanted your head on a platter. But it wouldn't have changed anything." He stares into the distance, unblinking. "I was just trying to remind Alex who she really is. But we've gotten to a point where she can't hear that from me anymore. And believe me, *that* is not your fault."

The setting sun plays shadow games on the sand-colored bluffs that rise from the river. I watch the colors shift, second by second.

"Well, thank you anyway," I say.

"For what?"

"Being there when I needed you most."

He laughs. "Unlike the rest of the week, you mean."

Now I'm laughing too, which seems completely impossible. "You mean the bill from Egghead Kegs? And the fancy hotel room for Alex and Fran? Oh, yeah, and the thousand dollars from the bank? No wonder you haven't been answering the phone." I'm practically peeing myself now. "Sheesh! We're like Butch Cassidy and the Sundance Kid. What the heck did you do with a *thousand dollars* anyway?"

Matt wipes away tears of laughter. "Nothing. I've still got it. But I was afraid Colin would block the credit card as soon as the Egghead Kegs expense showed up, so I took the cash to make sure we could pay for the rest of the tour. I should've taken the cash first, and used that to pay for the keg. I'm not exactly a natural-born criminal, I guess."

"Me neither. I've just been acting like one."

That sobers us up quickly.

"I'll give Colin the money, Luke. And I'll pay him

back for the hotel and kegs too, as soon as we get home. I promise. But I had to get that money straightaway—try to make everything a success."

I stare at him for a moment and then bust out laughing again. "Well, that thousand bucks must've been the clincher then. 'Cause this trip couldn't have been more perfect."

"Hey, it could've been worse. Colin might've come with us."

"Can you imagine? Hey, that reminds me, he wants a ride— Oh, crap!"

"What is it?"

"We're supposed to give him a ride to St. Louis tomorrow morning."

Matt looks sympathetic for all of a second before he laughs again. "Oh, man. He's gonna be really pissed."

"And to think," I say, choking up, "everything was going so well."

Matt doubles over and starts slapping his hand against the iron railing. We must both look completely insane. When the laughter finally runs out, a comfortable silence replaces it.

"So what's in the envelope?" he asks.

I'd forgotten I was still holding it, the paper fused to my hand as though my guilt has been branded onto me.

"Teresa gave it to me this evening."

"Who's Teresa?"

"The woman who announced that Fran was my girlfriend."

"Oh." He thinks about this. "Wasn't she also at Saturday's signing? The born-again one."

"Yeah. Except she's not a born-again Christian; she's a reporter for a magazine. Tried to seduce me earlier this week—had someone outside taking photos."

Matt's eyebrows shoot up. "Why didn't you tell me?"

"I was embarrassed."

He eases the envelope out of my hand and opens it. He only looks at the photos for a moment, and then he's back to staring at the river again. "I guess this was last night."

I glance over to see what Fran and I are doing: me lying on top of her, breathless, hopeless. It looks inexcusable, but at the time, neither of us needed an excuse. It had felt right. Innocent. God-given.

"A week of trailing you around, and she's hit pay dirt," concludes Matt.

"You think she's going to publish them?"

His look of surprise quickly morphs into one of pity. "Oh, Luke. Six TV vans don't tag along because of a bust-up at a book signing." He bites his lip. "She's published them already."

I won't cry. I can't give Teresa—or Chastity—that victory.

"Then why did she come to the signing at all?" I shout. "Why give me these if she was just going to publish them anyway?"

Matt rests an arm across my shoulders. "I guess she wanted you to know she'd won."

I can't hold it in any longer. I just throw myself against him and sob. He wraps his arms around me and doesn't let go.

"I am so stupid. I am such an idiot!" I yell, and the words torture me.

"No. This is not your fault, bro. What she's done is wrong. It's *evil*."

I lean back. "I'm not talking about the photos. I'm talking about Fran." I wipe my eyes with the back of my hand. "She's all I've thought about for years. I love her. I really love her. And I screwed it all up."

SUNDAY, JUNE 22

Realizations 8: 12–17

12. But yea, there were those who said "No!" And others who said "No way!" And some, even, who spake thus: "No freakin' way, dude." 13. But yet did the boy realize they were mistaken. 14. For though they had heard, they had not listened. And though they had read, they had not understood. 15. And so did the boy grasp the book and say, "This once was mine, but now is yours." And he held it aloft and waited for someone to take it from him, to claim it as their own. 16. Yet no one did, because they all knew that the story ended somewhat inconclusively, and was thus really, really irritating. 17. And besides, the cover sucked.

9:50 A.M.
The Dorsey Residence, St. Louis, Missouri

Sunlight floods into my bedroom, though the curtains are drawn. There's a poster of Gandhi above my desk. On the mantel over the blocked-up fireplace, framed certificates and awards fight for space. Somehow everything looks familiar and strange at the same time, as though I've woken up in another period of my life. Come to think of it, I sort of have.

I hear my parents' voices on the other side of my bedroom door, so I roll out of bed and stand beside it.

"You take the coffee, I'll take the muffins," says Dad.

"Sounds good," replies Mom.

"Remember, no responses. *Please.*" This from someone whose voice is out of place here.

Colin.

I can't face explaining to Colin what happened last night, and why I left him behind, and why I'm probably responsible for getting him fired. Since that means I can't leave my room, I figure I'll just wait here until—

The door flies open and stubs my big toe. I stifle a cry.

Matt peers around the door. "Oh," he says, somewhat apologetically. "Well, good to see you're up already." He barges into my room and throws some clothes on the bed. "Colin says you should change into these. It'll be easier for you to go unnoticed if you don't look like . . . you know . . . *you*."

There's a criticism hidden in there somewhere, but I can see Colin's point. So I throw on Matt's oversized T-shirt and sport shorts, and pull the drawstring as tight as possible.

"There's something written on your arm," he says, pointing helpfully.

Colin appears in the doorway, cup of coffee in one hand, muffin in the other. "Looks like you spilled some black stuff on your arm, Luke." He holds out the muffin. "You hungry? There's about fifty more where this came from."

I'm starving, so I take it. "Fifty?"

"Uh-huh. Seems your mom likes to bake. And being the kindly soul she is, she thought it would be a nice gesture to feed all the press gathered outside."

"Fifty? For the *press*?"

"I know. Not enough for everyone, but I told her she has to draw the line somewhere."

I'm not hungry anymore.

"Come on," says Colin. "We need to talk."

He leads me into the living room. *My* living room, though I don't feel at home here. Newspapers and magazines are strewn across the coffee table; he gathers them up and carries them away. He's pretty slick about it, but I know he's just hiding the evidence, unaware that I've already seen it firsthand in glossy 8x10.

"How did you get here?" I ask.

Colin sits down on Dad's La-Z-Boy and points at the sofa as though he's inviting me to join him.

"There are these handy things called *rental cars*," he explains, narrowing his eyes. "I was going to get a Hummer, but then I discovered how expensive they are. Certainly don't want to bankrupt my employer, do I?"

I cringe at his sarcasm. "I'm sorry about the ride. I forgot about you."

"Evidently."

He downs his coffee and helps himself to more from a carafe on the table. I wonder if he slept at all.

"Okay, moving on," he says decisively. "Last night was not your greatest moment, not by a long shot. And this morning, well . . . things aren't looking good. The *National Enquirer* has run the story about your extraordinary alcohol consumption. Now, your brother has explained the whole situation to me, so I know *you* didn't touch a drop. He's also promised to take full responsibility, so that Fran won't be implicated either." He takes another swig of coffee. "Speaking of your brother, he's returned the thousand dollars, and made arrangements to repay me for other unauthorized expenses. So we're putting all that behind us. I'm sorry I blamed you for it yesterday; he told me you didn't have a clue what was going on."

"That's okay." Actually, it's better than okay. I can handle everything he has mentioned so far.

"Now the bad news: There are photos of you and that girl doing something. Some magazine printed them first, but they're in the newspapers too."

I want to disappear. "We were kissing."

"Hmm. I worked out that much." He rubs his thumb along the edge of his cup. "Listen, it's none of my business what you two were up to. But last night you told the audience you didn't know her, and that puts us in a bit of a pickle, see? You've got some pretty vocal opponents now. Looking on the bright side, you'll be relieved to know that in spite of your behavior—or perhaps *because* of it—book sales have gone through the roof."

"I couldn't care less about book sales."

Colin is adding milk to his coffee, but pauses. "Well, I do, thank you very much."

"So as long as you make your thirty pieces of silver, everything's just fine. Is that it?"

"My what?"

"Thirty pieces of silver. You know, like Judas."

"Judas?"

If he's kidding, he's keeping a really impressive poker face. "Have you actually read the Bible?" I ask.

"Is that relevant?"

"I think so, yes. I mean, my book is a spiritual self-help guide, and you were the one who bought it."

"Not exactly. That would've been your editor, the executive editor, and the acquisitions department, not publicity. But coincidentally, I am an expert on self-help guides, so I'm halfway qualified."

"Are you even Christian?"

Colin sighs. "To tell the truth, Luke . . . no, I'm not. I don't even qualify as agnostic. But your book was a sure-fire best seller in the current market—"

"So it really was about *money*?"

"Let me finish. I *asked* to be assigned to your book, because I felt you had something to say. Your writing is honest and refreshingly humorous. So many books on religion are dry and preachy, and most people can't relate. But even I could relate to your book."

"But you just said you're not Christian. That's so hypocritical of you to take it on."

"Hey, O Holy One, if the only people you want to

read your book are the ones who already agree with everything in it, what was your point in the first place? Isn't the goal to reach non-believers? Trust me, I love to see thousands of people clamoring to buy your book—strong sales make for a happy publisher—but what *you* should be concerned about is not how many people are buying your book, but *who* is buying it."

He finishes pouring the milk. He trusts that his words will sway me, or at least make me *think*, because he has a point. More than that, he's right. Trouble is, I just don't care. Right now I want to step outside and give the press a sound bite they won't forget in a hurry.

Colin sips his coffee with one hand while sending a text message with the other.

"I guess your bosses want to know how it's going, huh?"

"What? No, I was just gloating about the fact that golf got rained out. Serves them right for going ahead without me." He slides the phone into his jacket pocket and leans back in his chair. "Luke, I know what you're thinking. You want to say *screw it*. You want to bail on this afternoon's signing. It'd be nice, wouldn't it, to do that just once?"

That's exactly what I'm thinking; I just know I shouldn't be.

"Don't go there, Luke. It's so much easier to let people down than to stay strong. And once you change, even for a moment, it can take a lifetime to find your way back again."

"I've *already* changed. You were there last night. You know what I did."

"No. You panicked, and you made a mistake, but I could see how bad you felt about it. There was nothing calculated about last night. But if you don't show up today . . . well, that's a different story."

"What if I don't want to find my way back?"

He takes a bite of muffin. "Of course you do. Or you will soon. Everyone does. I could've lied to you, told you I'm a devout Christian, but I want you to know who I really am. I have no intention of spending my life playing the role of someone I'm not."

The words are aimed at me, but I can only think of Fran. We've forced her to play a role all year, and just as she was emerging from it, I shot her down. Who will she be now?

"What should I do, Luke? I don't want to pressure you, but I've been working through the night to get books ready for sale. I have to know if I can count on you to be at today's event."

I close my eyes and imagine Fran lying beneath me, our bodies pressed together. I hate feeling ashamed of that night. I hate that anyone feels they have the right to judge me for it.

"Luke?"

Her kisses—soft, lingering. Her hair, tickling me. Her breath, warm. Her body coiled up against me, sleeping, calm, complete. Her entire being, mine. Just for an instant.

"I'm sorry," I say finally. "I don't have anything left to say."

There's a long pause. "I see. Your parents will be disappointed, but . . . I understand."

"Thank you." In my mind I'm still picturing Fran; still wishing I could hold her. When I open my eyes at last, it's because I've made a decision: "I have to go see her. I need to apologize."

"Are you sure that's a good idea?"

"Not at all."

Colin downs his coffee and reaches for another refill. "Take the alley out back," he says. "There might be photographers there too, but probably not as many."

He hands me his sunglasses, and furrows his brows as he looks me up and down. "Although, on second thought, I bet you'll make a clean escape after all."

10:45 A.M.
The Dorsey Residence, St. Louis, Missouri

I grab Matt's Cardinals baseball cap from the stool beside the back door. I'm about to slip out when someone taps me on the shoulder.

"You're going to see Fran, huh?" Matt asks.

"How do you know?"

"I was eavesdropping."

"Oh."

"Yeah. So, can you give this to Alex?"

He hands me an envelope. Not just any envelope, mind you: It's the manila one Teresa/Chastity/my destroyer gave me. He scribbles through the message on the front. "Sorry, bro. I couldn't find another envelope. And it's really important that Alex gets this letter."

"Why can't you give it to her yourself?"

"She doesn't want to see me. Anyway, this is the only way I can trust myself to say the right thing."

I still hesitate. "I don't think she'll be ready to forgive you."

"I'm not trying to get back together with her. I just want things to end with the truth."

So it really is over between Matt and Alex. I guess I ought to be sad, but Matt seems more relaxed this morning than he has all week. As I take the envelope, he gives me a hug. A real hug.

Outside, the sun is already high, the temperature soaring. In seconds my armpits prickle with sweat. I imagine frightening off the paparazzi purely through the stench of my body odor.

If only it were that easy.

The alley at the end of our yard is hidden behind a tall wooden fence, and I'm no longer naive enough to believe the coast will be clear. Sure enough, as I creep beneath Mom's decorative trees I hear voices outside; they're discussing the heat and the smell from the Dumpsters, so I figure they've been camping out for a while.

Since I can't exit through the gate, I grab the sturdy metal post at the side of the yard and hurdle the low chain-link fence that divides our yard from the neighbors'. For good measure, I hurdle the next fence too. Conveniently, there's even a bag of trash left at the end of this yard. When I open my neighbor's gate, I'm fifty feet from the photographers, with a trash bag slung over my shoulder, partially obscuring my face.

"Hey!" The voice is loud and demanding; pretending I don't hear it would be ridiculous.

I turn around. Slowly.

Five guys with cameras slung around their necks stand huddled together, shrouded in smoke. One of them raises his cigarette in greeting. "The kid that lives in this house," he shouts. "You know anything about him?"

I wait for someone to recognize me. I have *guilty* written all over my face in Route 66 neon. But no one seems interested in me. It's like the sunglasses and baseball cap really are a disguise.

"He's a total dork," I say. "What do you want with him?"

The guy takes a drag and smiles. "Haven't you heard? He got caught doing the dirty. The kid's finished, man." He points a thumb at the guys around him. "We're here to finish him."

I believe him. He has the look of a bloodhound, all sagging jowls and dog-tired eyes. He'll probably camp out for days without food and water for that one perfect shot he stands no chance of getting. Meanwhile, my poor parents are imprisoned in their own home, baking muffins for the enemy. I glance at my house, two doors down, and pray they'll get through this with their faith intact. Which is how I notice Mom standing by an open window on the third floor, scanning the alley.

Or at least the part of it she can see.

"Luke, what are you doing out there?" she shouts. "Come on inside."

My eyes shoot back to the five guys, but Mom can't see them, as they're directly behind our fence.

"I'm serious," she says. "We really need to talk."

There's a moment of complete stillness. I hear cicadas, the rush of distant cars, and through it we all remain bolted to the spot.

Then I twitch.

The jowly guy is first to come at me, camera raised. He's in attack mode, so I throw my trash bag in the air and run. I hear feet clattering behind me, but these guys are slow. They have shoulder bags and cameras with long lenses, and they're middle-aged and even more out of shape than me. Plus, they probably don't want to waste their cigarettes. But they're also shouting, so we'll have company before long.

I sprint around the corner and double back through a narrow passage between the redbrick warehouses. At the end I turn left and lose myself in the sea of pedestrians and diners at the sidewalk cafés.

From here it's only a quarter of a mile to Fran's house. I'm pretty sure I've lost my pursuers. I'm as good as free.

So why do I feel like the worst is still ahead of me?

11:05 A.M.
The Embree Residence, St. Louis, Missouri

I press the doorbell to Fran's house. It's a beautiful door: an old oak frame surrounding a large sheet of crystal glass in which I can see my own hideous reflection.

I take off the baseball cap, attempt to flatten my lopsided, spiky hair, and then realize there are letters on my T-shirt that I hadn't noticed before. I stretch the shirt and work out that the letters spell *Beer: not just for breakfast!* I was already anticipating a beating from Mr. E., but this pretty much seals the deal. So I drop Matt's envelope on the ground, whip the T-shirt off and turn it inside out. I'm in the process of putting it back on when the door opens.

"Why, it's Luke Dorsey," Mrs. Embree announces. "And he's topless."

I'm not topless—not completely, anyway—and I'd have preferred it if she'd said bare-chested, but I agree that the situation is kind of awkward. I force my hands through the sleeves, adjust the collar, and feel the telltale smoothness of the label at my Adam's apple.

Inside out *and* back to front. Who could harm someone so pathetic?

Mrs. Embree retreats—either because she'd like me to enter, or because I've freaked her out—and I step into a pristine, dust-free, climate-controlled oasis.

She directs me to the living room, where Mr. Embree is watching a Cardinals baseball round-up show on TV. He raises a finger to indicate that he'll be with me soon.

The room is a shrine to Alex and Fran—framed photos adorn every inch of wall space. There's even one of me and Fran, taken straight after the debate championship; her arm is wrapped around my waist, while my eyes burn into her, unaware of the camera, aware of nothing but the girl beside me, holding me, smiling so wide I wondered how the whole world hadn't ground to a halt to take in something so perfectly beautiful. But that was the *other* Fran: the pre-punk Fran; the Fran who could do no wrong. Punk-era Fran isn't recognized on these hallowed walls. And she never will be.

Mr. Embree turns off the TV. "You've been busy, Luke," he says, peering over half-moon glasses.

"Yes, sir."

He acknowledges my reply with a subtle nod. He's

about to follow up with his patented bone-crushing handshake when he sees my arm. He squints at the letters. "Someone's scrawled something on your arm. Says: 'She loves the one who sees her.'" He snorts. "What the hell kinda nonsense is that? Doesn't even make sense."

I hate the way he dismisses Fran's heartfelt words so casually, but what can I say?

"Well, take a seat." He points to the chair across from him, clearly having strong opinions on which seat I should choose. "Tell me what brings you here this fine morning."

I'd prefer to remain standing, but sit anyway. My mouth is dry. "I, uh . . . came to apologize to Fran."

He laughs at that—a real laugh, which confuses me. "Oh, Luke, you're so . . ." Apparently he's not sure what I am, so he leans forward and whispers: "Alex told me something happened between you two, and that it's over now. But seriously, I know about hormones, okay? I was young once too, believe it or not. And while I'm sure it was difficult for you to end things, it was all for the best. Tough love, you know? I always said that's what'd bring her around."

I have no idea what he's talking about, although I'm fairly certain I'm not about to get beaten up.

Then Alex walks in on our conversation and the air of forgiveness evaporates. She folds the newspaper she has been reading and slaps it against her arm. "What are you doing here?" she asks.

"Oh, hi, Alex. I'm—"

"You need to go. I'm serious, Luke. If you have any decency, you'll leave. And you won't come back."

Mr. Embree keeps his attention on me. "As you can see, a year of college hasn't tempered Alex's sense of drama."

"This has nothing to do with you," she tells him.

"What about Caltech tuition? Does that have anything to do with me?"

It's a lame comeback, but Alex backs down. "You should go, Luke," she says, newspaper still bouncing against her arm. "My father doesn't know," she adds enigmatically.

"Sure I know," he says. "You told me yourself he dumped Fran. Luke doesn't even deny it. But everything has come full circle now. All's well that ends well." He laughs again, a grating sound like nails against metal.

Now I realize what Alex is really saying: Mr. Embree doesn't know about the *photos*, the damage to Fran's reputation, the way I convinced her to trust me, and cut her loose in the cruelest way. He's sticking to the simplified—and perhaps most plausible, in his mind— version of events. And he's doing it because, unlike

Fran, I haven't completely changed my appearance to undermine his opinion of who I am.

Well, maybe it's time he learned the truth.

I snatch the newspaper from Alex, open it up, and hand it to him. I know there'll be a photo of Fran and me on the front page. After all, it's the *St. Louis Post-Dispatch*—our hometown newspaper—and if I'm making waves in Amarillo, Texas, it's certain I'm getting top billing here.

Mr. Embree's eyes narrow in concentration, and then widen in surprise. Not satisfied with gawking at the picture, he takes a moment to read the story too. Finally he folds the newspaper and places it beside him.

"Sit down, Luke."

Again, I don't want to sit. Again, I do exactly as I'm told.

"I've always had the highest respect for you," he begins, slow and measured. "I'll admit I was a little surprised you'd be interested in Fran. But this . . . this was *stupid.*"

"I know. I'm sorry."

"People have invested a lot of money in your book, and you have an obligation to them. That's business, son. This"—he picks up the newspaper—"could've ruined you. If I did something this damned stupid, I'd be out of a job, we'd be out of this house, and Alex would be transferring to community college. All I can say is, thank God you had the smarts to turn the situation around . . . deny knowing her."

It takes a moment for the words to sink in, but there's no question he's excusing me. More than that, he's applauding my quick thinking. I can't believe it, and judging from her response, neither can Alex.

"I lied," I say.

Mr. Embree rolls his eyes. "You did what you had to do to salvage a bad situation."

"I let Fran down."

"Yeah, well, none of us is perfect. Since no one'll ever find this girl anyway, it doesn't much matter. You're home free, trust me. Get the right lawyer and you might even be able to claim the photo isn't real." His hands become more active as his speech accelerates. "It was taken at night. It's grainy. Hey, maybe you should go proactive—you know, sue for damages."

"I *lied*," I repeat, and this time I'm almost shouting.

"Don't raise your voice at me, boy."

"I'm sorry. I just . . . I hurt her."

"And thank God you did. We've suffered through a year of her nonsense—a *year*. It's just about destroyed her mother. And I know it sounds harsh, but if I'd realized you could turn her around so quickly, I'd have paid you to do it months ago. I told Frances, none of us gets this year back. She won't be able to hide it on her college applications. One way or another, she'll end up paying for what she did."

"What *she* did? You mean, what *you* did to her."

"What are you talking about?"

Alex steps forward. "Stop, Luke."

"No, I won't." I stand now, because I need to show him I won't be intimidated. "Why do you think she changed in the first place? It's because all you cared about was how she looked to other people. You have the smartest, most amazing daughter, and you don't even know it."

Mr. Embree doesn't say anything at first, just watches me with stone-cold eyes. "You can go now," he hisses.

"So that's it, huh? You hear something you don't like and you just shut it out. Pretend it isn't happening." I want to scream, but I don't. "How's that worked out for you this year?"

Now he's standing too, and he is at least five inches taller than me. I think he's about to pulverize me. "How dare you!"

Suddenly Alex's hand rests on her father's arm. She's trying to calm him down, to protect me. "It's okay, Dad," she says. "Luke is leaving."

"I'm not leaving until I apologize to Fran."

Alex spins around. "For hurting her now? Or for hurting her a year ago?"

"What? That wasn't me. It was . . ." I point a shaking finger at Mr. Embree.

He eases himself away from his elder daughter. He's smiling, and it scares me.

"You know, I think Alex is right about you, Luke," he says, suddenly calm again. "When she read your book, she told her mother: Innocence and naivety are often indistinguishable. I thought she was being pretentious, but I get it now."

He pats Alex on the back, and she flinches. When she glances at me, I can tell that she loathes us equally.

"You were the reason Fran changed," he continues. "Not me. She put on some stupid clothes, dyed her hair, tried to piss us off. So I told her if she wanted to lose every friend she had, she should just go on looking like trash. And she said I was wrong, spouted some bull about how sad it was that her own father couldn't see past the surface to know who she really was." He licks his lips. "Ten days later we drove her to the church retreat, and she saw the same damn look on your face she'd seen on ours. Hell, you turned away like you didn't even know her. Not that I blamed you at the time. I kind of thought it might even be a good thing—bring her to her senses. Instead, she went crazy: sticking holes in herself; drawing on her arms. She hasn't been the same since."

"But . . . why?"

No one speaks for a moment. They both want me to work it out for myself.

"You were her best friend," says Alex, breaking the silence. "Everyone feels let down at some point, but your friends stand by you, help you get through. Especially your best friend. That's what Fran thought anyway."

They're watching me now, and I hate it. I'm grieving inside, and I want to be alone with my pain. Alex said I was Fran's best friend, and I blew it. A year later she was my girlfriend, and again I blew it. How can anyone be so stupid, thoughtless . . . naive?

"It doesn't matter." The voice comes from behind me, soft and tired. I know that voice so very well, which I why I'm frozen to the spot. "Nothing really matters," she says, even quieter.

I turn to face her—this friend and girlfriend and stranger—and my breath catches.

Fran is wearing a peach-colored dress that hugs her body and whispers around her knees. If she's wearing any makeup, it's too subtle for me to tell. She's been reborn as the new-old Fran.

Except her forearms, of course. And her hair: still purple, but pulled back apologetically into a ponytail.

She follows my eyes. "I've got an appointment tomorrow," she says, as though I deserve an explanation. "Mom thought . . . blond."

I'm almost crying now, tired and confused and elated and distraught. I hate how much I adore this version of Fran—so beautiful, so . . . *presentable*. A part of me wants time to fast-forward so I can behold her with blond hair. I want the entire world to see her like this, to be reminded that she can be this person. More than that, I want to be seen *with* her. But as soon as that thought arises—settling in my stomach like a satisfying meal—I hate myself even more.

Then I notice her upper arm. She's scrubbed it so hard that it glows red, but the imprint of my words is still there, a ghostly reminder of another lifetime.

"You can't change back," I say, my voice barely a whisper.

"Yes, I can."

"It's not who you really are."

"Don't pretend you know me."

Her words strike deep. I *do* know her, in spite of what she thinks. It's me I didn't know.

"I'm so sorry for what I did to you, Fran."

She shrugs. "Doesn't matter. It's just the way things are."

"Don't say that! This isn't fate. I screwed up, and I'm sorry. But you can't just give up."

Fran snorts, but she's clearly not amused. "Oh,

so wearing army surplus gear is giving up, and so is wearing a dress. Okay, Luke, why don't you tell me exactly what I *can* wear? How I *can* look. In fact, you and my parents should vote on it. You know, to make sure I get it exactly right."

"I don't want you to get it right. I want you to be happy. I . . . want you to be *you*."

"You look pretty, honey," her father says without really looking at her. He turns to me. "And you're leaving. You've done enough damage already."

I don't want to leave. I want to tell Fran to be strong. But for once Mr. Embree has a point.

Besides, I have the whole of junior year to prove that I can change. And the whole of junior year to persuade Fran that she doesn't need to change at all.

11:15 A.M.
Half a block away . . .

I'm only twenty yards away from Fran's house when I hear footsteps behind me—the rapid cadence of a runner. I know it's her, so I wait.

Fran stops a few steps from me. She's not wearing

shoes, and I find myself checking the ground for glass or stones. I'm afraid she'll hurt herself.

"Did you leave this on our doorstep?" she asks, holding up the manila envelope containing Matt's letter.

"Geez. Yes. It's for Alex."

She shifts her weight from foot to foot as though she can't decide what to do next. "Where are you going?"

"Anywhere the press can't find me."

She tilts her head to the left. "Mrs. Amberly's porch swing is hidden."

"Do you think she'd mind me sitting there all day?"

"I doubt it. She died three months ago."

Fran leads me along an overgrown pathway to a wide wraparound porch surrounded by rhododendrons. Only a few rays of sun penetrate this place. She sits down, and pats the swing to show that I'm allowed to join her.

"Why did you come to my house?" she asks.

"To say sorry."

"What if my dad had killed you? Or broken a pinky finger or something?"

"I kind of hoped he would, actually. I figured that actual physical pain would be better than what I'm feeling right now."

"Hey, you want physical pain, just let me know. I'll go grab my needle."

I glance at her ears. "Point taken."

"Good. Fifteen–love."

"Yeah . . . Fifteen–love."

We sit in silence for a moment. She's pressed against one end of the swing, and I'm pressed against the other. There's enough empty space in the middle for two more people. The air is heavy, humid and charged, and I don't know what to say. Meanwhile, Fran fingers her ears, where the rows of hoops have been replaced by small silver studs.

"So not everything has changed," I say, pointing to her ears.

She brings her hands down. "No. I like them. Plus, I figure if I'm going to dress like this from now on, I need to have something that's all mine."

The Band-Aid has gone, but there's still an angry red hole from Monday's misadventure. She catches me staring.

"It got infected," she explains, "so I have to let it heal. I shouldn't have done it in the first place. I was just crazy and upset. And drunk."

She pulls at the hem of her dress until it reaches her knees. Yesterday she would have wanted me to see her completely. Now she feels uncomfortable and self-conscious. It just about kills me.

"So, signing's at one o'clock, right?" she says, breaking yet another silence.

"Signing's off."

"Why?"

"Because everyone hates me. Plus, I doubt anyone will even be there."

She frowns. "Oh, I think they'll be there, even if it's just to throw things at you."

"Exactly."

"But you have to go." She folds her legs under her. "People deserve a chance to vent, and you need to show them you can take it. That you still believe in what you wrote."

"I don't believe in it, though. You know I don't. I wrote most of it when I couldn't stop thinking about you, and the rest when I was mad at you."

"But no one else knows that. To them, *Hallelujah* is about your ideas, not about you."

That makes sense, but it's still not enough. "What I did last night went against everything I wrote."

"Geez, Luke. Get over yourself. I just told you: *Hallelujah* isn't about *you*. That was the whole problem. Now everyone knows what the book really is, you can start all over again."

"They'll lose interest now."

"Why? Because you were an idiot?" She shakes her head, and her ponytail swishes gently behind her. "Luke, some truly idiotic people have said some truly inspired things. Are we supposed to ignore their words because they couldn't live up to them?"

"Actions speak louder than words."

"Then go to the signing."

"That's not what I mean."

She sighs. "Listen, I can't make you go, but I want you to know that I saw something this week—people lining up for two hours just to shake hands with you. That book of yours means something to people, Luke. But it's not really your book anymore. It belongs to everyone, and means whatever the heck they want it to mean . . . or need it to mean. You have to let go of everything—the praise and the guilt." She shifts on the seat, sits a little straighter. "So you're a sinner too. So the stories aren't about *you*. If that's enough to shatter people's faith, well . . . I'd say their faith was on rocky ground to begin with, you know?"

Fran is energized now. She conveys each point with the confidence of a lawyer reprising a winning argument. When I don't respond she seems amused rather than annoyed, as though I've conceded defeat.

Seeing her like this is enough to make me forget how awful I feel. I spent a whole year never seeing her smile, and her face suffered for it. People are meant to smile. It's like food and water—nourishment for the soul.

"No counterargument, huh?" she asks. "Then it's thirty–love."

"Who said you were on serve?"

"I've spent the whole of the last year returning serve. For once, I want to be in control."

I look at her dress, the strands of hair that have escaped from her ponytail and now frame her face. So beautiful, and yet . . .

"You're not on serve, Fran. Not like this, you're not."

She looks away, and I know I've crushed her once again. I don't mean to hurt her, but every fiber of her appearance screams defeat. Being a better person than her parents and friends, she has given up, gone back to being the girl they'd prefer to see. But it's just another mask. And I'll bet she knows it.

"I'm sorry," I say. "It's none of my business."

She doesn't answer, and she won't look at me. Why couldn't I have kept my mouth shut?

"Just do the event, Luke," she says finally. "Do it to show you're willing to take responsibility. And to show you're not afraid." She points to the sky. "There's a higher power than us, remember? If you can't face up to adversity now, are you really sure you'll be able to face Him?"

12:05 P.M.
United Christian Church, St. Louis, Missouri

I'm a couple hundred yards from the church when I see the photographers. News of my daring escape must have filtered through to the media masses, and now they're gambling on me showing up for my signing. Which is stupid of them, really. I'd be crazy to go through with it. Certifiably insane.

Unfortunately, they've guessed right.

I take a detour along another alley and approach the church from the back. There are about a dozen news vans in the parking lot, but everyone is so busy that they don't even glance at me as I weave through them. I even filch a clipboard from a deck chair, and when I barge through the throngs outside the church office door, scribbling on the clipboard, no one stops me.

I knock on the door, and Andy opens it immediately. He looks flustered—his robes are too heavy for a sticky summer day—and when he sees me his eyes grow wide. Before he can say my name, I hand him the clipboard. "I need your signature," I say. "Maybe you could do it inside?"

He nods blankly. "We'll, uh, go into my office."

I'm through the door before the words are out of his mouth, and it's not until I turn around to close it that someone recognizes me. The door shuts with a resounding clunk, followed by a chorus of frustrated shouts outside.

"Wow," says Andy. "You're pretty cool about this, huh?"

"No. I just can't let them win."

He gives me a hug, but pulls away quickly. "Do you smell something?" he asks.

"It's me. Sorry. There wasn't time to shower."

"To *shower*? How long do you take? And why is there writing on your arm? Never mind, the important thing is that you're here. Your publicist said you were having second thoughts, but that you wouldn't let us down."

Huh. Score one for Colin.

We walk to the church office. The dark oak cabinets and the tiny squares of glass in the window look so familiar, but somehow so different. I always felt as though I belonged here; now I feel like an imposter. I don't even sit down until he points to the armchair beside his desk, on which a copy of *Hallelujah* has pride of place.

"It's good to see you, Luke. Kind of a crazy week, huh?"

310

I actually laugh at that—a wry, angry laugh. "Yeah. Crazy is right."

He sits across the desk from me and presses his palms together in prayer pose. "During your interview with Pastor Mike, why did you say everything in *Hallelujah* is true?" he asks.

"I don't remember the interview. I was really nervous, so before I went onto the set, I prayed; after that I got into this kind of zone where everything just happened."

"But you've seen it since, right?"

"No. But you obviously have, so why didn't *you* call me out on it?"

"How could I? I didn't know it was made up."

"You thought I'd spent a month alone in the desert?"

"No. I just didn't know that was in the book." Andy picks up a pen, spins it around, and puts it down again. "See, I didn't actually get around to reading *Hallelujah* until this week."

"*What?* But you gave it to Pastor Mike."

"Because of the response it got from our youth groups. They loved those first few pages, and I thought Pastor Mike would too. He took it from there."

"You critiqued the whole of the first part—covered it in red pen. You practically rewrote it."

His expression is caught between amusement and concern. "That wasn't me."

"Then who was it?"

He may only be in his thirties, but his expression makes him seem a hundred years older and wiser than me. "It was Fran."

It takes me a moment to remember to breathe; even then, I don't understand. It makes no sense. And yet it makes total sense.

"When you gave me the first part of the book, I passed it along to her," he continues. "I knew something weird was going on with you two when she bailed on the church retreat, so I didn't really expect her to read it. But she did. Liked it too. Said it was funny and heartfelt, but there were problems. So I told her to fix them. I had this plan that when she was done we'd all meet and discuss it. Then she told me she wouldn't even hand over the manuscript if you knew she'd had anything to do with it."

He takes a sip from a tall glass of water on his desk. Then he runs it across his forehead.

"I told her I wasn't going to lie to you," he continues. "But then you never asked who'd made the comments, and so I respected her wishes and didn't tell you. I figured sooner or later you'd come back to me and follow up on the ones you disagreed with, and then I'd be able to tell you I had nothing to do with them. But you never did."

"That's 'cause they were great changes." I stare at

the copy of *Hallelujah* just in front of me. How many of the phrases in it are Fran's, not mine? "What about the second part? You didn't give her that too, did you?"

"Yeah. But she didn't critique it. I'm not even sure she read it." He shrugs. "It was around the end of the summer, and things had gotten bad for her, remember?"

Yes, I remember. I remember everything. And now I think I understand everything too—not Fran's fictional version of events, or even her father's simplified account, but the cold, hard truth.

"Hey, Luke." Andy interrupts my thoughts. "It's a good book, okay? I read it this week. Haven't laughed so hard in years, and I mean that in a good way. What you said in the interview with Pastor Mike was the mistake, not writing *Hallelujah*. The context may have changed, but the text is the same. Don't lose sight of that." He pats my hand. "I'm going to check on things in the church. I'll come back when it's time."

I'm already sobbing by the time he closes the door— big, fierce tears that shake me. I thought the puzzle had been solved, but I was only seeing half the picture. Now that the picture is complete, I can hardly bear to look.

But if I'm going to change, I must look: at the day I turned away from her at the church retreat, and showed her I was no different than her parents; at the day she read the first part of *Hallelujah,* and saw in verse after verse just how happy she made me; at the day she read the second part—an angry monologue aimed like an arrow at her heart. What could her parents have said that would've hurt as much as those words? Nothing at all. No, if I want to uncover the culprit here—the one who drove Fran to hurt herself over and over—all I have to do is look in the mirror.

I take off Matt's T-shirt and look for something less pungent to wear, but I can't find anything. So I put it back on correctly, my chest proudly proclaiming that beer is not just for breakfast. At the very least, it'll distract people from all the other reasons they hate me.

With nothing to do but wait, I open *Hallelujah* and begin to read. I expect to loathe it—almost *want* to—but instead a strange thing happens: I laugh through the tears. I recall how great it felt to write during those first inspired days. A few pages later, the mood shifts, and I remember how this felt too—the confusion and frustration. It's painful to read, and even more painful to know that Fran read it too, but I still find myself nodding after every few sentences, as though what I wrote in that fevered state a year ago still hits home today. I'm older now, sure. Wiser too, I hope. But I can't help feeling that my fifteen-year-old self has something to tell me: perfect or not, this is all just life. And whether or not I face up to my critics, life will always be beautiful and messy. *Always.*

Maybe that's a lesson worth sharing.

12:50 P.M.
United Christian Church, St. Louis, Missouri

The door flies open and Andy bursts in. "Sorry, Luke, but I need you to start now."

The clock on the wall reads 12:50.

He follows my eyes. "I know it's early, but the church is already full. Police are holding back the crowd outside. And . . . well, there's a problem." He tries to smile, but just looks deranged. "A *serious* problem."

I'd figured that police trying to hold people back was a problem. If there's something worse than that, I'm not sure I want to hear it.

"Look, just go in there and do your stuff, okay?" he says. "Will you? Please?"

It takes more than a little effort to stand up. At the doorway I hear the first telltale signs that things aren't going well.

"I love this church," says Andy. "It's been here

a hundred and eight years. I really don't want it destroyed."

"Destroyed?"

"You know . . . pews broken, stained-glass windows shattered, hymnals on fire."

I try to stop dead in my tracks, but he wraps an arm around my shoulders and presses me onward. Above the door there's a painting of Jesus carrying His cross to Calvary. I hope it's not an omen.

Beyond the door the noise is extraordinary, and I'm still only in a corridor; I haven't entered the main church yet. I figured no one would bother to show up, but instead a lynch mob has been summoned.

"I'm praying for you, Luke," he says.

If that's supposed to reassure me, it's not working. I'm even a little ashamed at my lack of faith, but really, I'm just being realistic. I mean, it's not like things got a whole lot better for Jesus when they finally nailed Him to that cross He'd been carrying all around Jerusalem.

At the end of the corridor, Andy opens the door with two hands, knuckles white as though he's fighting a stiff breeze. "Nice T-shirt, by the way," he says, but I can barely hear him now. In the church the rumbling noise shifts to booing.

There's a raised platform at the front, and I focus

on not falling over as I walk toward it. It distracts me from the verbal assault, these words that have no place in a house of God. But I still catch occasional highlights: "Liar!" "Disgrace!" "Traitor!" "Satanist!" That last one puzzles me. Would a Satanist really hold an event in a church?

The crowd falls silent as I take my place behind the lectern. A copy of *Hallelujah* is sitting on it like a joke that's fallen flat. It's mocking me, this book, but Fran was right when she said the problem was with me. So I hold it up for everyone to see, and elicit a fresh round of booing.

I wait for the noise to die down, which takes a long time since there are a thousand people here, quite a few of them from the press.

"Um . . . this is, uh . . . difficult," I mumble, my words amplified by the microphone just in front of me. "Awkward, you know? I think . . . no, I *know* that some of you are really annoyed at me right now."

I expect to hear people murmuring agreement, but most of them are laughing maniacally instead. It's not a good sign.

"Yeah, so . . . to start with, I don't know exactly what I said on *The Pastor Mike Show* because I haven't actually seen it."

The crowd boos. A projectile flies through the air,

lands on the front of the platform and bounces harmlessly toward me. I pick it up and spread it out. It's just a piece of paper—specifically, a page from *Hallelujah*. Why anyone would try to take me out with a page from my own book is beyond me, but I'll need to be on my guard from now on.

I raise my hands and wait for the noise to settle back into a low-level drone. Before I can continue, a man I don't recognize stands: "Did you really empty your hotel minibars?"

Halfway down the church, Matt is shaking his head from side to side.

"Well," I begin, "it's true that alcohol was taken from a hotel minibar. But I never actually drank any of it. Honestly."

More laughter. It's clear no one believes me. Matt just rolls his eyes.

"And what about that photo in the paper?" someone else shouts. "What do you have to say for yourself?"

I pretend to give this some thought. "That it was the best night of my life."

Predictably, several people cry out at once—such a melodramatic response, but I'm getting used to it.

Another woman leaps up. "You're a hypocrite! On the radio you promoted abstinence. Now we see you rolling around with a girl you say you don't know."

"It's true. And I'm sorry."

"Sorry doesn't cut it."

"I wasn't apologizing to you. I was apologizing to *her*. I'd do anything for her forgiveness. Yours I can live without."

The woman slaps her hand across her mouth like I've committed blasphemy, and I wonder why she doesn't just leave. Maybe she wants to hang around in case everyone starts rioting. Who can afford to miss out on something like that?

There's a bottle of water by my feet, so I take a swig. "I think I know what I must've meant when I told Pastor Mike the book was truthful," I explain. "See, it started out as a five-page assignment, but I was living every page. And so it grew. And when it was over a hundred pages long, it kept growing. I was in every moment, every situation. I was living it, breathing it, feeling it. It felt so real. Now for some of you, that won't be enough. But before you cast the first stone"— I look at the creased page—"okay, the second stone, remember this: Faith means trusting in things you can't know for sure."

The debater in me knows I'm on solid ground here, but I'm beginning to think that people don't want an explanation or apology at all; they just want me to know that they hate me.

A new projectile flies toward me: another torn-out page from *Hallelujah*; the same page, in fact. Someone must really hate that page. There's even a message scrawled along the margin: *Read this, silly boy.*

A few rows back, Fran is waving her hand. She's wearing a sleeveless white T-shirt instead of the dress, and her purple hair hangs loose around her shoulders, which makes me really happy.

Fran mimes reading from a book, so I flatten the page and read: "For though they had heard, they had not listened. And though they had read, they had not understood. And so did the boy grasp the book and say 'This once was mine, but now is yours.' And he held it aloft and waited for someone to take it from him, to claim it as their own. Yet no one did, because they all knew that the story ended somewhat inconclusively, and was thus really, really irritating."

I chuckle at that last bit, and in the quiet that has suddenly enveloped the church I feel something shift. Everyone is still on edge, withholding judgment rather than forgiving me, but as the sun pours through the stained-glass windows to my left, I feel . . . *something.* A peacefulness, maybe.

That's when it hits me: I'm in a church. And not just any church—*my* church. This is my home away from home, a place where I belong, where I should always feel welcome. And the people who know me best—Fran, my parents, Matt, Andy—are still here for me, rooting for me. One week—even the worst possible week—hasn't changed that. As for the other people here, they didn't know me before, and they don't really know me now. And that's okay. In fact, it's better than okay.

I throw another glance Fran's way and hold up the piece of paper. This time I'm actually smiling, because there's a light at the end of the tunnel, and I'm ready to embrace it.

"That passage I just read reminds me of something really important—something I need everyone to know." I crumple the paper between my fingers and feel the crisp edges of the page digging into my palms. "The boy in this book isn't really me. You all know that by now. He's similar, sure, but better, because the things he says and does have been edited over and over. I'm not him. I'm going to need to screw up sometimes. And I'm going to feel bad about it, and ask for forgiveness. But not from you . . . from the person I actually hurt."

There's a faint murmuring, like this sort of makes sense, so I afford myself a moment to scan the church. My parents are smiling and holding hands. Matt is beside them, looking bored but awake. Best of all, Fran is nodding. That, more than anything else, tells me I'm doing okay.

"But we also need forgiveness," I continue. "Over the past twenty-four hours I've betrayed my best friend, and let down the people I love most. But they're still here now, supporting me. And I ask you: What can be better than that?"

More murmuring—louder this time—but no consensus, I think. This is a lot for everyone to digest. I'm not even sure it makes sense to me yet. But I have to keep trying.

"I may not be the boy in this book, but I think I know what he'd want me to say to you today. He'd say: Tell them, read the book or don't read the book. Like it or loathe it. Just make sure that idiot Luke doesn't profit from it."

Someone twitches to life in the front row: Colin, startled and clearly confused.

"I'm serious," I continue. "This project was never about making money; it was just something for the kids in Sunday school. Now, I can see that most of you already have copies of *Hallelujah,* but if there's anyone left who actually wants to buy one, I'll be donating all royalties to the downtown homeless shelter."

Colin leans forward so far that he topples over and ends up kneeling. It's a highly appropriate gesture, though when he rolls his eyes he looks far from reverent.

I stare down the aisle at the thousand-strong congregation. I don't really believe I've won them over, but then, I don't care either. I just squeeze Fran's page in my fist one last time and launch it into the crowd. I want to return to them what was theirs all along. It's a symbolic gesture—and probably pointless—but it makes me feel better.

"Ow!" A boy my age is rubbing his eye. "What the heck was that for?" he yells.

"I'm sorry," I shout, but he's already throwing the paper back at me—a direct hit on my left arm.

As soon as the shock passes, I can't help myself: I bust out laughing. And when I'm over it, I pick up the paper ball and toss it toward Fran, who sniggers as she lobs it straight back. Another throw from me, and suddenly the air is filled with the sound of laughter and tearing paper, and a barrage of fist-sized paper balls are arcing toward me. Everyone wanted a riot, and for once, I haven't let them down.

I hadn't realized how many copies of *Hallelujah* were out there, but I don't mind this new use for a worn-out book. And so I spread my arms wide and let the pages rain down.

3:10 P.M.
United Christian Church, St. Louis, Missouri

Incredibly, at least two hundred people ask me to sign their copy of *Hallelujah*, and I don't complain even once about my aching hand. At least three hundred more line up for the privilege of hurling their copy on the floor and saying just what they think of me, and I accept that too. Amid the noise and confusion, I'm still at peace in this place, and it's enough to pull me through.

As soon as there's a break, Andy ushers me away. The photographers who have been held back dart forward, but Andy blocks them well. When we get to his office he pushes me inside, shuts the door, and remains outside like my personal bodyguard.

I lock the door. I need a moment alone. Several moments, actually. Maybe a day or two—just long enough for the press to get bored and move on.

"What are you doing?"

I spin around. Fran is sitting cross-legged against a wall, reading *Hallelujah*.

"I didn't know you were in here," I say.

"Well, that's a relief. Be kind of weird for you to lock me in otherwise, wouldn't it?"

"No weirder than what just happened in there." I point my thumb in the direction of the church.

"True." She laughs. "Heck, if I'd known services had gotten so exciting, I might have come back before now."

"Hmm. I think you bring your own excitement. You cast the first stone, remember?"

She closes the book. "I thought you needed some help."

"I did. Thanks for that, by the way."

"No problem. Felt good, actually. I've been wanting to throw something at you all year."

An uncomfortable silence follows her remark, which makes the noise in the corridor seem even louder. Maybe the reporters are planning to riot too. Heck, why wouldn't they? Everyone else is.

I cross the room and sit beside Fran. She shuffles slightly like she's about to pull away, but then stays put. She places *Hallelujah* on the floor between us.

"Andy told me you critiqued it," I say. "The first part, anyway. I'm sorry you ever saw the second part."

She keeps her eyes trained on the book. "Why? It's how you felt, right?"

"Yeah, but I wasn't thinking straight. When you didn't come to the retreat, I got upset. I figured it was because you'd changed your mind about how you felt about me."

She snorts. "No, you didn't. Come on, Luke. No more lies, okay?" Finally, she turns to face me. "I saw the way you looked at me that day. You were horrified. Couldn't turn away fast enough."

"I was surprised."

"So?"

"So I needed time to get my head around it."

"Around *what*? We were *different*—remember? We could look beyond the surface. We refused to judge by appearances. But then you turned away from me. From *me*." She takes a deep breath. "If you couldn't face me, then who the heck could, huh? Who?"

I know she's right, so I say sorry again. I've used that word so much today, I'm afraid it doesn't mean anything anymore, but it's all I have left.

"Hey, you want to get out of here?" she asks.

"Sure. If you can convince the reporters to leave, I'll be right behind you."

She *tsks*. "Where's your imagination?" She walks over to the window, unlocks it, and pushes it open. Before I can ask what she's doing, she's halfway out. "You coming?"

When I reach the window, she has already jumped. I want to follow her, but the drop to the ground is at least six feet.

Fran rolls her eyes. "Don't worry, I'll catch you," she teases.

I slide my legs over the windowsill. It's so much quieter outside, and my heartbeat slows down just a little.

"Hey!" A guy leaning against a TV van points a finger at me. "There he is!"

I push off and hit the ground, but a battalion of reporters is already converging on me. My instinct is to run.

Fran seems to know it too, and grabs my arm. "You're not thinking of leaving without me, are you?" she asks.

Within seconds a dozen microphones are shoved in my face, questions fired so quickly I don't understand a single word. We begin walking briskly, and the photographers surround us.

"A hundred years ago, we'd have had a chaperone," says Fran airily. "Now we get thirty paparazzi instead." She puffs out her cheeks. "My, how times have changed!"

"You can say that again."

The photographers jostle for position. I can practically feel their breath on my neck. I'm about to turn around when Fran locks arms with me and keeps me facing forward. "Don't," she whispers. "It's not worth it."

I wasn't going to say anything, actually; but she

doesn't know that, and I'm amazed that her instinct is still to protect me. So I keep walking, eyes fixed on a distant chimneystack.

"I'm proud of what you did today," she says, breaking the silence. "Going in there. Facing them."

"You were right: It was something I needed to do."

"Yeah, but that didn't make it any easier. A week ago you never would've had the courage."

Is this conversation being played out for the reporters, or for us? I wish I knew.

"Speaking of difficult," she continues, "some of what people said to you in the signing line . . . it isn't true, you know."

"Yeah. But some of it is." A microphone bumps my left ear. I ought to feel angry, but I don't. I feel almost nothing at all but her skin against mine. If only our arms weren't so stiff and awkward.

"Okay, some of it was true," she concedes. "And I guess a few people have a right to gripe. Like your publisher, for instance." She leans closer, as if she's sharing something confidential. "You weren't thinking of writing a sequel, were you?"

I actually laugh. "What? And go on tour again?"

Fran chuckles too, and releases my arm. I'm glad; I couldn't have walked another block like that. But then she squeezes my hand, and her fingers brush my palm. It feels so natural. It takes me back to a better place, a place without paparazzi and rejection and failure.

I squeeze her hand back, and she lets me. So I try to twine my fingers with hers. This time she pulls her hand away.

"No," she whispers. "I'm not trying to . . ." Her voice trails off. "We're friends now, okay? That's what I want. . . . All I want."

For a moment I feel the full force of her words. Even though it's what I deserve, it hurts—it *really* hurts—and my mind fast-forwards to tomorrow's newspaper headlines, the ones that confirm my rejection in print: *Dorsey dissed! . . . Pilgrim punked! . . . Hellacious ending for* Hallelujah *boy!*

Then my mind clears and I realize that's okay too. Because as I feel Fran there beside me—partner in my walk of shame; my guide to a future full of hope and forgiveness—I know that simply being friends is a priceless gift. Life without her felt empty; life with her feels full. And somewhere between yesterday and today, I've learned to value whatever I can get.

We break into a sprint at exactly the same moment, reading each other's minds.

Acknowledgments

Thanks . . .

To Audrey and Clare—my go-to readers. I'm so fortunate to have you on my side.

To the many booksellers who have worked diligently to get my novels into readers' hands. A special shout-out to the St. Louisans who've kept me so busy: Melissa Posten and Nikki Furrer at Pudd'nHead Books; Vicki Erwin at Main Street Books; Danielle Borsch and Sarah Pritchard at Left Bank Books; and Deborah Horn at the Fenton Barnes & Noble.

To the librarians of St. Louis Public Library, especially the Schlafly Branch; and to Patty Carleton, Director of Youth Services. And a tip of the cap to all librarians—I've come to know firsthand the enormous contributions you make to schools and communities.